HARD TIMES OF CHILDISH MATURITY

Greg
Zimmerman

Dedicated to my dad, Richard Adam Zimmerman. Thanks for 35 years of wisdom and love that I sprinkled throughout these pages.
- gipper40

"It was long ago and so far away, God it seemed so very far.
And if life is just a highway then the soul is just a car; objects
in the rear view mirror may appear closer than they are.
- Jim Steinman

∞∞∞

Prologue

All through my childhood I was bullied by my older brother. You may remember the type - the bad news that arrived at the front door the moment you were born without any real assurance that things would change in your favor. Doomed to live an early existence of constant beatdowns, wedgies and verbal assaults channeled by the annoying feeling that you would always lose by such physical strength already held against you.

Playing out the never ending game of cat and mouse where you got chased around the house repeatedly until mom or dad unknowingly made their presence shown by saying, "Cool it kids, dinner is on the table." or "Behave yourselves or else I'm cutting your curfew and lowering your weekly allowance."

I guess to some degree, I had certain advantages over him, that in hindsight, made it justifiably okay to overreact against me the way he did. What did I know back then, anyway? Mom always played her favorite, allowing me to get away with things that he couldn't, leaving me vulnerable for punishment when nobody was looking.

It wasn't easy growing up the youngster of the family but then maybe too it wasn't easy being the oldest. In my opinion, looking back now, having an older brother that was too old would have been harder to examine and less of a memory to share.

If you think about it, I was able to coexist inside a sibling rivalry structure getting my own fair shake of the "hard knocks" that life threw my way. Knowing, for instance, that there would always be challenges out there to overcome; that life wasn't filled with rainbows and peach cakes. That enemies awaited around the corner ready to pounce out from the shadows left to survive on my own.

They say blood is thicker than water and a brotherly bond is a push and pull of human emotion. One moment you lay down your life for the other while the next you bounce around like silly jack rabbits showing dominance like you were flirting for the attention over the same pretty girl.

My brother and I existed without the luxury of an older sister, leaving the two of us to fend for ourselves when we could. We weren't exactly the picture perfect poster children for a particular age but we did find ways for making the most of our childhood days.

Especially since we grew up in the 1990s, so by contemporary standards, the upbringing we shared was quite unusual with the fact that our family unit was not a broken home of deadbeat parents who were aloof and cheated on one another with the marks on their body for proof.

That's not to say they didn't have the occasional fight that we overheard while alone in our room managing our time away from schoolwork. Dad would come home early while mom being a working woman would struggle for a working wage. It wasn't like we didn't have money but we weren't exactly floating around in a pool of dollars and cents, either. Although the thought of that just now makes me want to smash open my old piggy bank and pay back my parents for all the times I was not in bed sleeping but out galivanting with my friends at the local bar during the midnight hours of those early high school nights.

Anyway, I'm getting off track here, back to my brother.

I should let you know now that only three years separated the two of us. At least that's what our birth certificates proved when we found them lying around in Dad's cellar. Growing up under the same household, our parents, like most of the other kids we knew, combined us into one little domain with the simple joy of bunk beds.

I was forced to take the bottom bunk, where I would be a slave watching his feet slip down dangling into my space during restless nights when those storms were heard crashing from the outside. Making me want to consider why he never changed his socks. Spraying out that rancid smell of an unpleasant odor made me want to jump in the shower to examine my own personal hygiene whenever I could. Something I would do quite often even before girls invaded my life.

As we got a little older, our habits began to change. I was an avid reader while he was the type who would just rent the movie. He enjoyed Stephen King, as did I, but I would always clash with him about why the books had more meaning with the movement of words and pacing of thought than what the screenplays could ever show on screen.

I would say to him, "An actor only acts to the lines on a page; a writer has to dig deep and create them with his own mind." He, of course, would just stare at me funny, call me a loser, all the while pretending everything I said had no merit.

People are funny. They know how to live in denial where I tend to accept reality for what it is. And trust me, it's not often a pretty sight when you're able to see things for yourself.

I guess I never considered myself a deeply religious person but the more you begin to age, the more the wisdom just flows. I overheard a preacher once say, "Wisdom is only gained the moment you begin to fear God."

It's crazy but I just met the actor Wil Wheaton at one of these comic conventions. He portrayed one of the characters

Mr. King wrote in the film adaptation of his novella, *The Body*. I was instantly reminded after meeting him that I was turning into my own writer of sorts, which is where I am now in my life; an old man just trying to piece together the puzzle that was my life and the mystery surrounding the many events that have conspired throughout. You never really know yourself until you take a self-reflective mirror and hold it up against yourself for judgments made during those instances that appeared fuzzy.

Which brings me to the story that I'd wish to share with you. Only the passage of time can pull up a clearer perspective on things that once were and I think now more than ever is the best time to explain what went down that autumn weekend back in 1999.

Chapter One

"*B*arry, I need a ride to school!" I yelled, bunkering in the bathroom putting on a clean face for the day ahead.

This usually came with the uniform ritual of brushing my teeth, shower bathing the body and rinsing mouthwash around the gums. All of which took place in a span of thirty minutes after the annoying buzzer woke me every morning.

I had become a creature of habit since my brother and I were allowed separate rooms, after begging dad to move his den into the garage, leaving the two of us with more space to live and roam. We were getting older; it was only necessary for our authority figures to give in.

"Just because I have my license doesn't mean I have to chauffeur you around like some kind of personal lackey *for cryin' out loud*!" he voiced in anger. "You need to take your lumps like the rest of us did in our youth and ride the stinking bus."

"In our youth?" I retaliated. "You're only three years older than me. What nerve do you have saying that?"

I spat out the toothpaste, flushing it in the sink, as I eyed him in the hallway walking in.

"You're like a woman you know that? Always wanting your way. I just get sick of it. Move it so I can take a leak, will ya?"

Maybe I was but sometimes you had to fight hard to get your way or you'd get run over. It didn't matter if I was the youngest that was just the way the world worked.

"You should really put yourself in my shoes." he acknowledged, hoping I'd see things from his perspective.

"***Stop your bickering or else I'm not making either of you breakfast!***" Mom warned, overhearing us from the downstairs.

"Mom," Barry whined. "We're too old for that nonsense. I'm going to pick something up when I get to school. You don't have to bother."

"Okay, fine, that's your loss." She answered, waiting for my reply.

"I agree. I'll get something too."

"And with what money?" Barry laughed, knowing he trapped me into the old poor boy routine.

He had recently finished his summer job, basking in the riches of what looked like $1,000 to his credit. Now he floated around town like Mr. Big Shot with his own car at his side and a burst of personal freedom.

I, on the other hand, was only a freshman, which meant it was becoming harder to make a name for myself inside the hallways of Brookside Senior High. I was a nobody with the fear and stigma of someone writing: *this locker belongs to Barry Chase's younger brother - the dillweed who wanders alone and never made it far."*

Let's face it: I had no money, no respected following; all I had was the same goofy friend I've had since I was in grade school. And he never wished to grow into maturity at any rate. I was shit out of luck waiting for my ship to come in.

"So Barry, are you going to give me a lift or what?"

"Fine," he finally answered. "But I have to pick up Jill on our way there."

I guess this is the part in the story where I tell you that Jill was Barry's girlfriend. How he was able to hook up with her is still anyone's guess and a mystery that to this day remains unsolved.

She was a complete knockout. Gorgeous blond hair, boobs that stuck out like flashlights hidden for their protection under her tight jacket and buttoned-up blouse. All with that curvy waist that screamed out: *"Bang me!"*

It was possible that Barry was hitting it but he never gossiped about her in a sleazy way. In fact, Jill - even with her good fortune for blissful beauty, treated the two of us like we were the nice guys. It was possible that she might have had a few bad past experiences that our type looked innocent in comparison. Whatever it was - we were grateful. She was good to us and we respected that. At least I did.

"What are your plans for the day, boys?" Mom remarked as we made our way into the kitchen.

I put a pop tart in the toaster eager to eat something quick.

"Not much." I answered, waiting for my instant breakfast to pop up.

I never really understood why my parents - or at least my mom - gave a shit about our personal lives in the matters of our academics and schooling. It wasn't like I was concerned with her daily activities at the insurance company where she was employed.

"What about you, Barry?" She asked rhetorically knowing the answer was most likely the same as mine.

"I have to go see Jill." He answered, confusing mom's train of thought.

"What for?"

"She's my girl. That's what we do, isn't it?"

"I get it but please don't make me a grandmother quite yet. I'm only in my forties for pete's sake."

"I know what I'm doing."

"That's the same thing your dad said and look what happened to us."

I always admired mom's charm. She had spunk and knew how to play a room.

"Are you coming or what, butthead?" Barry asked, wanting to clear out before mom completely had her way with him. "If we don't leave now we're going to be late."

"Wait a minute, you actually want to go to school?"

"No, but if we don't go now, I won't have the time to drop you off so you can get the valued education you need."

"Boys, no dry humor around the house, please." Mom replied.

"But you're the one who raised us, remember?" Barry laughed.

"Maybe I did," she agreed. "I guess I do deserve the blame for that error in maternal judgment."

Chapter Two

There was a reason why some kids my age didn't date during high school.

For one thing, and I'll tell you this straight out of the gate: It wasn't worth it.

What do you mean by that, you say?

Simple: From the perspective of where we stood, it wasn't like we were living in our parent's generation; an era of *going steady* where innocence was glossed over by simple sentiments and promises kept looking as if they came straight out of an idea for a 1950s wholesome family sitcom.

Don't get me wrong, those same baby boomer youths who grew up on that level of ideal utopia manipulated their own culture once they got older by attempting to erase it with the harsh reality that life brought their way. Albeit the Vietnam era, sex, drugs and of course rock and roll.

Leaving future generations of kids disillusioned with nothing but heavy unemployment, inflation, bad parenting and an unwelcoming epidemic of unwed mothers that sprouted up like weeds from the deadbeat dads who wanted no part in the "adulting process" for raising their offspring.

What was once thought up as The American Dream became nothing short of a nightmare on steroids shoving the few who remained honest with themselves hiding into some sensible salvation cult.

In a nutshell, society created chaos and the crazies were winning.

But there was, of course, a less sociological reason.

It came with the unfortunate circumstance with how we traveled. If you wanted to impress girls, owning a bicycle wouldn't do and it couldn't get you far.

Without owning or at least having possession of a car, what was the point?

Especially where I lived. School was more than twenty miles away from the house. Which only forced you to either be a sardine on the bus with the rest of the fishes waiting to breakout or a bum begging for a ride from someone you knew who was older and had that significant driver's license in hand.

Which, as witnessed, was the way most of the conversations with my brother started during that Freshman year.

Allowing me, on this particular morning, to sit shotgun as he took control of the wheel jamming to the music playing on the CD player he recently installed.

"Can you believe you got this car after Ms. Harris passed away this year?"

"She left it in her will but her son didn't want it so he sold it to me." Barry answered. "One person's loss is another's triumph, right? Plus, I think the guy needed the cash. I always figured Patrick to be some kind of deadhead stoner, anyway. Selling a car just so he could spend it on dope or something."

"I guess." I said, shaking my head, trying to understand this neighborhood's odd sense of goodwill.

"He gave me a good deal on it too. So far it hasn't acted up but I have a feeling things might happen in the future. You never really know with these types of cars."

This type of car was a 1994 white chevy Cavalier. So

far there was only 34,000 miles on it, which wasn't bad at all. One could still consider it quite new. But with teenagers around, that analytical data was completely useless once the speedometer meter inched higher and the blood alcohol level raised.

"Do you have any better music to play? I'm getting sick of listening to grunge. I mean Kurt died, what, like five years ago? Isn't it time we move on and away from the Seattle scene? I hear boy bands are the rage these days."

"Kurt is a God. You have no idea what the hell you are talking about. He's the John Lennon of our generation."

"Our generation? Need I remind you that we are mere millennials. We missed the cutoff to be Gen Xers by a few years. Also, your car stinks!"

"Stop complaining or I'll kick you out right here and you can walk the rest of the way."

"Okay, okay. I'm sorry, don't have a cow!"

"It ain't my fault mom and dad won't let me smoke in the house leaving me this cheap motel as my last resort."

"This cheap motel?" I questioned, with my eyebrow raised, looking around what could be considered the classic piece of shit car.

"Can I least open up a window or something? It's as if something up and died in here."

"Suit yourself," Barry responded, heading towards a drive thru window. "I'm making a pit stop before school. Want some breakfast, you dope?"

"Are you buying?"

"Of course. I'll just put it in on your tab for the next time I have to show you tough love or I need an excuse to blame you for something."

We waited until we heard the voice on the other side

grant us the opportunity to speak.

"Welcome To *Swiftys*" the intercom spoke. *"May I take your order this morning?"*

"What do you want, man?" He poked, trying to get my attention.

"I'll just take an egg muffin or something. Oh - and an orange juice."

"Living life in the fastlane, huh?"

"I'm just being cheap on your ass."

"Sure, you are."

"Make that two!" He yelled into the speaker hoping the employee heard.

"So, what's Jill been up to, anyway?" I asked, making simple small talk. "I haven't seen you guys around in awhile."

Barry took a moment to collect his thoughts before filling me in.

"She is still having some issues with her previous boyfriend. I think the guy is some kind of a stalker. He's been calling her up and stuff trying to get her back."

"Has she contacted the police?"

"I don't know, I think she's too shy to ask for help. So far it seems like nothing. Let's just hope it stays that way."

"And is that *why* she now has you?" I laughed, entertaining myself. "What is this guy's name again?"

"Brett Andrews, I think he's a student at the junior college nearby. He's a little older then both of us. They met last summer and things went south fast."

"What did he do?"

"I think he tried to have his way with her. At least that's what's implied when she tries to bring it up."

"Well, I guess that's what you get for dating a pretty girl." I giggled. "What was it that Dad always told us? If you want to be happy for the rest of your life,"

"Have an ugly woman be your wife." Barry finished. "That wasn't dad you moron, that was from an old song he sang to us. You know Dad was no philosopher."

"Does it matter? It's the truth." I snarked. "May I ask how'd you even got with Jill in the first place?"

"A magician never reveals his secrets." He gloated, passing me the food that was handed to him.

"Maybe I should give her a call."

"Maybe, you should." I agreed, munching on my breakfast in front of his face. "You can test out that new flip phone you just bought. How much did that baby ring you up again?"

"More than you'll make this year, buddy."

"You're just floating around in cash these days, aren't you?"

"Jealous, much?" He winked, loving his seniority over the situation.

"Just be thankful Dad gave you a discount on it since he works at RadioShack."

"Yeah, whatever you say."

"It's ringing." Barry announced, holding his finger up at me waiting for someone to pick up.

"Hello?" A man answered sounding concerned. It was assumed that it was the father speaking.

" Yes, this is Barry. Barry Chase. Is Jill there, by chance?"

"Hold on a minute."

"*Jill - someone is on the phone for you!*" the voice shouted, making me aware of the commotion on the other end.

"You better be nice or her dad will hunt you down."

"Shut up, jerk!" He responded, belting me in the chest. His behavior spilling some orange juice all over me.

"Look what you did now, nice going."

"Get yourself a few napkins out of the bag and wash up. Don't be a baby about it. Do I have to do everything for you?"

Barry continued to hold until someone came on the line.

"Yes, Barry? What's up?" Jill finally answered, picking up the phone and sounding a bit pained and clipped.

"I was on my way out this morning. I figured I'd stop by and pick you up. We're heading out your way now."

"We?"

"Oh, it's just my brother with me. You can take shotgun when we get you. He'll move!"

"That's sweet of you, Barry, but I'm not going in today."

She was hesitant to reveal why, giving the classic female response.

"It's just that time of the month."

"Oh, okay. I totally understand. Is there anything I can do for you in the meantime?"

"Nah, I'll be alright. You just come by afterwards and get me caught up if you'd like."

"Sure, I can do that." He said with glee. "But wait, your dad won't be home, will he? "

"No. We'll be fine," she laughed, before hanging up.

Barry took a second to reflect upon the news.

"So how'd that go?"

"Looks like it's just me and you this morning."

"She's not coming? Why?"

"Female problems, those were her words."

"I guess you're just going to have to get used to that behavior if you want to please her."

"That's a lesson we must learn from the opposite sex."

"Come on, let's go! Never mind her." he said shifting gears and heading back onto the road. "She'll be alright."

"Yeah, let's get this day over with."

"Something we can agree on."

"By the way, how much do we have in the tank, anyway?"

"Just enough to get us to where we need to go." He answered, looking directly at the dashboard and ignoring the speedometer or his right foot pressing down attacking the gas.

Chapter Three

"**S**hit!" Barry uttered under his breath thinking I wouldn't overhear.

"Wait, what's going on?" I asked, looking out the rear view, getting a good look at lights flickering on top of the cop car ready to pull us over.

"They just caught me speeding."

"I kinda figured that out, moron."

"Then why did you ask in the first place?"

I shrugged without a verbal answer.

"Didn't I tell you to slow it after we left the drive thru?"

"Oh, give me a break," he revolted with a punch to my arm. "Put on your stinking seatbelt before the cop notices and I get in more trouble."

"Hey, hey, now, now, don't be touchy." I snickered. "It's not like this is your first speeding ticket."

Barry became pale, looking as if he was about to vomit next to me.

"Holy shit it is!"

"I've only been driving for a few months. It wasn't like I had this on my agenda or something you asswipe."

"You didn't? You mean you weren't trying to piss off the fuzz after hearing Jill ditched us?"

Barry didn't answer, keeping his frustration to himself.

"Anyway, don't worry, look on the bright side, you're not a virgin anymore."

"Oh shut up, man. The cop is coming. Be cool, don't say anything. Just do what you're told, 'kay. Maybe we can get out of this without a ticket."

"License and registration please," the officer demanded, watching the two of us squirm in our seats trying to avoid eye contact with authority.

"Here you go, sir." Barry obeyed, handing him the information asked for after stealing it directly from my freshly stained sticky fingers.

"Do either of you boys know just how fast you were going?"

"I thought I was driving the speed limit, sir." Barry giggled, becoming condescending.

"Well, you weren't, son. I clocked you at about ten miles over on my radar. The speed limit here is only 45 which means you were going above and beyond what the state requires. This could be considered reckless."

"Oh, so sorry sir. It's just that I don't like traveling with these school buses around. You know how that is? They hold up traffic making everyone go slow. You can understand that, can't you? All we're trying to do is get to school on time. We kinda left the house later than usual. Our parents would be ashamed if they found out this happened."

The officer remained silent, looking annoyed, not appearing in the mood to hear upper lip, basically playing the part of the patrolman who was getting a little too old to hear every sad pathetic excuse.

"You boys do know you're traveling down a one-way road, right? Of course we're going to be hanging around spotting for safety precautions. Especially during the end of the month. These are the craziest times in the year for such behavioral trends."

"You're saying we're not going to get off with just a warning?"

"Today is not looking like your lucky day, if that's what you mean. Hold on while I write you up. Don't move."

"We won't."

The cop headed back, leaving the two of us to fend for ourselves.

"Nice play, Shakespeare!" I mocked, taking a cigarette out of his pack, instigating him.

"What the hell are you doing with that?"

"We're already getting grounded, might as well make it permanent and die of lung cancer while I'm at it too."

"Not with the fricken cop outside you idiot. You're under age. He'll issue me another ticket for influencing a minor or something."

"Give me a break. That won't happen. But thanks for caring big bro."

Barry rolled his eyes, swiping the cigarette from my mouth, placing it on his ear like some poorly dressed James Dean figure, awaiting the cop as he made the encore back to the vehicle with salty news.

"Here you go, son." he gestured to Barry from the window, as he reached out to take the slip.

"I just want you boys to know that what you just did is dangerous, and driving is not a right but a privilege that cannot be taken for granted. I've seen one too many horrendous accidents in my lifetime by people about your age and I don't want to see either of you two again, do you read me? Next time things may play out differently."

"Yes, sir, we understand." We said in unison hoping it would butter him up to leave on good terms.

"Good then, have a good day and remember to stay in school."

We both looked on with stern faces hiding out our laughter, waving goodbye.

"Do all cops talk like they have some sort of stick up their ass?"

"Who knows," Barry laughed. "It could have been worse, I guess. He looked old enough to suggest he was trying to do us a favor. If he was younger, he might have been the type that wanted to reach his quota or something. Y'know - be arrogant and all."

"Yeah, that makes sense."

"Whatever you do, don't tell mom or dad about this. What they don't know won't hurt them, right?"

"I guess, it's your funeral, anyway. You're the bozo that got caught. I bet if Jill was with us we would have gotten off the hook."

"I wouldn't have doubted that for a second." Barry sighed. "She would have made up some good excuse to sway his mind otherwise."

"Yeah, a little eye candy never hurts."

"You're telling me."

"Let me see the ticket."

"What for?"

"I'd just like to see what it looks like."

Barry's eyebrow raised with curiosity. "Dude, it's just a ticket."

"True, but if you notice closely, the ticket is only $25

dollars. The fee to have it disputed in court is $65. What a ripoff."

"I guess that's why it's called highway robbery. He suggested. "Sad, the way the world works, ain't it?"

"Yeah."

"On the other hand, it looks like we're still going to make it to school on time."

"Well, that sucks!"

"Sorry about that, bro. I'll drop you off in front so you won't miss the morning bell."

"Ah, shut up. I don't need to hear more of your wise cracks."

"But the day is still young."

"Maybe, so, but doesn't it already seem like it needs to end?"

"I hear you, you learn more about life on the open road then you ever could in a classroom."

"That's for sure." I acknowledged, preparing to finally head our separate ways.

Chapter Four

1999 could be considered a bridge between what was and what was waiting to come.

I remember it well if my memory still serves me correct. Before the Millennium Rush or the war on terror, our world - at least the teenage population that inhabited it - compounded itself with news. Story after story about the corruption of teenage youth. All over the media: film, television, music, we were the scapegoats being force fed an agenda that as Radiohead put it, turned us into nothing but "Fake Plastic Trees".

All leading to that fatal day in April when two losers dressed up in trenchcoats, decided to go nuts and infamously change the way school systems handled topics as gun control and violence on school campuses.

Our school wasn't one that was in lockdown that Fall but we did get the paranoid glances anytime inconspicuous characters came walking into the building roaming the hallways.

"Our society is so fake," my best friend Mark said as we swiped books from each other's lockers. "I'm starting to think Fiona Apple was right: this world is bullshit."

"You're telling me. I can't bother listening to someone like Marilyn Manson without judging how annoying and stupid looking that contact lens is. I, mean, seriously, what idiotic kids listening to this shit think any of this crap is real, anyway?"

"No idea." Mark agreed, hearing the bell, as we headed to our first period class. "You have to admit, though, that Fiona chick is pretty hot, did you see her "Criminal" video?"

"Indeed I did. She's a bad, bad girl." I sang in an off key voice that could possibly ruin a moment.

"Oh, stop that." Mark cringed, covering his ears. "Hey, by the way, did you hear about Joey?"

"No, what?"

"I heard he got kicked off of the bus this morning and is getting suspended after one of the kids saw him writing some poetry on a sheet of paper. One of the lines was talking about wanting to slaughter the popular kids in his class."

"I wonder how we stay so sane in this environment."

"You're telling me." he answered, slapping my hand, putting us in agreement.

Mark Collins was my most trusted ally. We'd been friends since grade school where we met under unfortunate circumstances after he slid into second base trying to rough me up during little league tryouts. He apparently had learned a move after watching the movie *Cobb* and wanted to try it out by "spiking" me in the chin with his cleat, seeing how I would react.

A fight soon ensued leading to both of us rolling around on the dirt being huddled away by our parents. The next day he was told by his mom to apologize and the next thing I knew we were playing video games, eating pizza and watching Ty Cobb play chicken with the train being reminded that the scene looked oddly familiar.

"Didn't I already see this in another film?"

"Maybe, but this is real life. Ty Cobb was a crazy son of a

bitch!"

"Boys, language!" His mother hollered, walking into his room oblivious to know that we were watching a movie that was rated R and full of racist slurs.

"So, did you get your homework done for Mr. Barrera's class?" Mark asked, snapping me back from memory lane.

"Shit! I knew I forgot to do something last night. What was the assignment on again?"

"We're reading *To Kill A Mockingbird.*"

"Oh, yeah, that." I remembered, as Mark held the book right up to my face. "I already read that." Shoving it away, accidentally knocking it to the ground. "I watched the movie last year after AMC played it and figured I'd get a head start."

"Was the movie any good?"

"It was in black and white so what do you think?"

"Why can't they modernize these books?"

"If they did then they wouldn't be considered classics, right?"

"I guess." Mark frowned. "One thing always plagued me about the story."

"What's that?"

"Is Scout a boy or girl?"

"What?"

"I mean the character acts like a boy but dresses like a girl."

"She was ahead of her time in her androgyny." I chuckled. "I think the term is called tomboy."

"It's really hard to tell, ain't it?" Mark questioned. "She sure likes to pick fights and also what kid calls their Dad by his first name? She sure had some nerve. What kind of name is

Atticus, anyway?"

"We better hurry." I dismissed, knowing Mark could go off topic at moment's notice. "The second bell is going to ring any minute. I don't feel like being tardy again like last week, remember? "

"What is it? Three tardies and they write you up or something?"

"I think so." I answered. "My brother actually knows more about ditching class than me."

"I bet. Did he drive you in today?

"Yep."

"That's why you weren't on the bus then this morning."

"That would appear correct."

"Don't get smart with me."

"I'm sorry but you had that one coming. I didn't miss anything? Did I?"

"No, not really. I was too busy taking a nap to notice. I hate having to get up early. I still say someone in the stinking school department needs to build a school closer to us. It ain't fair."

"You're telling me. It was easier when we were the big fish in a small pond back in junior high."

"Well, what about you?" asked Mark. "Did Barry give you any trouble with the ride?"

"No, we were going to pick up his girlfriend but she declined the offer."

"I wonder why."

"She said she wasn't feeling up to going in."

"I wish I could say things like that and make it happen. I always think girls have it easier than us."

"Gentleman!" A man's voice rang as we reached the classroom door. "Enough chit chatting, class is set to begin."

"We'll be right in, Mr. Barrera." I said, trying not to get myself into too much extra trouble.

"Sometimes you really can be a kiss ass. You do know that, right?"

"Wanna kiss mine? I just saved us both from getting another warning. So behave and thank me."

"Whatever, you say master." mocked Mark, as the door slammed behind us.

Chapter Five

I think Mr. Barrera liked his job. From what I could tell he did what he did not because of need but out of want. He was a rare breed in that respect. When it came to influencing the mind of the young he was an educator who wanted to educate and not indoctrinate.

In this upside down world that we grew accustomed to living, the only way that one could spot the difference between the two was in the method in which one taught their pupils; either they drew up the lesson plans that told their students "what to think" or they rebelled against the status quo with a reactionary spirit of teaching kids simply "how to think".

I enjoyed learning from the latter even if most of my fellow classmates were clueless in what it took to passing the class.

"Can anyone tell me the significance in this story?" He asked, holding up Harper Lee's novel.

He was greeted with the usual blow of dead silence. First period always welcomed the nappers who felt it best to use this time as an excuse to catch up on the previous night's lack of sleep.

"Come on class, *wake up!*" He yelled, slapping the book against the desk startling the room.

Some heads began to show life as they stretched back and forth.

"So, now I have your attention. That's good to see."

"William," He pointed to the kid in the back. "What do you think?"

Everyone locked eyes waiting for an answer.

"Well sir," he began, "It's my belief this story is strictly about the end of innocence from a little girl's perspective."

Mr. Barrera waited to respond hoping someone would comment over the response.

No luck was achieved.

"And who then would you say is the tragic figure in the narrative?"

Blank stares showing embarrassment were shown all around as if nobody bothered to finish the book.

"Jesus, do I have to explain everything?" I thought, raising my hand.

"*Kiss up!*" coughed Mark under his breath, seated next to me.

"Yes, Mr. Chase. What say, you?"

"After reading this book and watching the film, I think the author chose Tom Robinson to be the tragic figure."

"Good, but do you suspect anyone else?" Mr Barrera added, knowing he really wanted someone else to answer.

"*Calpurnia!*" A voice shouted with little hope for a cheap laugh.

"Really, Trey?" Mr Barrera asked, looking displeased with his answer while trying not to crack a smile.

"Maids in those days were always getting the short end of the stick, right?"

"Maybe so, but not the answer I'm looking for."

"Well, whatever happened to the phrase there are no

right or wrong answers, only opinions?"

Mr. Barrera refused to give in to Trey's juvenile sentiments.

"Come on you guys. Let's be serious, here." Mr Barrera pleaded. "This is a story about being scapegoated. Who would you say other than Tom Robinson got blamed in this story unjustly?"

Nobody was brave enough to answer leaving me wide open once again to discuss my own feelings on the subject matter.

"I was disappointed Mr. Raymond was not in the film. I thought he was very unique in how he handled himself. Pretending to be a drunk, only because he was judged early on by a town who already shared a strict prejudice against him."

Mr. Barrera looked amused that I beat him at his own game; answering honestly while boldly giving sound reasoning for my own thought that wasn't the one he was expecting.

"That's good, Mr. Chase." Mr. Barrera accepted. "One could say that same sentiment was given to the character of Boo Radley too. Wouldn't you say?"

"Yeah, I guess," I uttered under my breath. "That would have been taking the easy route."

"Boo Radley was the true innocence that was lost in the story which is why he hid himself in that house away from the gossip."

"All he wanted was a friend." added William.

"Indeed," Mr. Barrera applauded. "Friendships can be tough once we begin to age but he found it by the simple joys he shared with the Finch kids and the tree over those summers; returning the favor by saving their lives when they needed it most."

Listening to Mr. Barrera babble about the moral complexity found in the ending made me think that the chivalry shown in that moment of heroism was truly becoming outdated.

Nowadays one would see a lonesome loser like that roaming the streets in the middle of the night and alert the authorities immediately for fear of pedophilia or something. We were already one stop ahead of being lost in The Twilight Zone even by 1999 standards.

"Are there any other questions before the final exam next week?"

The class looked around unsure if they heard anyone ask one. Rhetorical questions had the ability to go over the head of my compadres. It wasn't that they were stupid but the times we were living in could suggest it.

The bell rang as the class filed out.

"Mr. Chase, can I speak with you for a moment?"

"Uh-oh, you're in trouble now." Mark said. "I'll meet you outside when you finish in here."

"Sure," I said, waving my binder for him to hold. "Here, take this."

"What for?"

"I don't want to accidentally leave it in here by mistake."

"You really can be quite anal retentive."

"Maybe, so, but did you notice that you didn't bring your copy of the book with you to class?"

"Huh?"

"I knocked it out of your hand in the hallway, remember? You didn't pick it up."

"Holy crap! You're right." He finally figured out. "I did forget to pick it up."

It was always fun to mess with Mark's head when he tried to give me shit for my own behavior. It was only necessary to spin things around on him for my personal enjoyment when all else failed.

"You better make sure the janitor didn't pick it up and throw it in the trash by now. You'll owe the school if you lose it."

"Screw you." He squirmed, rushing out the door retracing his steps.

"You know you shouldn't tease your friend like that." Mr Barrera said, noticing that I hid the book in my backpack.

"Where do you find friends like that in the first place?"

"People like Mark didn't exist in your time period?"

"You just called me old." he laughed. "I guess they did. I just tried to avoid them when I could."

"I guess it was easier back then, wasn't it?"

"Maybe."

"What did you want to see me about?"

"I just wanted to congratulate you."

"With what, exactly?"

"The essay that you submitted for the "English Final" reached the national competition. You should be proud of yourself."

"Oh, that thing." I teased. "That was nothing, really."

"Well, somebody thought it was something."

He handed me the paper showing the approval from the school board.

"You're on your way to becoming a solid writer one day."

"I appreciate it but I don't see myself becoming the next Harper Lee anytime soon."

"I wouldn't count on it." Mr. Barrera concurred. "With the way things are trending these days, you have to write your own story for your own times. That's where the magic happens."

He got up from his desk ready to shake my hand when the alarm sounded.

"Oh, God. That ain't good."

"What's that? What's going on?"

"We've been getting bomb threats the last week but it's been kept hush for the safety of the student body. I think somebody finally triggered a nerve."

I stayed silent, stunned.

"Get out of here, now!" He snapped.

With his permission, I did what I was told and headed out.

Chapter Six

"**B**oy, oh boy!" Mark jumped, watching me walk out of Mr. Barrera's classroom with a pep in my step.

"What do you think this is all about?"

"From what I heard we're under a bomb threat warning."

"What?"

"Mr. Barrera was just telling me about it."

"You're kidding?"

"No, we need to exit."

"Oh, wow! I'm not worried, these are normally false alarms, aren't they?"

"I'm not one to think about that right now. Let's just do what we're told, okay?"

"You don't think Joey had anything to do with this, do you?" Mark questioned, strolling down the hallway as the student body began to crowd the premises, attempting to separate the two of us.

"I doubt it. That dude is strange but not quite that insane. At least, I don't think so."

"Does he have any siblings that would be crazy enough to do something this stupid?"

"Beats the hell out of me. I hardly know the kid. I just had to sit with him last year after he fell behind in Algebra class."

"Like that kid really cares about school?"

"That's what I said. And Mrs. Bellows got upset with me for even suspecting that."

"Mrs. Bellows? Oh yeah, I remember her. That woman was a monster, wasn't she?"

"Don't you say that to just about every teacher we ever had?"

"Maybe, but it's true. Remember how she would humiliate all the kids in class anytime someone gave out the wrong answers to the problems?"

"That wasn't humiliation, that was tough love." I laughed, sensing a flashback coming.

"Whatever you want to call it, it got many people upset with her."

"I have to admit, she did have that stern look on her face all the time. She wasn't as bad as that student teacher we had, though. Remember?"

"No, who was that again?"

"Oh yeah, that's right, you weren't in my English class last year, were you?"

"Yeah, I was with Mr. Peterson. He was actually a good teacher."

"Shocker!"

"What did that student teacher do to you, anyway?"

"We were debating arguments and giving out oral presentations and under her breath during one of my responses I could hear her say, "I hate you.""

Mark laughed. "Jesus, I could say that about you too."

"Shut up!" I reacted, punching him.

"Hey, why'd you do that?"

"Because I could."

"You know what it is man?"

"What?"

"You're too smart for your own good, buddy."

I begged to differ. "She was from Harvard."

"They brainwash those types with their "Ivy League" education over there, don't they?"

"Especially, these days."

"You know, you shouldn't have let it get to you. Anyway, we should catch up with Tyler when we see him."

"He's in gym class right now. We'll have to catch up with him when we hit the parking lot." I said, heading down the stairs approaching the doors.

"If the school is going under lockdown then we'll be leaving early, right?"

"No shit, Sherlock."

"That's good news for me." gloated Mark. "I had a biology test coming up next period. I wasn't really in the mood to dissect the fetal pig they assigned me."

"Whatever ever happened to frogs?"

"I think only middle schoolers do them, not sure, really."

"Oh," I frowned, "What the hell are you doing taking that class in the first place?"

"My guidance counselor messed up my scheduling last year since I was new to the school. They didn't know where to place me so they stuck me in the classes nobody dared to take."

"Figures," I said, adding more insult to his wound. "Leave it to the board of education to tell us who they think we are."

"It's not like I'm trying to be the next James Watson or something."

"Who?"

"My point exactly. Nobody knows who the hell that is."

"I hear ya. If you don't play a sport or follow the arts, you're pretty much screwed for the rest of your life with gaining celebrity status."

"Not everyone can be an Einstein, right?"

"Did I tell you," Mark continued. "Last year I almost burned down the school by accidentally playing with the Bunsen burner in chemistry class."

"No, I actually don't remember that. Should I suspect you had some part in this bomb threat right now while we're at it?"

We both laughed at the absurdity of the statement.

"How's the weather outside looking?"

"I suspect it's still nice out. I don't think anyone was calling for rain today."

"*Hey, Marky Mark!*" A voice belted from behind, making us swing around.

"*Please*, stop calling me that." Mark sighed, as we were greeted by Jeff Gunther, our friendly yet annoying arch nemesis who enjoyed torturing the two of us with all the silly rock and roll cliches one could dig up from the grave.

"You do know Mark Wahlberg switched to acting, right?"

"Yeah, I know that. He should have stuck to rapping."

"Did either of you two dolts see him in that movie, *"Fear"* with Reese, what's her name?"

"Yeah, he played a pretty bad stalker in it." Mark answered. "I liked the way that he died in it, though. Maybe his acting career will follow suit?"

"I agree, next thing I figure is we'll be seeing him flipping burgers needing help transferring to a new occupation of sorts."

"He might need some assistance with his brother too. His career ain't going anywhere, right?"

"I can see them now, opening up the brand new *"Wahlburgers"* in a town near you!"

"Everyone's gotta make a living, right?" Mark snickered with a sinister grin.

"You two are crazy, you know that, right?" Jeff laughed, watching us ramble on.

"We can't help it. Society made us that way." Mark smiled with pride.

"Well, what are you two bozos up to? Besides being yourselves?"

"What do you think, idiot?" ranted Mark. "We're freaking out we might *die.*"

"Jesus, not so loud." I said, beginning to sense eyeballs wandering in our direction.

"Ah, this ain't nothing." Jeff giggled, bringing us news from the high school grapevine. "I heard someone called this in this morning, by the payphone near the 7-11, wanting the attention. It's just a red herring if you ask me."

"If you say so."

"How do you know that?" Mark frowned with disbelief.

"I got my sources."

"If by your sources you mean *my* idiot brother, Ryan, I would be highly suspicious."

"Your brother wouldn't lie to me. Besides, we're just living in the new normal. Paranoia is all the rage."

"Must we blame everything on the beautiful people?" I questioned, with smugness.

"Oh, that reminds me." Jeff recalled. "We got a gig coming up this weekend. Saturday night before Halloween. It's going to be a blowout."

"We?" I said, not knowing what he was talking about.

"My brother and this doofus hooked up with two twenty something guys and started a band."

"Oh really? What type of music do you play?"

"We're mostly in tune with a lot of that California stuff from a few years ago - Chili Peppers and Stone Temple Pilots."

"You're not trying to impress this Nu-metal crowd with Korn and that ilk, are you?"

"Nah, we're trying to be musicians and not horrible tattoo artists." Jeff laughed. "We're also trying to take it seriously. We have a few songs already written."

"You mean you're not doing it to feel up the girls at the bar and get wasted on school nights?" chuckled Mark.

"No way, groupies ruin all the fun."

"Thanks, grandma!" Mark remarked, sticking out his tongue.

"We're trying to work out some extra cover tunes in our set, do you want to request any that we can add?"

"The better question is, who is allowing you idiots into these clubs in the first place? Two of you are under age."

"That's actually how we met Darrell and Frank. They

placed an ad and Ryan and I got in touch with them. They also work at *HARD LUCK*. The biggest bar -"

"I know what it is." I said, interrupting him.

"So you're telling me these two couldn't find anyone better and chose the lowest of the low to start up with?"

"That's only because they work cheap." Mark chuckled.

"Ah, screw you guys!" Jeff roared, distancing himself away. "Just remember: when we make it big you'll remember the day you curse the name of *Silicon Honey*!"

"Silicon Honey?" I questioned, staring oddly.

"Yeah, beats the hell out of me how they chose that name."

"I wouldn't worry." he concluded. "I'll give the band one to two years before they eventually crash and burn from untimely failure."

Mark wasn't too far off with his prediction. The band disbanded the next year after Darrell knocked up his girlfriend, leaving our two underage knuckleheads unemployed and alone on their sad and pathetic quest for rock stardom.

With sincerity, though, Jeff went on to become an IRS auditor and a father of five. Apparently, his Catholic upbringing made it unfortunate for him to want to be a friend of the Devil.

Chapter Seven

Tyler Blackford was the third member of our tenacious trio. For Mark and myself. He usually played the odd man out in most cases since he was the only member of our group who actually lived near school.

Which only meant from our perspective, he could sleep in late and get away with not showing up to class until about five minutes before the bell rang every weekday morning. I wouldn't call him a lucky bastard but who wouldn't envy that ability to walk directly from one's own house without fear of needing a ride or getting punched by the school bully on the back of the bus?

I guess he was more of an acquaintance but we treated him with the utmost of respect when it came to helping with our class schedules and daily agendas. He was quick to pick up on our sense of humor making it easy to just accept him as one of us.

He too had skipped a grade after certain test scores were released showing a high aptitude in both Mathematics and English. He might have been a genius but for us, he was the guinea pig we used when we needed to amuse ourselves from the trappings of everyday teenage existence.

Long story short - I met him back in junior high after witnessing him fail miserably trying to impress Amanda

Pawkowski in the lunchroom. He was standing by his locker looking like he was about to cry, rubbing his eyes, making believe it was only the air in the room messing with his allergies.

Anyone with half a brain would know better and at least try to show moral support.

Of course, he denied the whole episode when I would recount the story back to Mark with the repeated line coming across - "that's not the way it happened".

Anyway, in all fairness, what the guy had was spunk. Certain characteristics that appeared lost at a time when everything was unraveling at a steady pace around us.

He almost seemed like the guy who accidentally got dropped off in the wrong period of time. The type of kid who needed friends to feel secure with himself and build self-esteem.

"So, do you see him yet?" Mark gazed, looking to spot him in the middle of the crowd of our fellow classmates.

"No."

"There he is!" Mark pointed. "He's wearing that Michael Jordan jersey. Let's go over and get him."

"Hey Tyler!" Mark waved, trying to get his attention.

He looked at us waving back, signaling to come join him.

We rushed over as quickly as we could.

"Why are you still wearing that jersey?" Mark noted, "You do know the Bulls dynasty is over, right?"

"I sprang out of gym class and threw it on after the alarm rang. What else was I going to wear?"

"Playing the denial card, already."

"Denial of what?"

"The idea that the team of the 1990s will continue on.

"I'm no bandwagon fan. I accept the fact that the team will suck for the next few years."

"Let's make it centuries." Mark laughed. "They'll be right up there with the Cubs before you know it."

"You're so full of shit, Mark!"

"You wanna make a bet? I have $10 in my pocket - "

"Guys, guys, guys, cool it!" I interrupted.

"Mark, I wouldn't be surprised if Jordan made another return. He's prone to silly outbursts that make one shake their head. And besides, the NBA was under lockout this past year paying up all those ridiculous salaries. None of this chatter means much so why the heck are we trash talking with one another about it in the first piece?"

Needless to say, I forgot to mention, here, that Tyler, albeit the least athletic looking among us, was the one fanatic who enjoyed talking about sports whenever possible.

One would think that it was his way of feeling like a jock, even if all the cheerleaders we knew didn't find a particular 5'2, four-eyed, pimple faced wimp appealing by any stretch of the human imagination.

Which brings our story full circle back to Amanda Pawkowski.

The female goddess around the 9th grade circuit that all the boys drooled over even if it was speculated in the rumor mill that she enjoyed stuffing her bra.

"Hey look! There goes your girl, Ty." Mark giggled, noticing she was with another guy. It was only typical for the freshman girls to hook up with the juniors and seniors who were too old for them.

"What's she doing hanging with Alex?" I asked. "He's not

on the football team, is he?"

"I'm not sure," Tyler responded. "I think he may have tried out but didn't make the cut."

"Amanda must be lowering her standards then." Mark suggested, humoring himself.

"If that's the case, then Tyler did have a shot with her last year, afterall."

"FACULTY, STAFF AND STUDENTS," the PA system broke in with an announcement for the entire student body. ***"THIS IS PRINCIPAL STRICKLAND SPEAKING. WE WILL BE CLOSING THE SCHOOL BUILDING DOWN AT 10 AM. STAY SAFE AND HAVE A PLEASANT WEEKEND."***

"Yes!" The three of us voiced with excitement.

"Nothing better than getting out of school free." Tyler said, high-fiving the two of us.

"Hey look, your girl is coming over here." Mark noticed, beginning to panic like a little boy ready to wet his pants.

"Hi Tyler. It was nice of you to help me with my basketball drills in gym class this morning." She spoke gently, with Alex by her side.

Mark and I refused to acknowledge any of the verbal dialogue between them, instead, gluing our eyes directly at the full amount of cleavage on display by her blue bra strap with the sweat still dripping off her body from the morning run.

It was possible Alex judged us but it was something he would have to get a custom to if he wanted to hang around with the popular crowd.

"Well anyway, I hope you have a good weekend, Ty. See you on Monday." She politely greeted before walking off.

"You, *lucky* dog! You might have a shot with her if things play and we can somehow ditch that loser she's with at the moment."

"Anything's possible." He agreed, fist bumping me.

"So, what do we do now?"

"I'm probably just going to head on home and sleep this through." Tyler responded. "Sorry, guys, but I can't be seen here, anymore. Gotta run."

"Get lost and *die!*" Mark yelled back, sarcastically. "We'll be stuck waiting for the *god damn* buses to come pick us up."

"I'm actually hoping Barry can drive me back."

"I guess we'll see about that."

"What do you mean?"

"Here he comes now." Mark noticed, as we both watched Barry's car inch its way towards us like it was ready to run us down.

"*Yo, butthead!*" He shouted, rolling down the windows in the Cavalier.

"I do have a name, you idiot. You know that, right?"

"I just called you by it. So be nice."

"Are you going to give me a lift back home or not?"

"What? I'm going to take a trip and see Jill later. You're on your own, turdface. I'll see you tonight, if I care to come home. Also, remember, don't tell mom or dad about this morning or else!"

He rolled up the window refusing to acknowledge my existence before storming off.

"Or else, what?" Mark asked, facing me, not knowing what he meant.

"It's nothing. Barry and I just got pulled over this morning."

" You what?"

"Yeah, but don't go spreading it around town, 'kay?"

" Sure, sure, you know me."

"That's the problem, I do. So keep it to yourself."

Mark remained quiet, keeping his oath.

"It looks like it's just you and me again, buddy."

"I guess," I said. "Don't you think life was a tad bit easier when everyone had to ride the bus and we all had to suffer together?"

"Not really," Mark thought. "I can't wait to get my license in a couple years and have some freedom of my own. Slavery is bondage and bondage around here sucks!"

"Fair enough, but one thing is certain, though."

"What's that?"

"On the bus you can just sleep and forget about all the drama at hand."

"You know what your problem is, you worry too much, man. Look on the bright side, the weekend is upon us and anything can happen, right?"

"Yeah, we can sneak in to see "Silicon Honey" tomorrow night if we want."

"Yeah, and maybe we'll see the break-up live on stage." Mark laughed.

" I wouldn't mind watching that."

"Same here." he assented, walking up the steps to greet our bus driver, taking our usual seats.

Chapter Eight

I 've complained about it long enough in this passage but the main reason why bus travel was so distant growing up was due to the county's inability to fund and build a high school within our school district.

The problem was simply this: I lived in a small subdivision that put everything in a pickle. On one hand, I was fortunate enough to have a grade school in the area but nothing ever transpired - or one could say, the politicians got in the way - when it came to building a facility for the junior and high school ranks.

It wasn't even until I entered my senior year when the blueprints were finally being considered, laying down the groundwork for the next generation of kids to never contemplate what life was like for the poor souls who had come before.

In retrospect - It could had saved everyone the hassle of traveling down that long stretch of highway many teenagers flew by with jubilee trying to pass around the school buses they found too slow for their own personal joy ride.

Leading, of course, to many premature and accidental deaths that left families voicing out their concerns.

Obviously, too young to partake in the red tape politics, Mark and I only did what we had to while silently venting out our own frustrations to one another about our journeys aboard our public school transportation system.

I never tried to make too much commotion while the bus was in motion. I'd sit next to Mark by the window with my portable CD player playing, resting my head against the window glass waiting for the bus to drop us off.

On days when it rained and the fog was apparent, I'd be the kid finger writing over top of it with my own signature, bored, with nothing better to do.

I tended to be more introverted but Mark was a talker. He'd be up in front discussing the issues of the day with anyone who dared listen.

"Can you believe our generation?"

"Not really," Mrs. Newman replied. "I mean with the way things are headed in our culture. I'm not too surprised by any of this nonsense going about."

It's funny how the bus drivers I had were nothing but old ladies, never shy to dish out their opinions when called upon. Age, I guess, was a familiar factor in simply not giving a shit about how other's thought.

"Would you see the day, though, when we'd be getting sent home early not because of the weather but due to a bomb scare?"

"Well back in my day, we settled our juvenile disputes with our fists and not in momma's basement concocting a deadly weapon. For pete's sake, what are these kids thinking?""

"I can't picture you as the violent type."

"I wasn't, but the boyfriends I had sure were. These kids these days don't even know the meaning of tough."

"I know what you -"

"Watch it, you damn hooligan!" she yelled, honking the horn, as a car cut her off.

"See what I mean, no damn respect for the laws of the road."

It was possible her tone scared him half to death.

"Well, anyway, I gotta get back to my seat. It was nice chatting with you."

"Hey!" Mark shouted, trying to get my attention. "What are you listening to?"

I did my best to ignore but he plopped down taking the headphones off my head.

"What is this? Prince?" He asked, looking confused. "What the hell are you doing listening to this shit?"

"It's 1999." I said, trying not to get offended by his strong offsetting demeanor.

"It may be 1999 but the song is like from 1984, right? What are you doing listening to that fool, anyway? I mean does he even go by Prince anymore? He's like a symbol now, right?"

"I think so. That was all publicity against his management."

"You really do like a lot of that old 1980s pop music, don't you?"

"The only one that I can stomach is Madonna. She's not bad looking for someone pushing forty something. I wouldn't mind having her to mess around with, if you know what I mean."

"No, I don't know what you mean. Explain it to me, why don't you, *wiseass*?"

Mark disregarded my comment, reaching down into his book bag, pulling up a copy of what looked like a VHS cassette.

"You want to see what I rented the other day?"

"You're going to tell me either way, so why bother even asking?"

"Good point." He stated. "*It's The Blair Witch Project!*" He gleed with teenage excitement, holding it up to show.

"That dumb movie!" I remarked, making him question his own taste. "When I was on vacation this summer, I heard a radio commercial for that stupid film, making you think it was all real and that they all mysteriously died while filming it."

"That was the genius of it!" He fired back. "It was all in the marketing. The next thing you knew there they all were on *The Today Show* making everyone look stupid."

"So you're telling me that true genius is nothing more than a trick one plays on their audience to snatch a dollar?"

"Right! What a way to become a millionaire, quick. Anyway, we need to watch it, once we get off."

"I'm not watching that-"

"Well, I'm stopping by your house anyway, when we're done here. Ryan and Jeff will be over at my house practicing and rehearsing for their big gig tomorrow night. The last thing I want to be is in their way bugging them. You know how they are. They're like old women when they bicker and fight."

"But I thought you liked being in their way?"

"I do, but I feel like I'm actually getting too old for that sort of thing."

"Really?"

"It's not really all that fun if I find out they actually are trying and they really do suck. You know what I mean?"

"I guess so."

"They're not going to have any groupies we can snatch up, will they?"

"That's actually a good question." Mark said, feeling happy about the possibility.

"Anyway, where heading up now to the gate to get in.

We'll be home in about five minutes. We're arriving early so I'm not sure if my dad is there yet."

"It doesn't matter if he's home, right? He knows me by now." Mark laughed. "We won't wreck the place in his absence, will we?"

"I guess not."

"Bring the tape. We'll watch the stinking movie, but you owe me one."

"Deal!" Mark said, shaking my hand.

"Don't forget to rewind it when we finish."

"No worries. My video store doesn't charge for that stupidity by the customer."

"That's good." I said. "Hey, did you hear that the internet is now getting involved with renting out videos on DVD?"

"I heard about that. It's called *Netflix.* You rent the movies online and they ship them to you based on what you place in your queue. Not sure how the DVDs don't get smashed in the mail, though."

"Maybe it's a flash in a pan? What do you think?"

"I don't think so." He said. "I see it as the next phase in the media revolution. Plus I'll back anything that can get rid of late fees. You do know that's the main revenue stream for all these corporations like Blockbuster. They bank big bucks off of it."

"Wouldn't it be nice if we could do away with them one day?"

"Sure, why not?" I agreed, making light of the subject.

The bus came to a stop as we got up from our seat heading down the aisle way to exit.

"See you boys, Monday." Mrs. Newman waved as we walked off.

"You too," we replied, walking out towards my house, allowing the weekend to officially begin.

Chapter Nine

The only scene that anyone remembers from "The Blair Witch Project" is that moment near the end when our lead heroine has the camera panned on her face with the stinging fear that she would be the next victim taken by the infamous ghost legend.

It would be plastered all over poster boards, sold to the masses and then fished back out to us as the biggest mislead ever concocted on film. Forcing Hollywood elites to take notice of this new hoax of documentary style filmmaking spawning countless knockoffs and spoofs for the many years that followed.

One could say it was ahead of its time in capturing an element of "Do It Yourself" theatrics mixed with complete insanity made by college kids who just wanted to have fun messing with other people's heads while their parents weren't around during finals week.

"Well, that was a complete and total waste of my time." I criticized, switching off the VCR while trying to reexamine my brain from the warped message the film was trying to convey.

"Im pretty sure this movie was nothing more then some cheap ripoff of a foreign film nobody's ever heard of before."

"What do you mean?" Mark challenged, feeling threatened.

"I see Oscar potential here." He debated, still munching on

the popcorn that was made specifically for the viewing.

"Are you like Siskel and Ebert? Want to give it two thumbs up while you're at it too?"

"All I'm saying is that it took some guts to produce a film of this stature."

"Rolling around and pretending to be chased by a ghost is held to a high standard these days? At least *The Usual Suspects*" had a good line at the end to give meaning to the madness. What was it, again?"

"The greatest trick the Devil ever pulled was convincing the world he didn't exist." Mark said using air quotes.

"And just like that - *POOF*! He was gone." I finished, stealing the last of the popcorn left in the bowl.

"Hey, that was mine."

"Don't be such a baby. I let you watch your stupid movie so be nice."

"You're just too critical." He said. "Maybe a second viewing will help change your mind."

"No thank you, I have better things to watch, like trying to make sense of whatever the hell George Lucas created with Jar Jar Binks."

"Now *that* we can both agree on was a total waste of -"

A knock pounded at the door interrupting Mark's train of thought.

"Who is it?" I asked, unaware and assuming that no one else was home.

"It's *only* dad. Open up."

"Dad?" I thought. "Come in, door's open."

"You have Mark over here," He noticed, "That's what the screaming I heard was coming down the hall was, wasn't it?"

"I wasn't screaming, Mr. Chase."

"Yeah you were." I teased.

"What are you boys doing home so early, anyway?"

"There was a bomb threat at the school this morning." Mark answered, filling him in.

"That's probably why Barry was trying to get in contact with me earlier then."

"Barry contacted you?" I said, unsure in Dad's answer.

"I needed some help at the store this morning and he called up saying that he was getting off early from school but was on his way to see Jill. He didn't really clarify why.

" Oh, I see. You didn't suspect he'd be skipping class?"

"No, when that happens, the principal normally calls up." He laughed. "He's a good kid, he just acts dumb sometimes. I was the same way."

"Oh, right," I said, smirking. "You were the rebellious type too, weren't you?"

"Sometimes," He answered. "Anyway, I'm only on my lunch break right now, I can use your help if you want to come along and stock up some shelves. We had a few extra orders coming in that need to get worked out."

"Work, Mr. Chase?" Mark responded. "You do know we're only teenagers, right?"

"I'm aware of that. I wasn't asking you, Mark."

"Good, because I have my own dad to get angry at when it comes to child labor."

"I'll go with you, dad." I said, trying to find my shoes which were hidden underneath my bed.

"We gave you and Barry both separate rooms and this is what you do to it?" He remarked, noticing the mess of dirty clothes all over the floor that were nowhere near the hamper.

"I'm working on it. Give me time. I'll eventually get to it."

"Be thankful I'm not mom," he shrugged. "She's more demanding."

"I guess I'm going to get ready to go." Mark replied, getting up, taking his book bag, beginning to feel un-welcomed.

"I guess I'll call you when I get back."

"Sounds good." he said, exiting the room.

"Be ready in about ten minutes, okay, kiddo?"

"Give me a chance to change clothes and I'll be there in a sec."

Dad left too, leaving me alone in the depths of my own dirty despair.

Chapter Ten

My dad wasn't the modern-day helicopter parent. That's not to say he didn't try to understand our lives and fly in when we needed him. He just opted out when possible and socialized with us only when it worked for his own benefit.

In such cases, this meant calling for further assistance at the local RadioShack, where he supervised downtown near the mall.

He treated Barry and me as his two little helpers which is actually a nicer way of putting it then some might suspect. Barry wasn't one to criticize the job since dad was able to pay him a wage for the work that he put in during the summer.

It was nothing fancy to say the least. We were basically stock boys able to get our hands on the coolest new gadgets the store brought in keeping us always in the loop and ahead of the game on such modern technologies that were springing up ahead of the new millennium.

The drive over allowed Dad to bounce around philosophies with the hope it could suggest building better communication with both of his boys.

It probably was his best effort to drill as much information into our brains when he had us inside his motor vehicle.

"So, what's new in school?" He asked, hand-knobbing

through the radio stations, searching for something to find.

Settling on the oldies station, as if there was ever any doubt. John Fogerty blaring out, *"Do-do-do - looking out my back door!"*

"My English teacher got back in touch with me today about the paper I submitted for the *English Final.*

"Oh, really?" He shrugged with amusement. "Are you still thinking you'll become a writer some day? You're going to need a scholarship because I'm not sure we can provide that."

"I really don't know." I answered. "I'm good at it but I'm not sure how much of a commitment I want to put into it. I enjoy doing it for fun but that's about it."

"You know what I mean?"

"Well," he cautioned, "If you want a job where you can work for yourself and be more independent, commitment is key."

"That's about what I figured."

"It's also problematic because everyone's going to turn against you in a heartbeat if you do that. We live inside this *"they hate you because they ain't you"* mindset."

"People can be cruel, can't they?"

"That's just human nature. It's either that, or work for a company where they tell you what to do and what to think without any hope of having a mind of your own."

"Jesus, that sounds like slavery, doesn't it?"

"Yep!" Dad chuckled. "Well that's sorta the way the real world works in a nutshell. You learn how to play the game. And sometimes it's rigged against you from the start. Education can be the only way out if you're fortunate to go that route."

"That's sad and yet ironic."

"How so?"

"School is the place nobody wants to go and yet you're saying that without it, common sense is dead."

"I guess I am saying that, ain't I?" He warned. "School sells us common sense that we then use in our everyday lives."

"I never thought of it that way. I always figured Common Sense was just something everyone had but never used."

"No," Dad chuckled. "It has to be sold just like anything else. And when you're young, nobody thinks about it, right? They just kinda assume it's there, never really knowing how to use it properly when they need it most."

"I guess I see your point. My generation is just so full of crap, playing video games and all that, simple things get in the way."

"You boys don't know how lucky you have it. Your mom and I tried to raise you right. You tend to be more of a realist about things, which is probably why you tend to think and be more analytical about things."

"I guess." I shrugged, "I'm not cursed, am I?"

"Anyway," He continued, ignoring my statement, attempting not to go off track. "We all have goals and ambitions. That's ultimately what keeps us going in life. If you want to pursue writing, I say go for it."

"Well, what about you? Did you ever want to be in retail sales when you grew up?"

"I enjoy the business but it is not what I'd thought I'd be doing with my life."

"What are you saying then?"

"I'm saying you have to find your own path but know too that you already have a good head start then some. Especially more so than your brother or me ever did."

"Gotcha," I pondered, putting on my headset preparing to escape the conversation. "I still have a few more years before I need to worry about that. I'll put it to rest for now. Wouldn't you say?"

"You should consider things ahead of time because you never know."

"Know what?"

"That life is filled with uncertainty."

"Huh?"

"You know what I mean, like something this weekend could change everything."

"Life can be unpredictable, like that, can't it?

"It sure can."

Chapter Eleven

A retail store can seem like a familiar paradise to the teenage spender. Cementing the cash flow into the economy sector from the money earned by their parent's hefty pocket books.

It was nothing to get spoiled over, as Barry and I discovered over the many years our dad worked in sales, it was the safest environment to play a part in when it came to finding personal nirvana with our closest peer groups.

In the feral world of 20th Century technology, where self proclaimed "nerds" shared a spot at the table, with the hopes to find the perfect toy to put inside their pocket protector, RadioShack was the gateway drug to all those common ecstasy's one could chase after, only appearing customary to get invited in by the electronic sliding doors, pampering their loyal customers with the personal welcome mat that could make Count Dracula blush.

"How's it going?" A greeter expressed with a firm handshake. A name tag simply reading - Ernie, on his proper dress attire. A name I was familiar with first-hand.

"Not too bad," I answered. "How's everything going around here?"

"Everything's fine." He replied while continuing to shake my hand off.

"How's Barry doing these days? I haven't seen him

around since school started up again. We had a blast last summer working here. I hope he's doing fine."

"He's good," I said, feeling he was going on with his open reception. "He's got himself a girlfriend. He's not really around much. You know that bit?"

"I did, but then my girlfriend just dumped me a while back so that may not be a pretty thing if you ask me."

"Sorry to hear that."

"Ahh no worries. She was a bitch, anyway. I'm actually glad it's over. Be safe and single while you can. Dating is not a pretty thing no matter what age you are. It can definitely be cold out there if you know what I mean."

"I'll consider that when my time comes." I said, not trying to be amused.

"What brings you by this afternoon anyway? Felt like skipping school with dad's approval?" He laughed, as dad walked in after parking the car.

"Something like that."

"Ernie, don't forget to check the money in the cash register before you leave tonight." Dad reminded, heading into the backroom.

Ernie Houston, for my story's sake, was dad's newest assistant, helping close up shop, doing all the clerical duties whenever the boss was away. One could think he was on the good side to be my dad's right hand.

A recent high school graduate, looking for any job to help kick start a career while putting anything "professional" on a resume that would be beneficial for the climb up the ladder of success. Hoping too to pay his way towards college doing double duty with night classes when his shifts allowed for it.

"So, what's really been going on with you, man?" He

asked, knowing we were finally alone to talk.

"School got a bomb threat this morning."

"Are you serious, man?"

"No, someone really called it in. Pretty sure it was all a hoax. It got everyone excited, though. Got us to leave early."

"Ah, that makes sense then. Dang! Didn't think that kinda stuff happened around here."

"I guess I'm not too surprised. We have a lot of shady characters lurking around campus these days. Some dude just got suspended for writing inappropriate things about people we know on the school bus. They're really cracking down on that type of behavior."

"I'm glad I graduated when I did. Even if it was only five years ago."

"We're kinda living in the belly of the beast these days. High school is no joke."

"I'm not too worried. I only have to put up with it for another three years."

"Hey, mind helping me stock up the shelves. Let's flip the script on the subject. I don't want to get too depressed."

"That's why I'm here, remember?"

"Oh yeah, right. I forgot."

"Anyway, we just got a new shipment of AV cables for these TVs in stock."

"Those juggernauts?" I questioned, looking directly at those old 30' inch heavy lifters.

"Yeah, those things. Wouldn't it be cool if we could watch television coming directly from the walls instead of having to carry those around?"

"What like a flat screen?"

"Something like that. It would save us on the costs to transport those damn suckers around."

"Maybe in a few years. The way tech is improving, I wouldn't be surprised. I'm pretty sure Circuit City will get them when they become available. They're more into home entertainment and all that junk, right?"

"Everyone wants to live like a millionaire, these days. Don't they?"

"Only in America, right?"

"That reminds me, you don't believe any of the shit they are saying about the new millennium, do you?"

"About what?"

"Y'know that the year 2000 will be the end all of society and computers as we know it."

"Dude, you got yourself watching too much of the nightly news. Don't turn conspiratorial on me now."

"Yeah, you're right. It's just nuts, entering a new decade. Besides, I'm thinking of becoming a writer. It's my job to think outside the box."

Ernie's eyebrow raised.

"A writer? Why do you want to be one of those? Don't they live alone and die poor with a pet or something?" He questioned, thinking he was dishing out sound advice. "Here, hold these."

"What do you want me to do with these?"

"Go in the back room and bring the rest of them out front, pronto!"

"Oh." I said, watching him quickly vanish from sight.

Figuring a lackey, like myself, did the clumsy chores while the honorary employee interacted with the customers coming into the store.

"Everything alright, son?" Dad asked, heading into his work zone.

"Where do you keep these hiding?"

"Over there."

"Where?"

"There," he pointed. "In those brown boxes."

"Okay, I see them." I said, as Dad continued to punch numbers into the calculator, looking a little frustrated with himself.

"Maybe I should ask the same to you?"

"Sorry. I'm putting in the data for last month's sales but the numbers are coming up short."

"What are you saying? Someone's not stealing from the store, are they?"

"What makes you say that?"

"I don't know, it just came out. Ernie doesn't look like the type that would sink the store, right?"

"Ernie, no way. He's a good kid. I'm probably not putting in the figures straight."

"That's probably it." I said, putting my arm around his shoulder trying to relax tension.

"Do you get a lot of customers in here on Friday?"

"The usual amount. Why do you ask?"

"Just wondering. I don't want to be here any longer then I have to be."

"I'm paying you to be here. You should feel blessed. There aren't too many other dad's who care enough to do that."

The telephone rang at the desk disrupting our conversation.

Dad answered with his usual greeting, gaining concern before eventually hanging up, looking as if a prize fighter had just jabbed him with a couple right hooks to the face. He became speechless.

"Who was that?"

"Ernie is going to have to bring you back home. I have to go."

"What happened. Who was that?"

"That was mom. She's been in some type a crash. I have to get her."

"Is she hurt?"

"No, I'll discuss details later."

"Oh," I said, as I watched him rush out, reminding himself to grab the *Notre Dame Fightin' Irish* jacket he accidentally left behind his chair.

The one he was seen wearing wherever he went.

Chapter Twelve

I never suffered any major medical setbacks growing up. The occasional checkup to the doctor's office, warning about my health was always touched upon but nothing ever screamed life or death when it came to matters with me or the family.

Which is why the sudden news of my mom's car crash left me tangled and worried.

I headed out of the backroom taking the AV cables, watching Ernie approach quicker than expected, not exactly knowing what to say but handing him the stuff he had asked for anyway.

"Dude, I just saw your dad run off. He told me to drive you home when I could."

"Yeah, that's what he told me too."

"He said that your mom was in a car crash but that she's alright. Apparently, it was a hit and run and she ran into the guardrail which protected her but the car got damaged on the passenger side pretty bad. There was a witness who saw the whole thing and she's going to testify if needed."

"That's good to hear," I replied, with a sorrowful tone in my voice. "He left before really explaining everything to me."

"I can drive you home now if you want. I have a few associates who can help around. You don't need to be here if you don't want to be, kid."

"That sounds good."

"I just need to go to the restroom real fast, I hope you don't mind. I'll come back to get you when I return. Just wait out front for a bit, 'kay? Look around - buy something!"

"Whatever you say."

Ernie exited, leaving me to browse the store deciding instead to swipe a drink from the break room's vending machine and head outside towards the parking lot where I could savor the taste while I waited.

The weather became passable for a typical late Fall afternoon while the spirit of the pending holiday was very much alive. Kids were geared up for the weekend's Halloween activities, acting out their parts, courtesy of the seasonal costume shop located on the other side of the street.

One boy, dressed as young Anakin Skywalker, another as Batman and I think I spotted a little princess, but she looked a little frightened, not wanting to be seen in costume, as if her parents had put her up to it.

"*Hey, Chase!*" a voice barked from behind, turning my head while losing nostalgia for the moment.

It was Ryan Collins. Mark's older brother, in the flesh. In route to give me a nuggie right on the head.

"What are you doing here, Ryan? Don't you have band practice with Jeff to get to or something?"

"Heck yeah! We just stopped by Guitar Planet real quick to get some equipment for our upcoming gig. We're getting a new amplifier. We're going to blow everyone away tomorrow night."

"Can't wait."

"Wait a minute, you're not old enough."

"Duh, moron! And if my memory serves me correct, you're not either."

"Oh, shut up!" He hissed, putting up a fist as if he was ready to belt me.

"What are you doing here, anyway?" He questioned, becoming more impatient, as I continued to sip my can of soda right in front of his face. "And where's my brother, Mark? Aren't you two always together like two peas in a pod?"

"We were at my house this afternoon after school let out but my dad needed help at the store so I left. He went back home, where *you* were supposed to be."

"By the way, my mom was in a wreck."

"You're kidding?"

"No, my dad just got news and left to go get her now. She's okay, though."

"Oh, man, you had me going there for a second. She's a nice lady if you know what I mean. I wouldn't want anything bad to have happened "

"Dude, she's my mom."

"Not like she's *my* mom."

It only made sense now where Mark gained a lot of his personality traits. A clash of heredity with simple stupid human nature never traveled far along the many circles of life.

"I hope she gets well. You'd know I would offer you a ride but my bullet is kind of packed with all this gear inside. I wouldn't want you to feel squished."

My eyes crossed paths with what looked like an old Ford F-150.

"That's not your truck is it?"

"Nah, it's Jeff's. His dad is loaning it to us for the time being."

"Dude, we gotta go." Jeff growled, barging in. "You again, Chase? You're always in my hair."

"I'll never understand why either of you guys don't call me by my first name."

"Why should we?" Jeff deride.

"It just seems proper. Dont ya think?""

"Kid, you gotta graduate to get name recognition around here."

"He's just a freshman so what does he know anyway, right?" Ryan butted, fisting his knuckles with Jeff, acting like they were training to be professional wrestlers.

"Where are your groupies at then?"

"Lexi is at the Halloween store getting her costume ready." Ryan answered.

"Wait, what? You actually have one?"

"You better believe it."

"Here she comes now." Ryan freely remarked as he whistled in her direction, getting attention.

I couldn't believe it. She was actually coming his way, dressed as the *Bride of Chucky*, which could only make sense in the horror show being played out right in front of my eyes.

"Wow!" Ryan screamed with childish excitement. "You look amazing. Just like Jennifer Tilly did in the movie."

"Thanks, my sister did all the makeup."

"So, who's the kid drooling over me?" She pointed, forcing to put my lip back into my mouth, showing uncompromising temptation.

"Just a dork we found lying in the gutter somewhere." Jeff joked.

"He looks pretty cute if you ask me."

"That's just my younger brother's best friend. His dad supervises the RadioShack next door. He can be a pain but we tolerate him when we have to."

"Oh, I see."

"I never knew you cared, Ry" I laughed, knowing they both were full of shit.

"If I were you kid, I wouldn't listen to either one of these assholes." Lexi smiled, having my back.

"Thanks." I complimented, as she placed a gentle kiss on my check before heading off with those two jerks at her side.

Chapter Thirteen

"**T**here you are!" Ernie shouted, looking exhausted, while waving his hands to get my attention. "I thought I told you to wait inside."

"I did but I needed fresh air."

"It's getting colder out here. You want to wind up catching the flu or something?"

"I just wanted to see the scenery. Besides, it's not even winter yet for that sort of thing."

"I suppose," he said, dangling his keys, as we headed towards his car.

"I just saw some kids with their costumes on. I can't believe how time flies."

"You can still dress up for that sort of thing, y'know. You're not that old yet."

"Yeah, my friend's brother is going to one tomorrow night with his girlfriend and their band."

"Oh yeah, that's right. *Hard Luck* has their annual thing going on this weekend, don't they? Are you going to try to sneak in? You need to be over 21 for that, right? I could hook you up with some fake "ids" if you want."

"Really?" I questioned. "I wasn't thinking about it."

"I'm just messing with your head, man." He laughed. "In all honesty, when they do those kinds of blowouts they never card, anyway. All they care about is the money they rank in from the live music. Just be part of a party crowd and they'll never notice any different."

"You sure?"

"Trust me, I've been there, done that before myself." He winked, showing affection. "Now get in the car so I can drive your ass home."

My hands reached the passenger door but nothing opened.

"Genius, the door is locked."

"Oh yeah," he remembered, electronically opening it with the button on his key ring. "Don't need to worry about manually doing that anymore."

"What kind of car is this, anyway?"

"It's a Pontiac Grand AM," he answered. "Still making the monthly payments on it. It gets me where I need to go. That's really all you ask for, right?"

"I wouldn't know but Barry enjoys his."

"I bet."

"So, are you ready for Notre Dame's game tomorrow against Navy?"

"I'm not but my dad is obviously. Why do you ask?"

"My family is military. It's always a big game for us even though we never win against them. Do you follow college football?"

"Not really but my dad does."

"I figured that." He said, smiling. "He's always sporting that jacket when he comes in every morning. Did he go to school there or something?"

"Nah, he was raised Catholic and they were the one team he wanted to root for growing up."

"Oh, I see. I guess it also doesn't hurt that they have that contract with NBC every year."

"Yeah, I mean what other team gets so much recognition? You either love 'em or hate 'em, right?"

"Your dad must have been pretty bummed when they lost to Boston College a few years back."

"You're talkin' about that 1993 screwjob, aren't you?"

"The what," he laughed, showing confusion. "If you want to call it that."

"Well, that's what *he* likes to call it."

"What was it, they beat Florida State in "the game of the century" only to lose to BC, falling out of contention for the championship while Florida State went on to win it all?"

"Yeah, basically. That's why they need a playoff system like the pros, he keeps complaining that to me."

"That makes sense. There's too much politics going about with the bowl committee and their panel of experts. I say let the teams duke it out fair and square and see who wins."

"Yeah."

"Lou Holtz could have won his final championship before retirement. I guess it wasn't meant to be. Bob Davie is a good coach but he's not really taking them anywhere."

"You know what's really funny?"

"What?" I asked, perplexed with the amount of trivial knowledge Ernie was dishing out about college football.

"I guess I never really thought about it but your dad actually reminds me a bit of Sean Astin from that movie."

"Oh yeah, he *loves* that film."

"I'm a big movie buff myself and that one is a classic. I love the scene at the end where he's coming out of the tunnel with all that joy. It brings a tear to my eye every time I watch it."

"Yeah, and that dude from *Swingers* shouting: *"Rudy! Rudy! Rudy!"*

"I agree, that and the Knute Rockne one are superb sport's films. Just win one for the gipper, right?"

"Jesus, it's no wonder why my dad likes you."

"I guess we kind of have the same personality." He gloated, coming upon a red light.

"Hey, look over there." He pointed, gazing and flaunting at the two college aged girls driving in the lane next to us.

"Dude, open up your window!"

"What for?"

"Seriously?"

"I thought you didn't want -"

"Shut up and do it!"

"Hey ladies," He flirted, as I watched the female driver become amused, blowing a kiss back in our direction, rolling down the window for a quick response.

"Wassup, handsome?" She teased.

"Yknow, the same ol' -"

"Sorry but we gotta run!" She giggled, as the light changed colors, leaving us in the dust.

"What did you expect?" I remarked, sounding a bit cold about the experience.

"It never hurts to mingle, dude."

"That chick was hot. Although, I think I heard Celine Dion playing."

"God, I hate that song. That was all my ex wanted to listen to. It may be one of the reasons we split up."

"Really?"

"Seriously, never date a girl who has a crush on Leo DiCaprio. What a waste of time."

"You're so full of wisdom, aren't you?"

"Yes, sir. Are we close to your house, yet? I'm kind of getting sick of driving you around. What are you, my Miss Daisy?"

"Just turn right after the next light and we should be good to go."

"Awesome, by the way, let Barry know if he wants to hangout sometime."

"Sure, I'll let him know when I see him. Thanks again for the ride."

"No problem. I guess I'll see you around too."

"More than likely."

"Keep me updated about your mom if you can."

"You betcha," I concluded, as his car finally reached the driveway to let me out.

Chapter Fourteen

I t was unusual for me to get home before everyone else on a late Friday afternoon.

The way the day was heading, I figured it wouldn't have been the least bit surprising walking into our golden nest to discover pity burglars searching the premises, tracing for riches to be found.

Thankfully, our lot in life was one that wasn't deemed too desirable for such common thieves to rummage through.

"I'm home!" I shouted, opening the door in front of me, knowing I was just playing with my childish instincts of feeling king to my father's castle.

The eerie calm of the room left only with the refrigerator running and the AC cooling off the living space leaving an atmosphere of peace for one to think.

The silence, being broken by the sound of barking, possibly someone eager to meet my acquaintance with the hopeful impression that her family hadn't abandoned her throughout the chaos at hand.

Some say dogs are man's best friend but this Australian Silky Terrier was brought to us simply by the loving care of our mother. I never had a pet growing up but when I entered junior high, mom felt it best to provide us with her own blessing of maturity. Dad obviously wanted the golden retriever but mom convinced him otherwise. "It looked so lonely and yet so cute."

she would tell us the day that she brought it home. It was love at first sight and dad had no real power but to obey. It became a classic case of "Happy wife, happy life."

"Hey, Ginger," I greeted, kneeling down to brush her back, feeling my hands softly glide across such gentle fur. "You're a good girl, aren't you?"

Her tongue sticking out, glossing over my neck, with a yearning to be fed or waiting a delayed walk.

"You wanna go out?" I asked, getting back up to stretch my legs.

Her sudden movements, suggesting she was in dire need to release her bladder.

"Hold on, hold on."

I walked over to the coat rack, grabbing the leash, spotting the telephone's answering machine lighting up with new messages.

"I'll answer them when I get back," I thought, thinking light about the matter. "Come on girl, let's get out of here while it's still light out."

Our neighborhood was relatively pleasant when it came to touring the community. Suggesting new ways for the locals to get out of their homes and socialize.

"*Oh, god,*" I shrieked. "*Not her!*"

Especially those who seemed unattainable and tempting by virtue of seduction like the promiscuous, Jennifer Leigh Murphy. Jogging in attire seeming very unconventional for the time of month.

She was twenty seven, recently married, fixing the eye of every male who spotted her.

"Oh, hey, Barry." She waved, crossing paths.

"Barry's my brother. I'm -"

"Oh yeah, that's right," she paused, stopping to talk. "I keep getting the two of you confused. You could be twins. Has anyone ever told you that?"

"Sometimes," I smiled, amazed she was chatting with me. "Isn't it a little chilly to be jogging out?"

"It's never chilly, gotta keep that heart rate going when you can."

"Your dog is so cute." She smiled, noticing the friendly companion by my side. "How long have you had her?"

"We've had her for a few years now." I said, sounding as manly as I could. "I guess I bear the responsibility of taking her out since my family is away."

"Dogs are a huge responsibility and they're good for kids your age to have. We have one ourselves but my husband normally does dog duty. It's a German Shepherd, a real man's dog."

"What's her name?" She wondered, petting the pooch.

"Ginger."

"That's such a pretty name."

"We named her after her color."

"That makes sense."

"What's your dog's name?" I asked, feeling foolish.

"Barkley," she answered. "Steve's a big sport's fan. I wanted to name him Trapper but he didn't want to listen to me. He's a bit stubborn."

"I'm sorry to hear that."

"Well, I hope you have a good weekend. I have to get going. I don't want my smell to offend you."

"Do you think I could ever be so lucky to find someone like her?" I thought, as she disappeared.

Ginger stared up with a look suggesting I was in over my head.

"Oh look, there's a bush over there."

Ginger rushed, as I waited for her to complete her business.

"Are you happy now?"

From the look on her face she couldn't have been more pleased

"Let's go home."

And in a flash, the race was back on.

Chapter Fifteen

I f there's one thing every pet owner should know it's this: it's never a fair fight when they battle for the attention to get you to do things. You simply let them, knowing, if you don't, they'll surprise you.

That was the current dilemma I was up against with Ginger.

Chasing her around the block included the dodging of at least two community sized trash cans on another's property, the verbal barking disputes with a fellow Jack Russell on the other side of the street, all ending with an infamous, *"Hey kid! Get your mutt off my lawn or else I'll tell your parents!"*

"At least no one called the cops." I thought, laughing it off, unleashing her back into her own domain.

"I think I need to take a shower after that." I figured, sniffing my armpits, heading towards the bathroom. Not making it far before the phone rang, breaking my concentration, beating me to the punch.

"Yeah, wassup?" I answered, sounding a bit agitated.

My brother's voice was heard on the other end of the line.

"Little bro, yeah, I'm just calling to make sure -"

"Are you at Jill's?" I interrupted him, not thinking.

"Actually, yeah, I am. You sound a bit tense. What's up?"

"Why is it that I'm the only one that ever walks Ginger?"

"Mom did give him to you on your birthday, *stupid.* So technically she's *your* dog."

"Don't get arrogant, jackass! By the way, did dad get in contact with you about mom, yet?"

"Yeah, he did," he answered. "That's what I called about, dude. He told me they were at the car doctor looking to fix up the damage that was done. Thankfully they had insurance so it won't cost them much. He also said they were going to go out to dinner afterwards, leaving us to fend for ourselves for the night."

"Are you coming home then?"

"Probably later tonight. I'm taking Jill out to one of those local cheesy haunted houses because it's Halloween weekend. I'm really hoping things will go further then that, if you know what I mean.""

"I get the picture," I said, rolling my eyes and strangling the telephone wire around my neck, attempting not to listen.

"Dude, you have to get a life. Don't be hating on mine. Go out with your *loser* friends if you want tonight."

"Talk with you later." I said, hanging up, tapping the answering machine before heading to the kitchen for a drink.

"*Son of mine!*" Dad's voice spoke loudly into the speaker. "*If you're there, pickup! I hope Ernie brought you back. Oh well, guess you're not there. Anyway, just an update on everything that's been going on, we're at the car doctor at the moment. Mom is talking with Kermit - you know how she is - paranoid they'll overcharge us for something. The car is going to need a paint job - the guardrail messed it up pretty bad, thankfully the motor and everything else is still working. Just the typical nut cutting into mom's lane - ruining her day and putting us out. Anyway - we're fine. I don't want to worry you anymore then you should.*

We called up the insurance and everything's squared away. We're going out to eat after this. There's leftover pizza in the fridge if you need something to eat. Also, Ginger needs her walk, I fed her before we both left. Oh, and by the way, in case I forget, I may not be home tomorrow, can you do me a quick favor and record the Notre Dame game on the VCR? The tape is already in the -"

"Message deleted." the recording abruptly ended, as my fingers threw it in the trash.

I took the leftover pizza out of the fridge, placing it in the microwave, giving myself time to do dad's command. Returning back into the kitchen until the telephone rang once more.

"What do you want now, *Barry?"*

"Barry?"

"Oh, it's just *you*." I said, realizing my mistake.

"Of course it's me, what, you can't remember the sound of your best friend by now? I've only known you since -"

"Sorry Mark - it's just been a rough afternoon since you left earlier."

"Wanna talk about it?"

"Not really. Are you like Oprah or something?"

"All I'm saying is you need to be more open and inclined with your feelings."

"You're not turning PC, are you?"

"If the chicks dig it, I may have to." He laughed.

"Anyway," I ignored. "My dad and mom are out for the evening. I need something to do or somewhere to go. I might bum and come over to your place."

"That's fine, you can come here if you want. My parents never care, anyway. I've actually been hanging out in the garage with Ryan and Jeff, apparently, there's a girl over at the house."

"Oh yeah, I know, I met her before - Lexi."

"How do you know her?"

"I saw those two idiots before when I was helping my dad. She came over dressed up for Halloween."

"That makes sense then. Yeah, she's hot as *fuck*!"

"She even kissed me." I gloated.

"You *frickin'* dawg!"

"Jealous?"

"*No*, it was a sympathy kiss. That doesn't bother me."

"Maybe so, but at least it was something."

"Okay, whatever you say," he whined, cackling into the receiver, sounding as if we were losing connection. "I'll see you over here soon, then, right?"

"Yeah, give me about an hour. I must wash up first. My dog and I took a long walk around the block."

"See you then." He remarked, before hanging up.

Chapter Sixteen

The visits to Mark's house were filled with those oblivious moments which lacked any parental guidance.

If I thought my family were aloof, it would only appear double in an environment such as his but maybe then that was just my perception since I was an outsider looking in.

In fairness, his parents were similar to mine, his dad was a route driver and his mother was a teacher, which meant that their time together was filled with non-existent mornings coupled with evenings where they appeared stressed enough to want to just relax and watch nothing but the nightly news in solitude, forgetting the fact they had children altogether.

On days when I came over, I'd notice that distance. His dad would open the door and simply say - "He's in his room," or "He's at the park, you can meet him there." Using very little dialogue, as to show they were nothing more than ghosts floating around the premises, unconscious of any other human existence.

Sometimes I'd bypass the cold welcoming and head directly to their garage, knowing if they spotted me hanging out with Mark, it wouldn't raise questions. They knew who I was, which I guess was a catch-22, being a teenager, it didn't fit well with any wannabe rebellious ego.

"Do your parents know that your brother is in a rock band?"

I asked Mark, welcoming myself into a loud ruckus of noise.

"Yeah - I think so, but they're old, y'know?" He answered, as the band continued to play, making it difficult to understand the words that were coming out of his mouth. *"Ryan soundproofed everything in here, so as long as the neighbors aren't complaining, I really don't think they give a crap."*

"WHAT DID YOU SAY?"

"I SAID THEY DON'T!"

The music stopped, as Mark applauded, showing gratitude to the musicians in the room.

Darrell and Frank weren't around. It was only Ryan, Jeff and Lexi, who was sitting on a stool with her makeup smeared, smoking a cigarette, looking a bit different since I last saw her.

"So where's everybody else?" I asked, waving.

"You again?" Jeff disputed with displeasure. "You're like a cockroach. We can't get rid of you."

"Now, now, he's my friend." Mark kindly addressed. "I told him he could come over. He had no other plans tonight so I figured he'd chill here with us."

"What's so wrong with a little constructive criticism, anyway?" I snickered.

"Why I outta -" Jeff retaliated, raising his drumstick ready to fire.

"Okay, okay, calm down everyone!" Mark hollered, playing peacekeeper. "I have to talk with you outside, anyway."

"What for?"

"Something big, now come on!"

Mark grabbed my arm pushing me out.

"Jesus, it's getting cold out here. What did you want to say?"

Mark looked at me with a grin.

"We found out who called in the bomb threat this morning."

Mark stopped, waiting for any response.

"Who was it then?"

"Do you know a guy named Brian Jenkins?"

"Not really? Should I?"

Mark's face turned puzzled.

"Oh wait, he's our brother's age so maybe not."

"Well keep going. What's this about, really?"

"A year ago there were rumors going around about him that he was the "lookout guy" in that murder that happened in the bathroom stall near the interstate. You remember, that robbery that went down last summer with that old man that made the news?"

"Oh yeah, I remember that."

"Well anyway, he dropped out of school about a year ago and guess who we found out was a close relative?"

"Joey, right?"

"Bingo!"

"It's all coming together, isn't it?"

"Nice to find solace, if you ask me."

"You think Joey was involved too with this conspiracy?"

"I don't know, but I don't think we'll be seeing him again anytime soon."

"Do you know if they questioned him about it yet?"

"I haven't heard anything, Ryan just told me everything he knew when he got back home."

"So this is all *"he said"* information?"

"Yeah, but I wonder what caused him to do it."

"Beats the hell out of me. Maybe he just wanted to be a copycat like the rest. These events are making front page hype. Maybe he wanted in?"

"I guess there *are* certain reasons why it's best not to live near school, right?"

"You're tellin' me. Too many weirdos around. Was that the big secret you needed to tell me?"

"You were expecting something else?"

"Nah, I guess not. It just seems out of our hands now, like the mystery is gone."

"I hear ya. I was actually hoping to get another few days off because of it. It looks like that won't happen now, right?"

"I doubt it."

"Anyway, let's get back inside before we freeze to death."

"I'm with ya," Mark replied, reopening the door in front of us as Ryan and Jeff were packing their instruments appearing to leave.

"Well little bro, we'd hate to pop your bubble but we're getting ready to head out of here."

"Where are you going?"

"We're going to meet up with Darrell and Frank up at *Hard Luck*."

"But I thought your big gig wasn't until tomorrow?"

"It is, but we're going to hang out with them tonight. It is Friday after all, douchebags. We also may go back to Frank's place to rehearse some more when we finish up there."

"Can we come with you guys then?" Mark asked.

"It's only for mature adults and not bratty kids, remember?"

"Oh shut the fuck up man. You know they don't card until after nine."

"What time is it now?"

I looked at my watch finding an answer.

"It's only a quarter after six."

"Good. We can get something to eat and then stay awhile. No one will tell, right?"

"How are you idiots going to get back home then?"

"I'll drive them," Lexi said, getting off of the stool making her acquaintance shown.

"What?" Ryan questioned, appearing dumbfounded .

"I'm serious," she demanded. "Drop me off at my house before you go so I can get my car and I'll bring them over."

"Really? Are you nuts?"

Mark and I remained silent as Lexi did our bidding.

"Ry, we only live once. Let them have this."

"Whatever you say," he sighed, caving in to the girl of his dreams. "I'm going to tell my folks I'm heading to Jeff's before they suspect anything. You two turds can just wait in my car. I'll be there in a sec."

Chapter Seventeen

"*H*ey now you're an All Star get your game on go play - hey now, you're a rockstar - get the show on - get paid!*"

"Gosh, I love this song!" Lexi howled as we huddled together in Ryan's ride with the radio on full blast.

"It's good to know somebody else does." I concurred, listening in the back seat, singing along.

"You know what Ryan," She insisted. "You need to play more songs like this in your set."

"No way!" He complained. "We want to be taken seriously. This is too pop for our sound."

"You're so full of shit, y'know that? Music like this is fun. I'm sick of all those Nine Inch Nails songs you cover. You kind of suck at them if you want my honest opinion. You're not an art rocker."

"That's an *alternative rocker*! Mind you."

Mark and I giggled, trying not to let it show. It was like watching doomed honeymooners with the fireworks already exploding right in front of our eyes.

"Didn't you guys use to tell me I looked a little like Trent Reznor?" Mark asked, laughing, while trying to ease the blow.

"Oh yeah, I remember, before you got your haircut last year."

"How come you didn't go goth?"

"*Can you two please shut up back there!*"

"It's still a free country, isn't it?"

"Yeah, but I'm driving. So sue me. And yes, I remember the long hair. You looked like a *damn* hippie!"

"Jesus, give a man some power and they think they rule the world."

"Not the world, idiot, just the car."

"We're so sorry if we're spoiling the ride." Mark sighed in defense to Lexi, who seemed to be enjoying the obnoxious banter.

"Nah, forget it. We're all good. What's a joy ride without bickering? I have sisters of my own at home. I totally understand."

"Good, because I didn't want you thinking we were the only ones."

"Really?"

"By the way, I liked the "Bride of Chucky" cosplay for Halloween."

"Thanks, it looked good until your brother started manhandling me in the garage messing up the makeup. I've never really done anything like that before. I want to go all out this year and have fun with it. "

"Are you guys doing anything for the holiday or are you "too old" for that sort of stuff?"

"We'd like to go to the thing tomorrow night but we're afraid they won't let us in."

"It's better that we're going tonight," I interrupted, "All the party animals will be out tommorow getting drunk and wasted."

"But that's why I wanna go!"

"Both of my sisters are going up to Mertle's Farm tonight. They heard about some Haunted House that's over there. They wanna sneak in after dark. They say the place is "spook central" during the night."

"I think that may be the same place Barry is taking Jill."

"Oh snap," Lexi jumped, "You're Barry Chase's brother, aren't you?"

"Yeah," I answered, as she looked deeply amused, like someone who just figured out the answer to final jeopardy. "What gave it away?"

"I don't know, I wasn't really thinking about it before now. You do look like him a lot."

"Well, we are only freshman. No one pays attention to us, anyway. We're just afterthoughts in the high school walk of shame, if you ask me."

"Don't worry about any of that. In a few years, all that age gap crap won't mean Jack shit."

"I hear ya," Mark agreed, kissing up.

"Don't listen to her," Ryan cutted back in, "You'll always be a loser in my book, bro."

"Is that anyway to talk about *your* brother?"

Ryan laughed, ignoring her question, continuing the drive.

"Do either of you guys *smoke?*"

"Those two, smoke? Get real." Ryan giggled.

"She wasn't asking you, nimrod!"

Lexi took out her pack of cigarettes, handing one to each of us.

"What's a little peer pressure, right?"

"My brother sneaks in his nicotine fits when he drives." I said, doing my best to sound mature. "Our parents don't want him smoking in the house. To be honest - I'm not even sure if they know."

"Typical parents, they never understand, do they?"Gasped Mark with anticipation. "Light me up, please."

Lexi took out the lighter, playfully shoving it back into her pocket.

"I'm sorry boys, I just can't do it."

"Wha-" groaned Mark, with the cigarette still dangling in his mouth.

"You actually believed her?" Ryan mockingly rumbled, giving her a high five while stealing the cigarette for himself.

"Everyone here is so full of shit. I want to smell like teen spirit too."

"Ha," I chuckled. "I don't think that's what Kurt meant when he wrote that song."

"No," Ryan added. "He was actually using the term because it was a girl's deodorant."

"You sure know your rock music, don't you?" Lexi suggested, still singing along to the radio. "Oh hey, you just bypassed my house."

"Oh shoot!"

"No big deal. Just make a quick u-turn around."

"You will have money when we hit the bar, right, Lex?"

"Seriously, you didn't just ask a girl that?"

Ryan dazed confused, as Mark and I bursted out with laughter.

"My looks always do the charm when it comes to that. You three are on your own, though."

"Rest assured, Darrell and Frank will cover us."

"That's good, anyway, give me about twenty minutes, okay? I'll meet you guys there when I'm ready."

"Sure thing," he said, not trying to get back on her bad side.

"We'll see you there then, right?"

"Indeed."

Chapter Eighteen

"What do you guys think of Lexi?" Ryan asked smiling, while puffing smoke.

"The better question is - what does she see in you, anyway?"

"Bro - I'm a sexy looking beast, it ain't my fault you can't see it."

"Oh, whatever. I can't wait till she begins to see more of you. Y'know, see what you're really like on the inside. She'll dump you faster-"

"Hey, knock it off guys!" I bawled. "You two sound just like my brother and me at times."

"So, what's wrong with that?"

"I don't know, maybe I figure you two could set a better example or something."

"Are you serious?"

"Nah, not really." I said, laughing it off.

"So, how long has your brother been seeing his girlfriend, dude? Since we're on this topic and all."

"I'm not sure. I think they hooked up a few months ago. I've never been able to figure out how, though. "

"Are you two boys jealous of us or something?" Ryan chimed. "Need a technique or two to try? I can probably teach one, if you want."

"Not really, Ry, I mean it's not like any of these stupid high school romances ever seem to last, right? Besides, Lexi is just a groupie you picked up, she would never be interested otherwise. Once the band disbands - watch out, it'll all be over faster than you can say *Silicon Honey*."

"If you say so, chap! But the point is simple, I got what I want and that's how the game is played, son."

"I'm not your son, idiot! I mean, seriously, do you even know what Lexi is short for dumbass?"

Ryan didn't answer leaving the question open for debate.

"If you ask me it could make for a great porn star name."

"Ha," Mark chuckled, beginning to think up ideas. "How about Lexi Belvedere or Lexi Munroe?"

"You guys are nuts. I want you to know this is the last time I try to do anything nice.

"It wasn't even you, it was Lexi who was kind enough to want to bring us back."

"Lexi or not, If anything happens tonight, you two are on your own. And one thing is sure, you better not squeal anything to mom and dad about this or I'll kill you myself!"

"Ry, you know you don't mean that."

"Wanna bet? I could stop the car right now and have you idiots walk the next five miles up to *Hard Luck* by yourself."

"You wouldn't -"

"Watch!"

"Ok, ok - I'm not really in the mood to want to hitchhike."

"*HEY RYAN - WATCH OUT!*" I screamed, as I noticed the momentum of the car inch closer to the one in front of us, rearing potential disaster.

"*HOLY SHIT! GOD DAMN RED LIGHT!*"

Ryan jammed the brakes before contact was successfully made.

"*JESUS, THAT WAS A CLOSE ONE!*"

"*DUDE - YOU ALMOST GOT US KILLED!*" Mark yelled, not partaking in any dramatic irony.

"You guys okay back there?"

"We looked at each other, a little bewildered, but still alive and well.

"Yeah, thanks for asking." Mark said, shockingly acknowledging a care from his elder sibling.

"Yeah, thankfully, there was no car behind us. That would have been bad news."

"Yeah, thank goodness. I'm so sorry guys. I have to pay more attention to the road."

"Well, we almost experienced our first accident together, buddy." Mark smiled, trying to make light of the matter.

"I wonder if this was how my mom felt."

"Your mom?"

"I'll explain later."

"*HEY BUDDY! WHAT THE HELL WAS THAT?*" A man's voice shouted as he turned and rolled down his window. "*I SAW YOUR HEADLIGHTS IN MY REAR VIEW. YOU CAME ZOOMING IN, YOU ALMOST REAR ENDED ME! YOU FUCKING BUFFOON!*"

The three of us remained silent trying to stay calm, not making any sudden movements, in fear for our own safety.

The light turned green, forcing the driver to storm off,

allowing the three of us feeling gracious about his exit from the scene.

"Pheww, that was close." Ryan uttered to himself, swiping the sweat from his forehead.

"Holy crap! I thought that guy was going to get out of his car and beat you half to death."

"Me too!" I agreed." Well, at least not the last part."

"You owe us big time for this," Mark demanded, spilling out his blackmail ransom quicker than loan shark could collect what's due.

Ryan remained quiet, not letting his emotions show.

"I'll find a way to get you guys a beer tonight when the time is right."

"You gonna be buying us a brewskie? You're not even old enough to drink."

"Don't worry, I have my connections."

The two of us shared in the delight with modest anticipation that the night had just gotten wilder by the passing aura of pretty girls, bad breath and lustful temptations.

"Who knew this guy had friends in high places?" Mark snickered, jabbing me in the elbow. "Remember I call dibs on any that come my way."

I did my best to stay chill without getting too overly excited.

"What the hell do you think is going to happen tonight? Ryan interrupted. "You're not getting laid. Jesus, is that what you have in mind?"

"Hey, we can dream, can't we?"

"Yeah, that's about it!"

"The way the day's been going, just a night out is fine by

me."

"Mark, you think anyone we know will show up?"

"Beats me, how many other people are like us in the first place? To be fair, I think we're below the radar when it comes to big crowds and social interactions with people our own age, anyway."

"Yeah, I'm hoping we don't recognize anyone, I wouldn't want this going about causing rumors in the halls."

"Oh, man! You know what that would mean for us, we would be legends. Although they'd probably kick us out if anyone narced on us."

"Yeah, especially with what happened today."

Mark nodded, coming to a complete understanding.

"Well guys, we finally made it." Ryan announced, driving into the parking lot, which looked pretty full for a Friday night crowd.

"What time do you got?"

"It's only 7:30." I said to Ryan, looking down at my watch."

"That's perfect, they're not carding yet. We can catch the cheap karaoke set before the night owls get in. After that, it's every man for himself."

"Is Jeff here yet?"

Ryan scanned the area looking for his Ford.

"Yep, there it is, on the other side. I'll leave with him when the time comes but I'll let you guys know beforehand, alright?"

"Sounds like a plan." Mark said, unbuckling his seatbelt. "*Holy crap* - I just realized I buckled myself up. I never do that. I just saved my own life back there and didn't know it."

"You're quite the character sometimes," I smirked ,

listening in on his own disbelief. "Don't be surprised if you wind up in one of my stories someday."

"You're a natural comedian, aren't you?" He replied.

"Not really, but I guess only when I try to be."

Chapter Nineteen

"**Y**o Ryan!" Jeff hollered, acknowledging us in the parking lot. "Come here."

"I see you brought Tweedle Dee and Tweedle Dum along with you."

"Yeah well..."

"Nevermind them, I got good news for us."

"What's that?"

"I heard that *Mudflush* is dropping out of the competition tomorrow night."

"Holy shit! They were the front runners, weren't they?"

"Yeah, so you know what that means, right?"

"One less band to worry about."

"Not only that, but with them out, we can steal one of their backup singers. I just received some contact info we could use to snatch one up."

"What do you mean?"

"You see that chick over there?"

Ryan's eyes rolled near the front of the building to a lady wearing denim jeans with red dye in her hair.

"Her?" he pointed.

"Yeah, her name is Tara Angela. I was chatting with her

about it."

"Sure you were.."

"Oh, shut up. You know you'd try to hook up with her too if she were available."

"That's probably true, but we don't have time, do we? The gig is a day away for God's sake. We can't teach her any of our original stuff."

"It doesn't matter. An extra person on stage can give us better credibility with the judges. We'll use her for one of the cover songs so that it won't be difficult. Heck, we can use all the help we can get, right?"

"Why'd she drop out anyway?"

"Creative differences, I assume. What difference does it make? This is our shot, man. We need to take it."

"What does Darrell and Frank think about it?"

"That's what I was going to talk with them about when I get inside."

"So they don't even know?"

"Not yet."

"Figures," Ryan said, shaking his head. "I say if it's alright with them then it's okay by me. They have more control over the say than either of us do."

"Cool, cool, yeah that's what I thought too. I'll see you guys, I'll let you know what they say."

"No problem, Jeff." Ryan declared. "And good luck trying to pick her up tonight. I thought you were raised Catholic."

"I was, but not tonight. We'll see what happens."

The three of us laughed as we watched him rush inside to distribute the news.

"So, what about you two?" Ryan asked, as we waited

with anticipation to check in.

"I'm going to wait for Lexi to show up," Mark said. "I wanna feel confident when being escorted in by a woman."

"You sly dog." I uttered.

"That's actually not a bad idea." Ryan said, winking. "I'm going to head on in and find us a table. If she doesn't show up, in say, fifteen minutes, come on in. I don't want you getting "carded" out accidentally."

"But we still have time."

"It doesn't matter, my rules, now play by them or get walkin'."

"Jesus, you're a little bitch!"

"Hey, I think I see my brother's car over there." I interrupted, removing myself from a potential war of words being splattered about in public.

"Oh yeah, it is," Mark replied, walking over to get a better look. "I wonder what he's doing over here."

"I don't know."

"I thought you said he was going to some haunted house?"

"Maybe he's doing that afterwards. It's not even eight yet. There's plenty of time to go to that, I suppose."

A horn honked from behind, scaring us half to death.

"Hey boys!" Two female voices shouted in our direction.

Our heads spun quick but the car cut to an angle where it was unrecognizable to see who was calling.

"Was that Lexi?"

"It didn't sound like her." Mark answered. "I didn't get a good look to tell, though."

The car pulled into an empty space, as we held our

breath.

"Well this is different?" Mark questioned, watching two women we had never seen before get out, looking a little intoxicated, as if they probably weren't even registered with the state to be behind the wheel.

"*You fellas looking for some fun tonight?*" The woman asked, freeing up a rhetorical response for someone like Mark to catch.

"We sure are!"

"*Nice!*" the woman responded. "*I'm Jesse Adams - this here is my girlfriend, Bobbie-Jo. She's a little shy but she won't bite. You boys look young -*"

"We're Freshman at State." Mark lied, attempting to underplay his hand.

"*You don't have to lie to us,*" Jessie responded, "*You two look like high schoolers - don't worry, we won't let the cat out of the bag. It was only a few years ago for us too.*"

"*Jessie!*" Bobbie-Jo replied with embarrassment. "*You don't have to tell them everything, do you?*"

Bobbie-Jo waved my way, reaching into her pocket, taking out what appeared to be a pack of gum.

"*Jesus, girl - what's a little small talk. It's not like we're hooking up with them or anything. We're just here for the excitement of the evening, remember?*"

I could sense Mark's heart beginning to pace faster by her bold persona.

"*So did you two fellas bring anyone with you or are you playing the field?*"

"I'm actually waiting for my girl to show up." Mark voiced with more dishonesty spewing from his mouth.

"*That's alright! I hope you boys save us a dance when the DJ*" starts spinnin'."

"You bet!" He replied back, feeling as if he had won some type of victory.

"Well - if you're waiting for your girlfriend to show, we don't want to -"

"No, that's not a problem." He bashfully explained, covering up his own misdeeds, while holding both girls by the shoulder. "I wouldn't mind escorting you two fine ladies to the door."

"Well, that's sweet of you."

"Well, are you coming or what?" He asked me, as I kept my distance.

"I thought you were waiting for Lexi to show up?"

"This is better my friend."

"I'll pass for now," I said, remaining vigilant with the growing nightlife. "I'll meet y'all in there after Lexi arrives."

"Whatever, dude," He said making his way towards the entrance. "I don't need you to blow my night."

Chapter Twenty

I t wasn't long after Mark ditched me when I witnessed it with my own eyes.

Lexi hadn't arrived, causing the wait to become increasingly unbearable until I heard sounds of a woman storming out of the bar as if being harassed by a predator.

Her voice was recognizable, familiarizing it with the recent memory that my brother was in the realm of the establishment where it followed.

I spotted her off guard but remained a phantom fearing any interference would look shady if caught.

It was Jill, she was outside of the entrance with a guy approaching appearing drunk, at best. Coming straight from his vehicle like he had phoned up with an attempt to patch things up.

My mind immediately turning to the possibilities of where Barry might be and why he wasn't in attendance for this unusual outing.

"Jill - we can work it out!" The man complained. *"You can't do this to me. Especially now, not under these circumstances!"*

"Why are you over here?" she panicked. "I told you to stop calling my house. If my father ever finds out he'll kill us. This isn't normal. You need to leave - *now!"*

The man remained frantic but with other people around, he attempted to pace the pavement not letting any excitement show.

"But Jill - I know that it's mine!"

"It's over, Brett. You have to go." Jill fought, hoping her words wouldn't cause a scene.

Security began looking, but at the moment they weren't moving.

"If you're drunk I can call someone to give you a ride. A taxi is always available." Jill insisted, holding up her arm to camouflage an otherwise awkward sequence of events.

"Please, I don't want you to get hurt. We can talk about this another time. This isn't the place, please?"

The man put his arms around her, collapsing into a brief bear hug, where what was being spoken underneath was untraceable back to my ears.

The moment abruptly ended, as the man made his way towards his car while Jill collected her belongings before heading back to the bar for shelter.

In a matter of seconds, everything got erased as if this lover's quarrel was nothing but a distant memory already drifting in the breeze.

Was it possible this "Brett" character she was referring to was the ex-boyfriend, the man whom Barry had replaced after they started dating?

I warned him not to get involved but he wouldn't listen.

In all honesty, I wouldn't have listened to myself if I was put in his position. A girl that gorgeous could not be frowned upon by any means necessary.

Even still - I was unsure what was meant by the line, *"I know it's mine!"* It kept aching at me everytime it got repeated in my head. Even at the age of fourteen, my subconscious could only connect the dots to some scientific theory that this meant a major problem that hadn't been resolved, leaving all parties involved a little unsure about the proper handling of the situation.

It may have been possible that Barry was blinded in a cover-up that wasn't revealed leaving him vulnerable.

Something was fishy. It just wasn't the proper place to piece the puzzle together. I had my own problems and at the moment the weather began to drizzle.

I was tempted to walk into the bar before it poured, letting the chips fall where they may but fortunately the good angels found my salvation as Lexi finally made her presence shown.

"You got here just in time." I said, putting my hand out to catch the raindrops.

"You're tellin' me," She answered. "The radio just said it's going to be a downpour any moment. It's going to be raining cats and dogs before you know it."

"Really?"

"That's what they were sayin'. We need to get inside soon before we get drenched."

"What happened to our posse?" She asked, noticing I was alone.

"They're already inside," I replied, beginning to sound a little impatient. "I felt like waiting for you."

"Awww, that's sweet of you." She giggled. "You really just need a girl to escort you in, right?"

"Well kinda."

"You look like you've seen a ghost or something. Is everything alright with you?"

"I'm good," I lied. "I'm just a little nervous. I've never really done anything like this before."

"What, like stay up late on a Friday night without parents around?"

"I am only a freshman, after all."

"Then I guess it's time you enter the real world of the wild and crazy."

"There was just this one thing that happened."

"What was it?" She frowned.

I wanted to open up but cowardly opted out. If the melodrama was going to be exposed, it would be best to let the key players play a part in telling it.

"It's nothing. It's really none of my business."

"Well good. Don't overthink, let's just have some fun. No need to worry about anything. Just relax, I'll have you covered."

"Thanks." I said, feeling a strong connection.

"The night is still young. Why waste it all with fear and anxiety? Let the rain wash all that shit away."

"Yeah, you're right about that." I said, tucking my head into her jacket for protection.

"I usually am," she laughed. "Sorry I didn't bring an umbrella. Come on, it's time to get our boogie on."

Chapter Twenty-One

I wasn't sure if I was going to bump into Barry when I entered *Hard Luck* that evening but my answer arrived when I saw him with Jill heading towards the exit while I was on my way in.

He seemed shocked to see me and a little perplexed about the female friend at my side.

"*WOW!*" He exploded, with eye candy all over Lexi. An unannounced gesture that could make anyone blush with jealousy.

"You're not going to tell mom or dad about this, are you?"

"I'll let you live this time but don't get used to it, pal."

Jill still appeared a little uncomfortable with my assumption she hadn't yet let the cat out of the bag about her recent encounter.

"What are you doing here, anyway?" Barry asked.

"I'm doing what you told me to do, bro, live a little. Maybe I should be asking you the same thing."

Barry judged me.

"Jill and I just wanted a bite to eat. We were going to go out to that haunted house but it seems to be raining out. We might just catch a movie at the theater or something if all else fails. What do you think, babe?"

Jill shrugged, as if not paying too much attention to what was being spoken.

"Whatever you want." She finally acknowledged, looking lost.

"Is something wrong?"

"No Barry, we'll just go to a movie. That works for me."

Lexi and I nonchalantly remained hush, hoping no drama would overspill.

"I guess we'll be seeing you guys then."

"Guess so, bro," I said, patting him on the back, with a consensus effort that the quicker he left the safer I could be.

"I have no idea where you found her but if she's real, you better keep her." He whispered into my ear before walking out the door.

My sudden smile caught Lexi by surprise.

"What did he say?"

"It was nothing."

"He probably thought we were together or something, right?"

"Something like that."

"I guess we fooled him then."

"I think so."

"I don't mean to pry but he seemed a little tense, don't you think?"

"I think all women turn men that way."

"Don't get too prideful or I'll ditch you myself."

"Okay, okay."

Lexi scanned the bar looking for our present company.

"Guys, over here," Ryan hollered, snapping his fingers to

motion us his way.

He was sitting with Jeff and Mark along with the two ladies who we recently met.

"It looks like the gang is finally here," Jeff spoke loudly, greeting Lexi with the last open seat at the table.

Leaving me to ponder the thought of having to stand alone.

"Oh, I'm sorry dude, it looks like we're all filled up." Jeff laughed, egging me on. "You're gonna have to try to sit someplace else."

"Just pull up a chair out from that table over there." Mark said, eye rolling over Jeff's juvenile remark. "No one is sitting there right now."

"Good idea."

"*Chase* - I forgot to mention, I saw your bro in the bathroom when I came in."

"I know Jeff, Lexi and I saw him walk out just now."

"Oh, okay, don't say I didn't tell you then. I was just trying to be considerate."

"Considerate, that's a big word for you to use. Did you bring your dictionary with you?"

I'm just trying to be helpful. You don't need to knock my IQ."

"Sure, Jeff. Whatever you say."

Jeff's remark gave me closure about Barry's absence, making it more understandable where he was during the time the melodrama unfolded outside.

"So, were you able to get your wish and gain another backup singer for tomorrow's show?"

"I think so. Darrell was talking with her. They seemed to hit it off too."

"I guess that's bad for you then."

"Huh?"

"Doesn't that mean he moved in on your girl?"

"Don't be such a wiseass."

Mark bursted with laughter as the waitress came by to finally take our orders.

"What do you guys want?" Ryan interrupted, "Frank and Darrell are paying so get whatever you guys want."

"Awesome!" Mark and I fisted, studying the menus carefully.

"Can we just get a round of bacon cheese fries for now as an appetizer?" Mark insisted. "And maybe a couple beers with that too."

"I'm going to need to see some ID." The waitress frowned, knowing she was getting short changed already by our offsetting behavior and youthful antics.

"That's no worry," Jessie said, handing her a driver's license for proof. *"Here ya go!"*

The waitress looked it over, paying no mind to it whatsoever before walking away. It appeared this most likely was not her first rodeo with underage customers.

"I guess it did pay to have you around." Mark gloated, wishing a kiss was due.

"Don't thank me 'youngin," Jessie backhanded. *"Bobby-Jo, here, is the one that likes to have a brew. I can't stand the smell of alcohol."*

"So then how come she didn't show ID?"

"I'm only 20," Bobby-Jo answered. ***"My birthday is next month."***

"Well, that makes sense then."

"Happy now, fellas?" Jesse countered, beginning to open up.

"I know I am," Mark responded. "Can this night get any better?"

"Well the night is just getting started, guys!" She declared, getting up from her seat letting her personality show. *"Anyone up for a little karaoke?"*

"What the hell, I'll test it out." I unapologetically accepted, treading my natural given fears of public humiliation into new areas of unknown delicacies.

Chapter Twenty-Two

The only place I ever rocked a tune was in the shower.

That wasn't to say that my voice was completely dreadful to the musical skeptic, there was just no need to destroy a fine working muscle in my body for the sheer sake of unabashed pleasure of annoying others.

Which was why karaoke was a joy to some degree. You could get away with sounding like trash with hope that nobody else gave a shit or noticed.

Especially during "happy hour" on a Friday when the regulars filled in early to route havoc on their own personal ills about society's problems.

"What song did you have in mind?" I asked Jesse, skimming through the playlist.

"It looks like there's a lot of boy band stuff on here," she said reading the options. *"You don't mind singing NSYNC or Backstreet Boys, do you?"*

"Wait a minute. I have to sing first? I thought we'd do a duet."

"That's not necessarily my cup of tea."

"Really? But I thought,"

"There has to be something else on here you can do. I know - how about you do Mambo # 5?"

"Mambo number what?

"Y'know the Lou Bega song that's popular right now."

"Oh yeah, the Clinton song."

"What?"

"The line about Monica?"

"Oh, right. I get it."

"It's not in a foreign language is it?"

"No silly, you're not singing La Bamba," she said, shaking her head, while handing me the microphone.

"Are you going to introduce me before I start?"

"Why?"

"To play with the audience a little bit."

"Sure, why not?"

We both took a moment to rehearse our parts as she began to play facilitator to the evening's semi main event.

"Fellow bar patrons!" She cheered to a somewhat doubtful crowd, *"Welcome to Hard Luck's karaoke hour, I'd like you all to greet our first act."*

She looked at me, unsure what to say next.

"What's your name again?"

With stage fright in front of me, I panicked. Funny looks began to float my direction with fears I would get shot down by promoting some kind of lewd behavior on stage.

"Well?" Jessie continued to ask, not getting a firm response back.

"It's -"

The microphone fumbled in my hand, losing all train of thought as she went along without me, making up some ridiculous stage name instead.

"Drunks and rednecks - I give you for your listening pleasure - Mr. Friday Night!"

The scatter of applause launched a stampede of potential constructive criticism.

"Her kid - you better not fuck up or I'm going to piss in your beer!" An aging onlooker shouted from the pool hall, appearing ready to rumble. Obviously, a man of very poor eyesight by any stretch of the imagination.

"He's right, though!" Jessie commented. *"Don't mess this up. You'd be letting the whole table down if you do."*

My focus shifted towards Mark who seemed to be enjoying it thus far by throwing up a sign of good faith before getting bitch slapped in the face by Bobbi Jo for overreaching his boundaries.

"Gee, thanks," I scorned, raising my eyebrow to her. "I'll do my best. Is that enough?"

"It better be!" She retaliated, making her way off stage, back to her seat, as the music began playing and the ball bounced on the monitor signaling the proper time for the vocal track to kick in and guide me with the lyrics.

My eyes remaining glued, with the pressure beginning to mount, I took a deep breath, relaxing, letting my inner Elvis Presley attempt to wiggle my nerves away.

"Here goes nothing," I thought as the spotlight grew larger on my face while the words flowed out of my mouth and into the tobacco scented world of cigarettes and chew.

"One... Two... Three... Four... Five..." I sang out, familiarizing myself with the next few lines on the screen. Thanking that most of the melody was spoken so an attempt to find the perfect pitch wasn't a necessity.

"Jerkface, you're not doing all that bad!" Ryan cried out with laughter, rallying others, showing his support as everyone around him began to sing along

It was turning into a raving success. I couldn't believe it, I had them in the palm of my hands.

I wanted to run down, join the excitement, instead kept my distance until the song came to an end and I got my round of applause.

"Encore, encore!" A woman yelled, wanting more. I couldn't help but catch a wink.

"Thanks, everyone," I said, feeling overwhelmed. "I just wanna give a quick shoutout to my table over there."

Ryan and Jeff were caught off guard as I signaled them to come up on stage.

"I'd like everyone here to know these two will be performing tomorrow in the *"Battle of the Bands"* Halloween contest."

Ryan and Jeff took a bow in acknowledgment, turning into rock stars.

"Do either of you two want to say anything?" I asked, handing them the limelight.

"Yeah, I hope you guys all come back tomorrow night!" Jeff preached to a hopeful faithful following. "Our band will blow the roof off of this joint. So be prepared and come ready to rock!"

Ryan waved to Darrell and Frank to join the party as the whole Silicon Honey crew united. It was the first time I saw the band together looking like a wild bunch of animals released into the wilderness hunting for prey.

"On behalf of Hard Luck's sponsoring the event," Darrell said, "All drinks will be half off tomorrow after 7 PM."

The crowd took a second to digest the announcement; soaring with both approval and skepticism.

"You're not rigging the competition, are you?" A man with a red trucker hat belched, throwing down what looked like his third bottle of liquor.

"Nah, Sam!" Frank answered. "You're one of our loyal customers. we'd never do that to ya or anyone else."

"I only come for the fun. Nothing about nothing means jack shit to me anyway around here. Just send me the pretty girls and I'm all alright. Good luck, fellas!"

"You bet," Frank replied, finger pointing to his waitress. "Susie, give Sammy another beer before the night is through. It looks like he's had a rough enough day as it is."

"Ha," Sam delighted with pleasure, "You guys know me too well!"

"We sure do."

"You know what they say," Frank declared to those still listening to the hype and banter. "This night must chug along and the train must never stop rollin'."

Chapter Twenty-Three

The atmosphere was a blazed as the fire continued to ignite.

Darrell and Frank went back to their job behind the counter as other contestants made their way up to karaoke.

"You were actually good up there," Lexi noted, as I retreated back to the entourage. "You weren't just pulling our leg pretending you sucked, were you?"

"It's not really up to me, I guess, to know." I said, sitting back down and finally getting my hands on the appetizer that awaited me.

"Yeah, doofus! I was like waiting for you to choke or something and it didn't happen. Although, you were a little clumsy with the mic."

"Sorry to disappoint, Mark." I laughed. "But if you really want to witness utter failure you have all night to show us by doing it yourself."

"Maybe you should try out for a position with Ryan and Jeff? You sounded a whole lot better then both of them combined. I should know, I was with them all afternoon. It was like fingernails on a chalkboard listening to them play."

"I think not," I remarked. "It'll ruin my image and besides, I wouldn't wanna embarrass them with real talent."

"Embarrass who?" Ryan overheard, returning back after a brief hiatus at the bar.

"Nothing, we're just talking bullshit about you guys."

"I don't need you two knocking our chances of winning tomorrow night. We worked really hard these last two months putting everything together."

"You know if you put just as much effort into your schoolwork, you'd be getting straight A's too."

"You guys are such asses."

"You know we're just pulling your leg?" Mark refuted, chowing down on the last of the cheese fries on the plate. "What's a little male bonding if we can't belittle one another around?"

"It looks like our food is here." Lexi observed, ignoring all the pity politics among the three of us.

"But I didn't order yet."

"No worries, we ordered you a bacon cheese burger while you were performing. You good with that, sir?"

"That's fine, I appreciate it, Mark."

"Yeah, we kind of figured that's what you'd wanted, anyway. What's a best friend for? You'd know I'd come through for you, right?"

"Yeah, thanks," I accepted. "What did you guys get?"

"Besides the brew in my hand, just the regular, a hot Deluxe Chicken sandwich with a taste of barbecue on the side."

"That looks delicious," Lexi gasped, captivating her mouth full of doggy drool. "Wish I had ordered that."

"You could try a little bit of mine if you want."

"Hey, back off Mark," Ryan shoved, thinking he was putting one on. "She's my girl."

"Woah, woah, woah, that wasn't my intention at all, bro."

"Whatever, you're no different than me. I know how your mind works."

"It looks like the truth is revealed." I intruded, laughing. "You guys are funny. You know that?"

"He's right. Sooner or later you boys are going to have to grow up." Lexi concurred, beginning to feel a little embarrassed.

"What happened to Bobby Jo and Jesse?" I asked, hearing an odd silence at the table.

"They went outside for a second to do something. I didn't ask." Mark replied. "I may have to take a leak myself, anyone care to join me?"

"You're disgusting, you know that?" Ryan voiced with contempt, looking unamused, attempting to show bravado towards his potential girlfriend.

"I wasn't even asking you." Mark ignored. "Lexi, do *you* want to come?"

Her eye roll pretty much sold his answer.

"I have to go, dummy."

"Once again I repeat what are good friends for?"

"You boys are crazy," She laughed.

"That maybe so, but we're just living out the philosophy Seal preached to us."

"Who?"

"The rock star, silly."

"You know you're never going to survive unless - you get a little crazy!" Mark sang, to the displeasure of everyone's eardrums.

"Jesus, what was that?" Ryan scowled. "It sounded like a cat getting attacked by a bus."

"That was the sound of someone winning first place, bro."

Ryan shook his head feeling a loss of words.

"Dude, get out of here, take your loser friend with you and don't come back."

Taking his advice, we got up, walking the short distance over to the restroom.

"I actually have to tell you something." I said, reaching the entrance.

"Not now, you can't believe how close I got too feeling up Bobbi Jo's tits before."

"I kinda saw you getting slapped across the face, if that's what you mean."

"Looks can be deceiving. I'm telling you, she wanted it."

"Which is probably why she avoided coming back to the table then, right?"

"Hey, shut up. You don't know that."

"I'm just piecing the puzzle together."

"Okay, then, what did you want to tell me, if it's that important to you?"

I opened the door, to our surprise a tall redneck man wearing a motorbike vest charged out alerting us about danger ahead.

"Guys, don't go into the stall, there - it's clogged up bad. It's beginning to smell too."

He ran off in a hurry as if to boldly say he was the culprit; leaving the two of us to second guess what to do next.

"What the hell did that guy eat?"

"He probably has a bad digestive tract or something like that, or he ate beans. That always does the trick, right?"

"Don't get me started. Barry once was in the bathroom all night because of something our mother made for dinner."

"That must have been brutal."

"You're telling me. I had to sleep in the guest room because he stank it up so bad."

"Well, what are we going to do?" Mark asked, still standing in front of the gateway.

"I say risk it. We only live once, right?"

"Okay, then."

We entered with the godawful odor still in the air as we reached the urinals.

For Mark it was like reaching Heaven's Gate, being fortunate enough to have St. Peter's blessing.

"All that alcohol I drank, wow! I needed to go so badly. Thanks for having my back, dude. I really appreciate it."

"So much for being able to hold your liquor, tough guy."

"That's not what that expression means."

"Yeah, whatever you say. But seriously, Mark - my problem is with Barry."

"Your brother?" He uttered with confusion, looking at the wall while zipping up his pants. "What about him?"

"They were here tonight."

"I know that, stupid. I thought we already discussed this with Jeff before?"

"That's not it."

"Then what is it?"

"Jill's ex looked to be stalking her when I was outside

waiting for Lexi."

"Hold up, where was I?"

"You came in with Bobby Jo and Jesse, remember?"

"Oh yeah, that's right. I totally forgot. You mean I missed it?"

"Obviously."

"Did Barry know about any of this beforehand?"

"That's what concerns me, I don't think so. I'm pretty sure he was in the bathroom when all of this was occurring, making him out of the loop."

"Well I guess that's just the price he pays for dating someone prettier than him, isn't it? I'm sure it'll work itself out."

"What?"

"I can't help you, dude." Mark hindered, taking the last of the paper towels from the dispenser after washing his hands. "If I were you, I'd leave it alone. You don't want to get involved with other people's bullshit."

"That's kind of my thinking."

"Yeah, don't be stupid about it. Let's just worry about ourselves for the rest of the night. As long as he's not ratting you or me out to our parents, you shouldn't let it bother you. Okay?"

He left, leaving me to think it over, clearing my head while silently filling me with guilt and a belief that I wasn't doing enough.

Chapter Twenty-Four

I left the restroom but not before getting a quick glimpse of Darrell with someone oddly familiar.

"Boy, he works fast," I thought, watching him lock lips with the "red-dye" chick over by the jukebox.

"Dude," he signaled, telling me to come over, " That was an awesome thing you did for us before. You got us some great publicity with the crowd, man. I have to give you credit, you did good."

"It was no biggie, especially with the way you're handling everything around here." I complimented, spotting his new darling, eyeing me closely like someone who didn't belong.

"How old are you, kid?"

"How old do I look?"

"You're a tall sucker, but no way you're 21."

"Hey," Darrell interrupted. "Don't mess with him. He's cool. He's on our side. Don't fight it."

"Sorry, babe. I didn't want you getting shut down for selling booze to minors."

"That's not going to happen, will it kid?" He googled his eyes, looking straight at me for an honest answer.

"No way, man. My posse would kill me if I squealed."

Darrell glanced over at our table noticing Ryan badly flirting with Lexi. Suggesting everything was legit.

"You can come back tomorrow, if you want, watch us win it all." He laughed. "We're going to wipe the competition clean now that we got our secret weapon."

"He's referring to me," the girlfriend snarled as they went back to making out.

"That must be fantastic," I remarked, although I could tell I was already appearing invisible as Darrell put his hands around second base.

"Hey - there you are!" Jessie returned, poking from behind, catching me viewing what to many would seem like softcore porn.

"Holy crap," I reacted fast, "You scared the shit out of me."

"Oh boy, you want some of that, don't you?" She tittered, laughing at my lustful hopes and temptations.

"What, no way! That's not me."

"What then, are you gay or something?"

"No."

"I'm just messing with you but if you really want to know, Bobby Jo was interested."

"You're kidding, right?"

"Kinda - but it's only for tonight, right? Don't forget - you're Mr. Friday Night."

"I thought I saw Mark trying to have his way with her before?"

"Who - your friend over there? That kid's an idiot, if you don't mind me sayin'."

"Don't remind me, I know but he's a good guy."

"Well, anyway, we just returned from outside."

"Wasn't it pouring out there?"

"No, it's actually letting up now."

"Oh, that's good. I mean it was coming down like buckets before."

"We just had to take a smoke break and clear our heads a bit. This place can be full of obnoxious animals, if you know what I mean."

"Yeah, sorta. But isn't that ironic?"

Jessie didn't answer, letting the question sink in.

"Well, anyway, we were thinking, did you guys want to come back with us after we leave here?"

My mind seduced itself with the endless possibilities that question posed.

"What did you have in mind?"

"Well, silly, that's for us to know and for you guys to find out."

"I'm not sure, I think it's best to pass. I'm actually trying to hook up with Lexi over there."

"I get it," she winked. *"You, at least, don't mind if we get a dance in tonight, do you?"*

"Yeah, that's no problem but are they still playing karaoke up there?"

Jessie looked up at the stage, getting a view of the club staff shifting displays.

"I think they're finished. I guess that means the DJ is ready to spin."

"How's everybody doing!!!" A loud male voice shouted cutting into Jessie's words as we saw the transition occur.

"Who here is ready to jam!?" He continued, watching the

lights dim - turning the atmosphere into a lava lamp of colors.

"It's FriYay and it's best that we all Party!" He screamed into the microphone, blowing up the amplifier as the round of applause became intense and contagious to everyone in the room.

"Best that we get back to our seats then." I sheepishly whispered, feeling an uncomfortable sensation that I would play fool once again.

"You don't want to get up on the dance floor?" Jessie asked grabbing my hand and pushing me in the opposite direction towards the disc jockey.

"It looks like we have our first couple here - come on up you two!" The DJ yelled, waiting to make small talk with the contestants.

"Oh wassup, man!? - He belted into my ear, recognizing me, *"You're the dude that kicked it doing Mambo before, aren't you!?"*

"If you say so." I said with a mocking tone, not knowing what would happen if I said anything different.

"Yo Everyone!! It's Mr. Friday Night - you may remember him as the karaoke kid - now he's busting his chops doing -"

He paused for a second as the crowd awaited which record would drop.

The sounds of something familiar came ringing to my ears in an unsatisfying way.

"Oh, Jesus, not this -" I whined, beginning to see nightmares of a dance craze my mom was giddy about only a few years prior.

"First the Cuban diddy, and now this?" I thought, as the rhythms bounced to the tune of Los Del Rio's "Macarena".

"You know the dance, right?" He chuckled, watching me fly into uncharted territory.

"I try not to."

"It's 90s night, man! Enjoy the decade before it ends in a few months."

"You do know it doesn't officially end until 2001, right?"

"Sure, whatever you say, dude - next thing you'll be telling me is this song was written about some church in Spain, right? Gimme a break!"

"Hey, Chase!" Jeff howled from the bar, "Lemme see you do it!"

"Oh, c'mon, really?" I yelled back.

"Yeah, come on, kid everyone's waiting!" The DJ continued to instigate, forcing me yet again to bust a groove, with hope that nobody would remember any of this nonsense come morning.

Chapter Twenty-Five

The lights went out as the rock star died, gracing an exit from the stage.

"Hey bartender - pass this guy a water," Jeff remarked, as I walked towards him at the bar. "You were hilarious up there, man." he laughed, patting me on the shoulder. "Just like that one time, y'know, you remember, right?"

"You're a complete asshole," I fired directly, taking my seat. "You do know that, right?"

Jeff didn't respond, possibly catching a moment for himself where he didn't have to think.

"Hey man, don't listen to his wiseass. I liked your rendition of the Macarena up there."

"And who are you?" I wondered, attempting to fill myself in with the locals.

"The name's Gene, glad to meet your acquittance." He answered, sticking out his hand.

"I'm sorry, but I really don't know where that's been."

"Oh, I see, you're one of them."

"One of who?" I asked, perplexed.

"A germophobe."

"I don't think so, dude. But I appreciate your comment."

The bartender, gazing at me hard, finally filled Jeff's request without mincing words.

"And what's this?"

"It's water, you idiot," Jeff chuckled. "I'm not stupid enough to buy you a beer."

"I wouldn't have wanted it, anyway." I replied, gulping it down, quenching my thirst.

"You enjoying yourself tonight, man?"

"So far, I have to say so. It's different."

"Yeah, I get it, just don't take anything we say around here, personally, 'kay man?"

"I try not to."

"I mean half the people around here are fake and phony, if you want to know the truth."

"I gotcha."

"Good, because we're only trying to have a good time, right?"

I couldn't help but notice Jeff appeared heartbroken, a position I don't think I ever saw him in during our time together.

"I'm sorry about that girl you were trying to hook up with. I saw Darrell having his way with her over by the jukebox. I hope she doesn't "Yoko" her way into the group somehow."

"Don't get me started about it."

"The breakup can be rough."

"What do you know about it?"

"I'm just sayin'."

"Whatever," He shrugged, pretending not to pay attention. "Besides, I never figured you as a Beatles fan."

"I'm gonna head on back over to our table, want to come along?"

"I'll be there in a sec. I have to pay my tab first."

"I guess you have to thank Darrell for something, right? He's giving you all this alcohol."

"Get lost will ya, kid!"

"Yo - Mr. Friday Night!" Mark bellowed, flicking his hands to maneuver me his way.

"You guys are never going to let that nickname go, will you?"

"I actually thought you looked handsome up there." Bobby Jo replied, persuading to get on my good side with hope I'd take her up on the offer to leave with them.

"Dude, did you here?" Mark whispered in my ear. "I'm heading out with Bobby Jo and Jesse in a few, wanna come along?"

"You're kidding, right?"

"No way, man. Why would I kid about this?" He gloated, beaming a fake smile as our two escorts sat watching with glee.

I could sense Bobby Jo fearing I was playing the part of the stool pigeon.

"Dude, we need to talk."

"What for?"

"Isn't this what we wanted?" He asked, begging for my approval.

"Yeah, I guess but you should've heard what Jessie was saying about you before. It wasn't nice."

"Really, what did she say?"

"I think they're only using us. I mean we're only

freshmen, aren't we? Besides, we don't even know them. And they're seven years older than us to begin with. Something doesn't add up if you want my opinion."

"Well, I don't want to hear it." He reacted with frustration. "I'm going, call me naive but I want this badly."

"Fine," I said, shaking my head. "I'm going back with Lexi, anyway. So, suit yourself with whatever happens."

He looked at me with disbelief while I remained concerned.

"Don't worry, we're still friends, I'll let you know what happens."

"Just be careful, okay?"

"Yes, dad." He scorned, before walking away and out of sight.

Chapter Twenty-Six

"**W**here'd everyone go?" Jeff asked as I sat alone. "Did you barf to get everyone to leave?"

"No moron, the night's just coming to an end." I answered. "Mark went out with Bobby Jo and Jesse and I think Lexi is in the bathroom washing up. I'm not quite sure what happened to Ryan."

Jeff stayed chill, listening, trying to be useful before opening his fat mouth.

"I see Ryan with Frank over there," He observed scanning around.

"Maybe you should go meet up with him." I said, showing some sympathy to help ease his distressed state of mind. "Weren't you guys going to do some rehearsing after this?"

Jeff, still beaten up, couldn't help but keep his emotions on his sleeve.

"That all depends, now. I think Darrell is still smooching with Tara over there. Those two need to find a room."

"Don't let them get to you, man. Your priorities should be on the band. You're going to win tomorrow night. Keep focused on that, will ya? Stop turning into a woman right in front of me. It's beginning to sound a little pathetic."

"Yeah, you're right. Who wants to be in a relationship these days, anyway? I think I'm just angry."

"Ya think?"

"Where did you say Mark went again?"

"Out with the two girls we picked up tonight."

"Is he nuts?"

"That's what I can't figure."

"Does his brother know that he's gallivanting with complete strangers out in the middle of nowhere?"

"I severely doubt it." I sighed, "We should let him know, though. Wanna come and tell?"

"Yeah, I'll follow you."

I got up, beginning to walk over but not before Darrell charged into the conversation, telling us his own plans for the rest of the evening.

"Hey guys," he greeted, looking very amused with the likelihood that everything was so ever in his favor. "I know I promised we'd rehearse but things just changed. If you know what I mean."

"But weren't we going to practice?"

"Don't worry so much about it, Jeff. You know that we got this. We've been practicing forever, right? We'll do fine tomorrow night. Just remember to bring along Mr. Friday Night. You never know, he may be our lucky charm."

He retreated without any further words leaving Jeff and I to question his true motives.

"See, I told ya!" Jeff cracked, heading back into another deep depression that for all practical purposes couldn't be saved.

"Dude, just wait here." I said, beginning to feel at a loss with his emotional baggage.

"Hey Ryan!" I shouted, trying to get his attention from six feet away.

"Yeah, what do you want?"

"Where'd Lexi go?" I asked, trying to soften the blow before laying down the real news.

"She said she was going to the restroom. Why do you ask? Are you ready to leave or something?"

"Kinda. It's almost midnight."

"Well, where's Mark, isn't he supposed to be with you?"

"That's sorta what I needed to talk with you about."

"Huh?"

"You see, he left a few minutes ago with the two girls we came in with."

"You're kidding, right? What do you mean he left?"

"I mean, he got up and walked out the door hoping to score."

"Ugh, geez!" He belted with disgust. " I can't believe he'd do this to me. He should know better than this."

"Frank, I'm going to have to go." He said, slipping down some money he owed before getting up and stretching.

Frank gazed at us, somewhat startled but nonetheless not really giving a fuck.

"That's alright, guys. Just remember to be here by 7 sharp tomorrow night. Hope your brother gets back safe."

"I appreciate it, man. Thanks for everything."

"No worries, no problem."

"Why didn't you warn him not to go?" Ryan asked me,

putting on his jacket while finding his keys.

"I tried but you know how he is. He's stubborn."

"Yeah, I know," he said in agreement, possibly praying that I'd say something different. "Thankfully, I gave him my pager. I'll get in contact with him when I'm out on the road. You'll be okay with Lexi driving you back, right?"

"Yeah, that was sort of the plan, remember?"

"Good, I really don't need to be in more trouble then I should."

"Well then what about Jeff?"

"Jeff?" He asked, sounding disarray with my question. "He can go home by himself. It's been a hectic night already, right? Let us all get some shut eye before we come back tomorrow night to channel more madness."

Chapter Twenty-Seven

The difficulties of having to wait on a woman plagued as midnight struck and my only companion became Frank - still dishing out last calls to the lonesome losers who craved one last taste of their of 40 ounces to freedom.

There were two guys seated but given their age and appearances - it was best to keep a distance until my chaperone arrived to save me from this desperate crew, who at face value couldn't escape this trauma of deprived happiness strained on them by the outside world.

"Jesus, what's taking Lexi so long?" I thought, sitting there, having nothing better to do but watch the clock on the wall inch slower and pray that both of my parents would be asleep by the time I got home with the inevitable horror of them ringing my neck being postponed until break of dawn when final judgements could be made appropriately.

Feeling alarmed inside a steep growing sense of paranoia, I took solace in knowing that my brother would suffer the same cruel fate when he returned.

"Hey kid," Frank called, noticing how the boredom had overtaken my brain. "How are you getting home?"

"The girl I came with is driving. She's in the bathroom. It'll just be a few more minutes, I think."

"Just like 'em, huh?" The man closest to me commented,

slurping down his Budweiser with a strong desire to dish out his own drunken wisdom. *"They always keep you guessing, don't they? It's all that men are from Mars and women are from Venus crap I keep hearing about on the news. It makes me want to vomit."*

"Tell me about," I reacted, "That's just the nature of the beast, ain't it? I mean you can't get what you want with them."

"Man, you got that right!" He hollered, raising his beer for a toast. *"You want a Bud or something? I mean don't leave me hanging, bro."*

"Nah, I'm good."

"Hey Frank, get my boy here a drink. I'll buy, okay? Put it all on my tab."

"But you still owe me from the last "tab" you haven't paid, Paul." Frank argued, rolling his eyes while glancing my way, knowing he'd be selling it to a minor. "This one's on me." He whispered into my ear. "You'll pay me back later, you hear?"

I nodded, making believe all was jolly as Paul looked on, pleased.

"What did I tell you, you deserve it - Mr. Friday Night." Frank laughed, feeling he did his good deed helping this poor sucker out.

"Oh, hey, looky there -" Paul said, glossing over at the pool hall, as footsteps patted on the hardwood causing everyone to turn - spotting Lexi, without any makeup on and appearing like her typical teenage self.

It was unusual seeing a pretty girl roaming freely in this part of town, especially late in the dark.

"So, are you ready to leave?" She asked me, becoming a bit antsy and nervous to head out, possibly fearful of these night owls, who remained glued to her every movement like sharks for a kill.

"You bet." I answered.

"Where's your friend at?"

"He's not here, he left earlier."

"Oh, I wasn't aware."

"Yeah, you only have to bring me back. Is that a problem?"

"No, that actually works out better for me."

Frank looked on, sensing possible danger afoot by the two drunkards at the table.

"Seriously, kid - you're dating her? Isn't she just a tad out of your league?" Paul obnoxiously observed, putting my whole reputation in doubt while sliding his arm around Lexi's neck.

"Hey, they'll be none of that." Frank fired back, hoping to keep these wasted wolves at bay before they accidentally turned violent.

"Chill, chill - I was just asking a simple question. Y'all don't need to gang up on me like this."

"Well, what makes you think otherwise?" Lexi rebutted straight to his face, pulling his arm off, eyeing me closely, with full armor on, playing her hand for mine and her own self-protection.

"She's a feisty one!" Paul eased, keeping the situation stable without blowing his top. *"I like that - you did good, hold on to this one."*

"You guys have a safe trip back home." Frank replied, keeping peace.

"Thanks, see you tomorrow." She waved, before strolling out the door figuring we wouldn't return.

"Oh, shoot," she remembered, clutching her wrist, detecting something was misplaced. "I forgot my mother's watch on the sink counter in the ladies room. I have to go back in and get it before someone steals it."

The shivering temperature in the parking lot escalated as my face turned colors causing a unique stutter.

"That's fa fa fine," I reacted, showing some concern, "Just hand me-me the keys, I'll wait in the car. It's getting cold out here, anyway. I need to warm myself up."

"Sure, here ya go," she smiled, throwing them up in the air as they immediately dropped to the ground.

"You were supposed to catch them, bozo." She laughed, before retreating.

Feeling the moon also howling from my stupidity, I couldn't help but get embarrassed.

"What a way to impress her," I thought. "You're batting 0-1".

I picked up the keys, unintentionally hitting the panic button causing a loud noise that had the ability to wake up the neighborhood.

"Crap!" I shouted, quickly turning it off as Lexi's car glowed brightly.

I scurried my way in, swiping the ignition on while channel surfing through the radio dials, figuring the only shows I would catch on the AM dial this late in the night were the talk show kooks whose lust for life included conspiracy theories for the endless search of Sasquatch and Nessie the Loch Less monster. I closed my eyes, letting the dreamscape of radioland snore me to sleep until Lexi's return.

"Good evening -" The host greeted.

My imagination quickly painting the picture of some deadbeat middle-aged college professor hiding underneath a desk in his radio studio as the microphone dropped and the spooky sounds of bumper music played in the rotation making one feel they were being transported to another universe of bizarre antics and intellectual thought.

"We are closing in on hour one here on "Places And Parts Unknown, my name is Peter Pirraglia and we are still here talking with my good friend and former colleague for the evening - Dr. Megan Killawock, about her new book just released this week entitled - "Understanding Aliens."

I have to say, after reading this, your subject matter was richly detailed in this volume, making me question how you do your own investigation on such topics on these paranormal activities and events."

"Well, thank you, Pete." Dr. Killawock expressed, feeling the weight of his gratitude overwhelm her. *"After releasing my last book, "Understanding Humans", it only seemed natural that I tackle something this mind boggling that I knew would lead many of my fellow readers asking more questions that we all want answers to about the supernatural and the outer limits of time and space.*

"... and what may I say is that, exactly? In your honest opinion." Peter questioned, as the radio turned dead air for a brief second.

"What we all want to know and figure out about our own species." Dr. Killawock finally answered. *"That through belief in God and the natural sciences of our universe, we can get a better glimpse into understanding the truth about our own existence, not only with ourselves, but with the many creatures that are already out there amongst us in areas we are seemingly afraid to explore without further ridicule and speculation about society as a whole. Our culture has turned vastly political thus sometimes it's often hard to factor what are the objective and subjective ways to think beyond anything anymore. That's always at the heart of my research and hypothesis."*

"Those are all such fascinating viewpoints, Dr. Killawock." Peter applauded, amused by her every word. *"Believe me when I say this: you are not alone in your search and quest and as Chris Carter reminds us every Sunday night to the Fox TV audience -*

The truth is out there!"

The car door opened - awakening me, as Lexi made herself comfortable in the driver's seat, turning the engine on while chewing on a candy bar she had stuck in her jacket pocket.

"Hey, you want a piece?" She asked, belting my arm as my eyes stretched open to read the wrapper.

"Baby Ruth? Nah, I'm not a fan of peanuts."

"Oh, really, I thought maybe it was because of your lack of eye-hand coordination I saw back there when I flipped you the keys?"

"No really, I actually like baseball, and for your information, the Baby Ruth candy bar was not named after Babe Ruth."

"Oh really, genius?

"No."

"Then who was it?"

"It was named after Grover Cleveland's daughter, Ruth. Go figure, right?"

"I'll say," she thought. "That's enough double meaning to confuse a whole generation of people not to know the difference."

"Yeah, it's all psychology, ain't it?"

Lexi shrugged her head in agreement.

"By the way, kid, what the hell were you listening to before I got in? It sounded like the news or something."

"Talk radio."

"Really, why?"

"I blame my dad, he's into that sorta stuff."

"About what exactly, UFOs? Little green men?"

"About life in general, I mean it's such an open book that If you don't try to understand it, you keep yourself closed to the possibilities of any existence outside of your own."

"Understand it, yeah, I guess, but we need to live it out too, right?" She suggested. "No one is that analytical about things. I mean we're not robots or something. We live in the "Here and Now" don't we? And that, I think, is what keeps us grounded in some functioning reality where we can all feel safe and sane with our opinions on things."

"I see your point."

"I didn't know you were an egghead."

"It's late, so maybe it's showing more than usual."

"You're a funny guy, has anyone ever told you that?"

"Not really, I'm mostly the annoying one in the bunch that gets laughed at when everyone is around."

"I guess that makes sense too," she snickered, while crunching down on her chocolate. "Oh well, you ready to go home?"

"Yeah."

"You know what?" She said, interrupting her own coherency.

"Why don't we just make out for a bit. It's not like we're really going anywhere else tonight, right? It'll give us both some time to warm-up and get our story straight when we see everyone again."

My mind began flickering out of control, unsure if what she was saying was coming out of her mouth correctly or being interpreted into my ears the same way.

"What did you say?"

"You heard me."

"But what about Ryan? Isn't he?"

"Forget about him. He doesn't need to know about this. You better not tell him, alright?"

My deep fantasy was turning reality and there was no way I wanted to fight it any further by saying anything that would contradict where I imagined this was heading.

Chapter Twenty-Eight

I woke up feeling like I achieved something monumental. Maybe it wasn't that historic in the long scheme of things but to any red blooded teenager - "making out" with Lexi (no last name is necessary at the present moment of this writing) for over fifteen minutes, would be hailed in high regard from my social network of delinquents by any stretch of the human imagination.

I'm not sure why she pursued me and I wasn't exactly sure what to make from it exactly in the aftermath. All I knew was, it left me lying in bed the next morning with a sensation that I couldn't resist or refuse to extract.

With my mind remaining focused that nothing dangerous occured - playing an offbeat Lothero was one thing, slapping the label "baby daddy" next to it could ruin reputations leading to questions that would have stifled me from here on out till graduation.

I could never handle that kind of pressure. I may have wanted the notoriety but an ego can only extend so far before it exploded and then you're just left alone to explain it - not only to yourself but to all those who would feel more than ashamed if you didn't think first about the problematic situation you placed everyone in.

I couldn't tell if I was simply grasping at straws or salvaging something that I knew wasn't truly there - It was only a onetime thing, right? What I needed was her side of the story but the trouble with that became the complications one traps themselves in when they effort themselves to understand the opposite sex, which always ended in a bout of utter failure.

I snuggled in bed not wanting the daydream to die, getting a crash course of reality blown away as the telephone near the bed began ringing, causing my hand to hover over it before it roused the house.

"Yeah, who is it?" I answered, trying to sound half asleep so maybe the caller would think they dialed a wrong number and go away.

"Dude, it's Mark." He answered, sounding agitated with himself and annoyed that I was pulling this trick.

I could only assume his late night had as much intrigue in it as mine.

"Those two bitches ditched me last night and stole my money."

"Huh?" I voiced, with a perplexing tone, attempting not to laugh directly into the receiver. His story already sounded too good to be true.

"What exactly happened then?"

"I got into their car, they said we'd make out at their apartment so I tagged along, right?"

"Did you?"

"No!" He yelled. "What happened before everything else was that we stopped for gas. I got out and Jesse gave me a nice sweet kiss on the lips before I told them I needed to go to the restroom. They seemed nice to us at the bar, remember, so I believed them."

"Let me guess," I sighed, ruining his innocence all in one lethal blow, "They left you stranded flushing the toilet, didn't they?"

"Not only that but they stole my wallet that I had in my back pocket. There must have been at least forty dollars stashed in that baby."

"They really did see you coming."

"What do you mean?"

"I mean, didn't I try warning you about them last night before you left. And like normal, you didn't want to listen."

"Oh c'mon, I call bullshit on that."

"Mark, calm down, you're beginning to ramble. And quite frankly not make any sense. Just tell me one thing: how did you get back home?"

"Ryan swung by and saved my ass after I gave him a beep on my pager."

"Lucky you had one of them on you, although I think the gas station would have allowed you to give someone a call."

"I'll say," he continued while coughing on the line, making it difficult to hear. "But our parents would have probably found out if I did it that way, right?"

"Possibly," I answered. "You okay, man?"

"Yeah, why?"

"I don't know, you just sound sick to me."

"I think the weather caused some of that. It was rough yesterday, wasn't it?"

"Yeah, that may be it."

"So what about you? What happened once I left? You went back with Lexi, right?"

"That's actually a story for another day." I gloated, teasing him like a mouse dangling a piece of cheese.

"Oh give me a break! I severely doubt you and Lexi

hooked up or did anything out of the ordinary."

"I guess that's for me to know and for you to find out then."

"Wait, are you telling me you made out with her or something, dude?"

"Jealous, much."

"I don't believe you."

"Mark, when do I ever lie?"

The conversation paused as Mark checked his memory bank which for most cases was always empty.

"I'm still waiting, Mark."

"Ok, you don't lie! But wasn't she going out with Ryan? Oh, crap, he's going to totally kick your ass when he finds out."

"She told me not to talk about it with anyone."

"It looks like you broke her promise then, Einstein!" Mark laughed, ready to send over his blackmail demand.

"I tell you stuff all the time, numbnuts. Come on, you're supposed to back me up on things like this. We are friends, aren't we?"

"Fine," he rudely complied. "We're going to see them tonight, anyway, right? You can't hide inside this pickle forever."

"That's right, yeah, maybe not." I answered, feeling a little of the weight on my back. "Yesterday just seemed so long with everything, didn't it? It's hard to believe we're going back there again."

"It's a long weekend, dude. We need something to do to make it all seem worthwhile. Let's live the adventure."

"We'll probably bump into your two lady friends again." I teased, knowing more than likely the statement would get under his skin.

"I don't want to hear about it."

"I figured you wouldn't."

"Oh, by the way, I forgot to mention, there was an accident on the road after Ryan picked me up last night. A vehicle was turned over in a ditch. We couldn't make out much because it was dark but it looked serious."

I listened, not paying attention, as the timing to get off the phone seemed in reach.

"What a brutal night it was for everyone then." I remarked, before hanging up.

Chapter Twenty-Nine

My friendship with Mark was a struggle of wills when it came to having bragging rights for who was more successful with girls.

It wasn't like neither of us had any experience in the area but hearing him speak over the phone filled me with joy knowing I surely had the upper hand.

It was just like him to play the part of the street wise romantic searching for love but in reality he was nothing more but the naïve sucker getting his heart stomped on by vicious nocturnal creatures who fed from their prey, leaving only leftovers for people like me to help mend once savagely ripped apart.

"Mark, Mark, Mark," I grinned, shaking my head after getting up from the bed, sniffing my undershirt, coming to terms with the fact that a shower was necessary.

With my clothes still stained from the smells of cheap liquor and cigarettes, it was best to toss them aside and get them washed before any questions arose.

I made my way into the hallway getting a clear glimpse of Barry's room - which was vacant, unsure if he hadn't come home, maybe, deciding to stay over at Jill's to help patch his own story together before returning with an alibi that was excusable.

I opened the bathroom door, trying not to disturb my

parents, whom I could hear snoring a couple doors down in their bedroom. Their door was wide open, leading to assume they knew their children had refused any curfew set, giving way towards punishment that although maybe strict, could still be reasonable.

"What a night." I whispered, closing the door behind me. Looking down at my watch getting a view of the time before placing it by the sink.

"Jesus, it's only 8:30." I thought, opening the curtain while undressing myself, finally stepping in and letting the water spray my body full as I hummed out a tune in my head. The relaxation of scrubbing away yesterday's odor was the perfect medicine to brace the new day ahead.

I dried myself off making more use of the morning ritual by brushing and flossing. It wasn't every day I had this much privacy. Barry would usually be the one hogging up the space during the weekend doing god knows what with his hair gels and other accessories scattered about, leaving me to clean up his mess and get blamed for never doing a good enough job in the process.

"You want breakfast?" Mom asked, knocking on the door.

"Oh, that's fine," I answered. "Sorry if I woke you. I heard you snoring and thought -"

"You didn't wake me, I've been up all night. That was probably dad you heard. I'm going to make eggs, how do you want them cooked?"

"Sunny side up, my usual."

"Did Barry come home with you?"

"I'm not sure." I responded, not understanding the question.

"Didn't you boys go out last night or something?"

"Yeah, we did but I was with Mark most of the night, he was with his girlfriend. We didn't really talk much. I think he said they were going out to a movie."

"Oh," she remarked, listening to me mumble my words. "I just haven't had any contact with him, so I wasn't really sure."

"Yeah, that's all I know."

Although, concerned after what I witnessed first hand, I remained vigilant about Barry. He had done things like this in the past. Maybe, to my mother, it seemed alarming with the growing responsibility of a motor vehicle being toyed with.

I tried to keep events with him at bay until I gathered further data. It wasn't like he was the only character in my life that garnered attention.

"Is that you, Ginger?" I asked, noticing her paws clawing their way into my free space. Figuring maybe she wanted to know what I had been up to since I ditched her.

"Sorry I left you by yourself, yesterday." I said, picking her up and brushing her hair back gently - dangling her up to the mirror as we both looked on at each other.

"We could pass as twins," I joked, styling her hair.

Ginger didn't bark, she just licked my face showing sweet affection.

"Ah, you're too kind." I smiled, feeling loved.

"*Hey!*" Mom shouted from the kitchen. "*Do you want your bread toasted or not with the eggs?*"

Her voice pierced like glass, scaring Ginger and rushing her out of my arms, leaving me with a light scratch on my chest.

"You'd think I own a cat." I thought, turning the faucet back on and sprinkling water on my wound.

"Yeah, mom just don't burn it, will you!"

"You'd know I never do that."

I snubbed her remark knowing any retaliation would end in some pointless argument that would leave me without a decent morning meal.

"It'll be ready in, say, five minutes then."

"Okay, mom, thanks!"

The phone began ringing again, chasing me out with only my bathrobe on, inadvertently forgetting to turn off the light indicating the many possibilities for my dad to yell my ear off about upcoming skyrocketing electricity costs.

"Mom, I got it in my room!" I yelled, thinking more than likely it was for me.

I picked it up, not expecting a female voice on the other end.

"Who is this?" I asked, with deep faith that it was Lexi trying to get back in contact.

"It's Jill." She answered, ruining my moment.

"Oh, hey, how's everything?"

"That's actually what I called to find out about?"

"Isn't Barry with you?"

"No, he dropped me off last night after the movie."

"What film did you guys decide to see?"

"We took in a showing of The Sixth Sense."

"I heard that was good, a twist ending."

"Yeah, it was good," she said, hurrying herself, not trying to be rude. "Is it alright if I talk to Barry?"

"He's actually not home."

"That's kinda what I was afraid of."

"What do you mean?"

"We got into an argument before he left."

"Oh."

"Can you let him know when he returns, to call me back?"

She hung up before I could complete my response, making me ponder if somehow he really was in some state of dire straits.

Chapter Thirty

I stumbled down the stairs, watching mom prepare breakfast with her curiosity to know who I was talking with. Not scaring her with the truth but opting to fill her in on Mark's misadventures, knowing if there was one way to enter this conversation, it was through common laughter.

"Where exactly did you boys go, again?"

My heart began pacing, feeling her eyes lasering into mine, deciding to come clean.

"Full disclosure - we went to *Hard Luck*."

She didn't say anything. Mostly finding a moment before taking the spatula and tossing the eggs onto my plate.

"Mom, where's my OJ?"

"It's in the fridge, get up and get it yourself." She voiced with annoyance. "I'm surprised you don't drink coffee yet like the rest of us. You're getting older, you should join the club."

Her demeanor, sounding strong, sensing anger, apparently seemed afoot.

"I keep telling you that it tastes like dirt."

"Your loss," she dismissed, filling herself a cup, before sitting down next to me at the nook. "So what else happened last night that I need to know about?"

"Are you looking to ground me?"

"I don't know yet. Let me hear what you got before I do."

I couldn't think straight. It was as if she had me controlled, playing a suicidal round of damned if you do and damned if you don't.

"We just went out to support Mark's brother. They're having their "Battle Of The Bands" tonight. We were invited back because they liked us so much. Do I need your permission?"

"Well," she pondered, framing her answer to hopefully fit my ambitious yearning to return, "You boys deserve some lease on life. I'll let you."

"Gee, williquors, mom, thanks!"

"Since when do you ever say that?" She gagged, nearly choking her food.

"I'm not sure. It just kinda slipped."

"Get yourself a better vocabulary." She teased, "You almost killed me there."

"I'm sorry."

Noises began screeching from the upstairs, leading to conclude my father had awakened.

"Is that you, hon?" Mom asked.

Dad didn't verbally answer, only the sounds of grunts were made before he made his presence shown.

"Hon, you want some breakfast?"

"I'm just going to have a bowl of cereal before I head out."

"Head out?"

"Yeah, I have to go back to the job. The branch manager is coming by on Monday for their monthly report and evaluation. He's a real stickler about the way things are handled at the store. I figured I'd get ahead of things by putting in some extra time this weekend."

"Oh," she smiled, handing him his cup of joe, sipping it with delight. "You'll do fine, just don't worry too much. You know your job is secured."

"Honey, you don't know Richard Sutta. He's a real pain in the -"

"So, when will mom's car be ready?" I jumped in before he went on his classic cursing spree against upper management.

"Oh, yeah, right, Kermit said the car wouldn't be ready for another week."

"So, how are you getting to work then, mom?"

"I'm getting a rental."

"Okay, that makes sense."

"I really don't need it until Monday, so it's really nothing to rush out over."

"By the way, son," Dad intervened, "Did you record the game like I asked?"

"Yes, dad, I taped it." I stated, watching him walk into the living room with his bowl of cereal in hand.

"Adam, you're supposed to eat your breakfast in here." Mom pouted, begging him to stay.

"Sorry, dear, just give me a second. I need to make sure he did it right."

"What are you talking about, dad? I know how to record your games by now. I've been doing it since I've been born."

"Yeah, I know, but last time you just forgot to put the video cassette tape in, remember? I missed the entire 1st half because of it."

"That wasn't my fault. That was Barry."

"You and your Notre Dame," mom sighed. "Is that all you think about?"

She looked at Dad then directly back at me.

"Only on Saturday." We answered in unison, signaling our unique telepathy towards the question in focus.

"Why did I marry a sports fanatic?" She shrugged, nodding with disappointment.

"Justine, you know you love me."

"I guess somewhere deep down I do, dear."

"How's the team doing this year, anyway, dad?"

"Okay, they're good," he answered. "They beat USC last week. They have a nice shot at making this a season again if they beat Navy. Which is likely going to happen since they always beat them."

"That basically means their record is .500, correct?"

"Yeah, but what can you do," he replied, staying on point. "When you're a diehard sports fan you have to take in all the lumps."

"Do you think they'll ever be great again like they were?"

"It'll be a while, Holtz was such a great coach that it makes it nearly impossible."

"So, you're saying maybe not?"

"I'm sayin, let's wait and see."

Dad flicked the remote control off, double checking that everything was set properly before heading back to the kitchen.

"It's best that I get a move on. I want to make it over there by 10:30."s

"Don't you think you'd look better with some clothes

on?" Mom signaled, wiping some of the milk off his nightshirt.

"That would make sense." Dad laughed, heading back upstairs.

"So what about you," Mom said, raising curiosity once again, "What are your plans, exactly?"

"I'll just hang out with Mark at his house. We'll figure something to do before tonight."

"That's fine," she said, staring into space, not paying attention. "I just wonder where your brother is off to."

Without completely compromising the phone call, I let it slip that he might be over at Jill's.

"So that's where he is." She sighed with relief.

"He did say something about if I didn't make it home that's where he would be."

"Now I feel a little better."

The look on Mom 's face guilted me.

"So, honey, how do I look?" Dad returned in complete dress attire - saving me from any more dialogue about the whereabouts of Barry.

"Handsome like a fox." She grinned, helping to tie his tie.

"I'll see you guys later." He waved strolling out the door accidentally forgetting to kiss mom goodbye.

"Okay, dear, we'll see you tonight then."

Chapter Thirty-One

"It looks like it's just you and me again." Mom expressed, judging the sincere grin on my face. "Why do you look so happy? Something must have happened last night that you're not telling me. Reveal it, mister!"

I stayed silent hoping she'd let it go. Knowing all too well that she'd never cave - causing me to confess, spilling out my guts, right there at the kitchen table.

"What is it, Sherlock?" She demanded, holding a fork up as a weapon, apparently in the mood to instigate violence.

"Well, don't get too upset, but I did pretty well last night with a girl."

"Hold it."

"No, it was nothing like that."

"That's good because I don't wanna have to worry about you too."

"Mom, you *do* know that I'm the good son, right?"

She rolled her eyes, smirking. "Okay, wiseguy, what happened?"

"Nothing, really, we just made out in her car after everyone had left the bar."

"And who may I say might this person be?"

"Just someone that I met yesterday when I was hanging out with Mark's brother."

"Mark's brother, you mean, Ryan?"

"Yeah," I remarked as she stared into my eyes, trying to come to her own conclusion.

"Are you then sayin' that she might be a little older than you?

"What makes you think that?"

"I'm adding up your story so far, it's a mom thing." She giggled.

"Fine," I moaned, giving in to her Jedi mind tricks. "Her name is Lexi. I think she's a Junior, but I didn't really ask. I think maybe it was a one-time thing."

"Lexi? What's that short for?"

"I'm not sure, maybe Alexa or Alexis?" I answered, irritated by the third degree. "Jesus, mom do you have to get all up in it?"

"Yeah, I kinda do," she laughed. "Don't worry, I'm on your side. What made her interested in you in the first place?"

"I'm not sure. Ryan was trying to hook up with her all night but he left early and I was all that was left."

"It looks like you lucked out then."

"I'll say, but what do I do next? Maybe I need some advice. Do you have any?"

"Well, I do remember that one time your father was stalking me right before we were officially dating."

"You're kidding me, right?"

"No," she remarked, "I guess it was more innocent flirtation back then but I need to make the story more hip."

"Dad, a stalker, no way, what happened?"

"I was on this blind date that I was hooked up with by a fellow girlfriend who shall remain nameless."

"It was Diane, wasn't it?" I interrupted knowing exactly who she was referring to.

She ignored me with a funny look, continuing the story.

"And unbeknownst to me or anyone else, your Dad, who I knew a little bit at the time, had the job of waiting on our table. It must have been his first job and, anyway, during our dinner he was sneaking in little love notes and side glances at me when nobody was looking."

"Really?"

"I mean he was cute and all but at the time it really was a bit hysterical. I couldn't keep a straight face and my date got so upset that he walked out, leaving me to pay the bill before your dad came by to apologize."

"Did dad help pay your bill?"

"Actually, he did. It's what got us talking."

"That doesn't really sound like dad, does it?"

"Your dad was a different person before you were born. I guess you should learn that now because once you start to have kids, they'll most likely be saying the same things about you."

"You think?"

"I don't have to. I already know."

"But what's the best thing I can do right now with Lexi?"

"Simple," she suggested. "Just be yourself. You're only a freshman. They'll be other girls during the next four years, I bet, right? Be lucky something happened and play it by ear."

"Yeah, I know, I was kind of shocked, myself, when it all happened. Especially with what I found out about Mark this morning after he called me up about the two girls that ditched him. I mean what was he thinking?"

"We all know what," Mom laughed, pacing around the kitchen as if she was looking for something. "Mark was just being Mark, your friend is quite the character, isn't he?"

"You're telling me." I agreed, as the telephone began ringing yet again.

"Who keeps calling us?"

"I doubt it's Mark." I answered, anxiously waiting for her to answer it, hoping for no bad news.

"Hello?" She responded, staying quiet while letting the caller speak, before raising her own voice to give them a piece of her mind.

"Kermit, what did I tell you yesterday!?"

I was relieved. It was a false alarm, only the car doctor.

"Mom, I'm heading back up to my room to change." I said, not caring if she heard.

"Okay, honey, that's fine," she replied, continuing to release hot air.

Chapter Thirty-Two

I retreated to my bedroom as mom yenta'd from below. There was no telling what kind of monster she'd create whenever she spewed her logic to any mere mortal who tended to disagree. The only solution was to get out before anything backfired and ricocheted in my direction. One would assume my family was a tight knit clan but at any moment the need for human survival could come to where you had to fend for yourself.

"Mom's a savage." I thought, locking the door behind me, getting a strange scent of a stingy odor surrounding me.

"What the hell," I screeched, detecting Ginger didn't want to wait for her morning walk to free her bladder. "Ugh, Jesus, Ginger, if you really needed to go you should have gone into Barry's room. You know he likes the smell of your piss better than I do."

I could see her hiding under the bed looking ashamed.

"Get over here," I commanded, glossing over my room. "My dad's right, my room is a mess." I said, reminding myself to scrounge through the clean clothes to pick out my shirt for the day. "Mom tells me to put my clothes away after they get washed but do I ever listen?"

Ginger crawled out from underneath, once again licking my hand as I knelt to rub her belly, possibly looking for forgiveness.

"You gotta stop doing this. I don't want to have to get you fixed. Trust me, you don't want that. Nobody does. Wait here while I find your leash."

I got up, forgetting exactly where I had placed it from the night before.

"Oh, there it is," I said, locating it by the windowsill, opening up the mini blinds letting light in.

"It looks like it's gonna be a beautiful day," I smiled, looking out past the driveway and onto the street corner discovering the pitch perfect view.

The morning was blooming - the sun was up, the sky was blue. The trees all had a colorful tint of Fall in the leaves. There didn't seem to be a care in the air as I spotted Jennifer Murphy walking her dog, wanting to wave but knowing it wouldn't matter since she'd never see me from the distance.

"Hey, Ginger, why don't we get a move on? It's possible I could accidentally bump into her outside and we could talk again. I'm on a roll already, let's keep it moving."

Ginger looked at me as any animal companion would - with complete bewilderment towards their human owner.

"Let's go!" I rushed, leashing her up in a hurry and heading downstairs, running into mom who was still having it out with Kermit over the phone.

"Mom, I need to walk Ginger, I'll be back in a bit."

She didn't answer but looked on with her eyes signaling that she heard.

I grabbed my coat and baseball cap located on the rack nearby then shut the door.

"It's actually cold out here," I thought, as Ginger looked straight up at me. "That damn sun can be a liar."

"Good Morning," Jennifer greeted, approaching my

street. "It looks like we meet again."

I waved back feeling like a complete dork, fumbling to make sensical words come out of my mouth. Yet again within reach of the prettiest girl on the block and having a hard time sounding coherent.

"Oh, hey," I mumbled.

"It's a little chilly out this morning, isn't it?"

"Yeah, but I can handle it." I said, building up some confidence. "I see you are walking the dog."

"Yeah, my husband came in late yesterday from work and is resting up this morning, I guess I'm doing him a favor by doing this."

"Are you a Notre Dame fan?" She asked.

I was unsure of her question until I noticed I had been wearing my dad's hat by mistake.

"Haha, actually, this isn't mine."

"I actually have a girlfriend who went over there."

"Over where?"

"To that college." she reminded me.

"Really, that's cool," I replied, nodding my head up and down like a bobble head doll. "She must have been smart."

"That," she agreed, "Plus her family was Catholic."

"Oh, I get it."

"Yeah, I was raised Protestant. I'd never go to *that* school If I had a choice."

"What about you then?"

"What about me, what?" She asked, confused, catching me tongue tied, attempting to sound plausible.

"I mean where did you go to college?"

"I didn't go," she remarked. "My grades were average and I didn't have the money for that."

"It's never too late."

"Yeah, but I'm satisfied with life right now. I mean who can't be happier than being a dog walker on a wonderful Saturday like this and just taking it all in?"

I couldn't tell if the sarcasm was directed at me or not.

"Thanks for the advice, though."

"Yeah, no problem."

The conversation died down as Jennifer noticed somebody on a bicycle fast approaching.

"Who's that?"

I looked closely figuring it was only my partner in crime racing to meet up.

"That's my friend, Mark."

"Oh, well, I guess it's best for me to be heading home then. I think Barkley did what he needed to do. It's been nice chatting with you again."

"Same here." I said, waving goodbye, mentally capturing another teenage fantasy to exploit for the purposes of my mind.

Chapter Thirty-Three

"Y'know, you could just steal a camera and take a quick snapshot." Mark scoffed, punching me in the back as we both watched in wonder as Jennifer graced her exit down the street.

"Boy, oh boy, that one's hell of a beauty!" He drooled, blowing kisses in the wind. "She's the type I'd like to nail down to the floor."

"Shut up before she hears you, you moron!"

"What are you, like, Mr. Sensitive or something about her? It's not like any of the shit we're saying means anything to anybody, dude."

"I'm just trying to be *mature* about it."

"Oh, really?"

"Someone has to, right?"

"Oh, c'mon, man, she must know she's the most attractive looking babe in our radius. I can only imagine what her husband does to her when no one is around."

"Do you think he's like a serial killer or something?" I laughed, making Mark think twice.

"She's too good looking for that. What husband would be that dumb to try something like that in the first place? He'd be out of his freaking mind."

"I mean Hugh Grant did screw a prostitute, didn't he? And he had Elizabeth Hurley by his side when he did it. What was he thinking?"

"Yeah, but that's only the Hollywood elite. He has the right to play the part of a scumbag. I'm pretty sure it's written somewhere in his contract."

"Hollywood or not it was pretty stupid, what he did, if you ask me."

"But that's just it. Nobody was asking you."

"You're one to talk, especially after that ordeal you pulled last night."

"I don't want to talk about that."

"I tried to warn you, man. You should have listened."

"Nah, it's all good," Mark reacted in denial. "I learned my lesson well."

"Sure you did."

"You bet, you won't be seeing me do that again."

"So you're saying the next time that something like that happens, you'll have better judgement over the situation?"

"You mean like when we go back tonight?" He smirked, knowing everything I was saying was going into one ear and out the other.

"Do you think those girls would show up again after what they did?"

"Who knows and who cares - screw them!"

"Hey, let's switch topics, okay?" I pleaded, sensing that Mark was getting too emotional to handle his speech without anger breaking through.

"Fine, how come you're always out walking the dog and not your brother?" He bitched, suckering me to small talk about the pooch.

"Apparently, to my family, she's mine, so I've gotten shafted with it. You want to make a federal case about it?"

Mark looked down, petting Ginger, acting like he felt sorry for me.

"I'm glad my parents never tried to stick me with all that responsibility. I would hate it."

"Yeah, it sucks at times, but I'm not one to complain about it. It gives me a way to get out of the house and get a little exercise."

"Dude, you're already sounding like some 50-year-old man who has a nagging wife and finds inner peace doing this."

"Hey, now, not too loud, don't blow my cover."

"How come you just didn't adopt a bunch of cats? I mean all they do is mope around the house all day and sleep. It saves you from actually doing any of the hard stuff, right?"

"Like, what, really, working?"

"Exactly!" He bolted, "Hey, I'm just being honest, here, man. Don't get mad at me for saying it. I know you're probably thinking the same thing too."

"No, I'm not! And stop trying to put words into my mouth. My mom got us a dog and I like her. Case closed.

"It's a shame she didn't give you a manly dog -y'know one that doesn't make you look like a complete - "

"MARK - DONT MAKE ME BELT YOU!"

"Okay, okay, hold your temper.. geez! I'm just messing with you, man, we are friends, aren't we? How far do you have to walk her, though?"

"Just around the block or until she poops."

"Do you carry a doggie bag for when she goes?"

"Most of the time she just lets loose on other people's property. There's really no telling what she'll do. You always have to be on guard no matter what."

"That must really piss them off."

"Yep, sometimes. You should have seen us yesterday; we were flying by the neighborhood."

"You say you walk her around the block?" That's about a mile. You do this every day?"

"Most of the time, yeah. I'm telling you, it's not all that bad the way you're making it out to be."

"Whatever, you say, dude. Just don't try to sucker me into doing your job."

"Why don't you just get out of here then?"

"Huh? Why?"

"You're not really adding anything to the conversation. You're just being a bit of a jackass. Turn around and go home, will ya?"

"Fine by me." He answered, turning his bike in the opposite direction.

"How come you're out here, anyway."

"I was on my way to see you. How was I to know you'd be out running errands?"

I stood there, waiting for more wise cracks to stream, however his ammunition was finally running low.

"You know what, I'll meet you at your house in, say, thirty minutes after I finish up here. Are you good with that?"

"Yeah, that doesn't bother me. What time is it, anyway?"

"It's almost a quarter to ten." I answered, looking down at my watch, holding the leash tight, fearing Ginger was about to run after the UPS truck zooming by around the corner.

"Ginger, down girl - stay!"

The leash slipped out of my hands - breaking her free, leaving me to yet again chase my way around the ol neck of the woods fearing potential disaster.

"You're right about one thing, dude." Mark chuckled as he watched my mishaps unravel in real time. "There's never a dull moment hanging out with *you*."

Chapter Thirty-Four

"**G**inger, come back here!" I shouted up the road as cars began passing by.

"Get over here, now! I'm warning you! Don't make me come over there and get you!"

She turned quick, losing track of her target, choosing instead to obey my orders before any real danger apparently struck.

"Jesus, do you always have to go chasing around anytime you see a mail truck? I'm only glad a car didn't run you over by accident. You know that's the last thing I want to have happen to you. I don't want to be attending the funeral."

Ginger stayed put, allowing me to tie her back; The drivers, on the other hand, were not so welcoming with their choice of language.

"*Hey kid, what the fuck,*" a teenager, looking no younger than my brother commented, pulling his car over and putting down his window. "*You got to do a better job of keeping a hold of your mutt.*"

"I'm sorry about that. She got loose and -"

"*I don't want to hear it.*" The boy continued, "*My insurance is already high enough as it is - having a dead animal on my track record isn't going to improve matters for my next policy renewal.*"

The absurdity of his tone made me giggle underneath but I remained wise to his game.

"I hear ya. It won't happen again. My mom's actually an insurance agent, she could help you out with that if you want."

"Are you some sort of wise ass?" He remarked. *"Hey, wait, I know you, don't I? At least I know your bro, your Barry's kid brother, aren't you?"*

I grinned, hoping it would maintain some peace.

"We went to school last year." He nodded, pointing his finger directly at me. *"I graduated before him. He's a cool dude. He helped me out on my finals. He gave me all the answers to the questions from his computer. I would have flunked out if not for that."*

"So you're saying he helped you cheat?"

"Yeah - I paid him what he wanted and he returned the favor. That's the way it works, isn't it?"

"Pretty much." I answered, knowing this guy was turning into nothing but a pretty idiotic simpleton right before my very eyes.

"Well, I'm glad it all worked out for you but I have to get going."

"You listen to what I said, man. I don't want to see you again, capeesh!?"

"Capeesh," I accepted, feeling any other response might ignite World War Three. "I don't want to cause any harm with you, either. Once again sorry for everything. Hope you have a good - ."

He pulled away before I could finish as his muffler sprayed out like a cat marking his territory.

"I think he has to get that thing fixed." I coughed, wiping the fumes away from my mouth.

"Can you believe that guy? What a douche. And he's telling me I have problems?"

I looked down at Ginger knowing she was the true culprit.

"What am I going to do with you now?"

"I have to take you home before you get me into further trouble. You're killing me this morning - first the crap you left in my room and now this."

Ginger looked at the ground without barking knowing punishment was afoot.

"I love ya but sometimes you can be a pain."

"Hey, cutie, cute dog!" A woman whistled, interrupting my mood as she drove by honking her horn.

I didn't catch her face thinking it was only someone from school noticing my existence or playing mind games with my heart.

"You're going to make me famous, aren't you?" I laughed, figuring out what to do next. Ginger stayed put, waiting for me to make my move.

"I have to keep my eye on you, you're a pesky pooch."

She followed my lead as we walked back together, remaining close.

"Sometimes I have to think Mark is right. Taking care of you is too much work and time on my part. Why do they say a dog is man's best friend, anyway? All you do is drive me nuts. I mean, seriously, look at me, right now, I'm out in the middle of daylight talking to myself hoping you can understand anything I am saying."

I panicked, if there were any moments in life where I worried too much about how others might judge me, this would be it. Keeping composure was always difficult when scatterbrained out in public.

"It looks like the cops are up." I thought.

The fuzz - driving down the street patrolling the avenue like they were preparing for some arrest.

"Something must have happened, or maybe they're only on a drive by?"

I didn't think too much about them before reaching home base, releasing Ginger into her corner of the house and letting mom know about the current plans for the day.

"Mom, I'm heading over to Mark's. Be back in the afternoon."

No response was heard but the shower was running, leaving me in the clear.

I went out by the patio, grabbing my bike with only the desire to pedal the few extra miles across town to meet up with my friend who for all practical purposes made my life more interesting.

.

Chapter Thirty-Five

"What took you so long?" Mark demanded, after entering his bedroom - a place reeking of dirty gym socks and bad body odor - not to mention stained clothes from the night before.

"Dude, I took Ginger home and then traveled around the block over here. Be grateful, twerp! I didn't have to come. Especially with the way you've been acting."

"Okay, man, I was only teasing you. Don't take it so personal. You need to get a hold of yourself and chill out."

"No, you weren't. I know you by now. And mind you, everything is personal. You can ask Michael Jordan about that. He would never have won all those championships if he didn't take it out on his haters."

"Besides, why does it always have to smell like cheap shit every time I come in here? You should watch your hygiene. I, at least, have an excuse - you don't even own pets - your stink is all you. And you don't even smoke yet. I'd hate to see you in a few years. This room will smell like a chimney by then, won't it?"

"Man, aren't you the woman this morning? What has gotten into your panties? We were both out last night, weren't we? I mean give me a break - the cigarette smell is stuck all over my clothes. It ain't my fault. If anything, it's *your* fault."

"Get outta here." I asserted, knowing this conversation was going in a spin cycle of utter confusion and nonsense. "I'll stop bickering - only if you stop being an ass for once in your life."

"Deal," Mark agreed, spitting in his hand and forcing me to shake it.

"You're gross. You know that, right?"

"I know, but you're the only friend who can tolerate me even at my worst."

"I wonder why that is?" I questioned, shaking my head. "By the way, I didn't see your parent's cars outside when I rode in. Where'd they go?"

"I'm not sure where actually, it's just me and Ryan over here right now."

"I thought that was him snoring as I was walked by. He's a deep sleeper, isn't he?"

"Yep. I hope he's trapped inside a nightmare, it would serve him right for the way he treats me."

"Did your parents find out where we went last night?"

"We came home late and they were sleeping, so, I don't think so. They're not like your parents; they really don't give a crap about either of us or what we do. As long as we don't die on them mysteriously, I think we're in the clear from getting yelled at."

"You know what this reminds me of, right?"

"What?"

"The song The Way by Fastball?"

"The what?"

"The Way."

"Never heard of it."

"Yeah, you have, you remember, the song about the children getting up and discovering their grandparents went missing?"

"Oh, yeah, right," he remembered. "That retro video we watched on MTV last year with that chick in the green dress who was tempting as fuck. That was a great video. Wait a minute, you're telling me that the song was about what?"

"Death, obviously."

"No way, really? Explain."

"I'm referring to the fact that your parents could be out doing god knows what right now and they may have disappeared right before your eyes without any one of us even knowing it."

"Get outta here," he dismissed, waving his hand at my face like I was a waning lunatic. "You have to have quite the active imagination if you want me to believe that mumbo jumbo."

"Hey, man, I'm just sayin'. You never know, it could happen. I've heard stories like that before. It wouldn't be the first time, if you know what I mean."

Mark began to hum the tune in his head trying to make sense of my logic.

"Oh right, I get it now - "*Where were they going without ever knowing the way?*"

"I always figured the people in that song were somehow abducted by aliens or something. Y'know - very X-Files-esque. I didn't take it too seriously. It had a cool rhythm and that's why I liked it. Thanks for ruining it for me."

"Apparently, the real story is they drove off a cliff or something after being intoxicated."

"What a way to go, right?"

"You're telling me. A bit Thelma and Louise, right?"

"*Can you two please shut the fuck up!*" Ryan shouted from across the hall listening in on our banter. "*I'm still trying to catch some shut eye from last night and the bullshit you guys put me through.*"

"We thought you were asleep, asswipe!" Mark yelled, knowing no one else would hear. "It ain't our fault your door is wide open. You should remember to close it next time. And what bullshit are you talking about, anyway? It was a fun night, wasn't it?"

"*It was until I had to pick your loser ass up at the gas station, remember?*"

"Oh yeah, that." Mark whispered, hoping I wouldn't hear.

The sounds of Ryan's bed began creaking as he got up

making his way towards our domain.

"You really got to do something about your bed man." Mark continued, still playing the instigator. "The box spring or something is fucked up on that thing. Every time you get up it makes strange noises like you're trying to wake the dead."

"Ah, shut up! You're just jealous I got a queen size and you're stuck with a little bitty full-size over there."

"No I'm not!"

"It's called growing up. Get used to it." Ryan gloated, thinking he was getting the final word in.

"No it's not, it's called being a prick while annoying your younger brother."

"Seriously, though, getting back last night was brutal after that accident on the road." Ryan said, brushing his hair back - looking like a shower was necessary.

"What accident?" I asked, forgetting Mark had mentioned it to me from the morning phone call.

"I told you, man, last night. You remember?"

"Oh yeah." I lied, thinking they'd fill me in on the details if I'd just shut up.

"A car was in the ditch turned over." Ryan revealed, giving me the lowdown on what happened. *"I think the driver died. The police were at the scene after they closed everything off. We had to drive the scenic route home, which cost us about 30 minutes. We couldn't really make out what happened. It was just one car that got totaled - we were guessing maybe it was a hit and run and the other driver was drinking or something and y'know accidentally knocked the other guy off the road without really caring. Y'know, one of those off-the-cuff tragedies that might make the nightly news and affect some local family."*

"Holy shit, for real?" I said in horror while my mouth hung open - believing every word.

"Yes, moron!" Mark echoed, "Did you think I was fooling you when I was chatting about it this morning? I am your friend, aren't I? I wouldn't lie to you like that."

"I don't know." I reacted, remaining stunned. "I had too

much stuff going on in my head at the time. I guess I wasn't paying that much attention to what you were trying to say."

"Oh yeah, that's right." Mark smiled, eager to watch the fireworks explode when explaining to his brother about my recent rendezvous with his potential girlfriend.

"Oh yeah, Ry, you have to hear this - it may blow your mind."

I looked at Mark with disbelief annoyed he was putting me on the spot yet again with someone who may have an ax to grind against me.

"You jerkface!" I said, punching him, hoping the hurt would sting.

"Ouch! Why'd you do that?"

"You know why. I oughta slap you across the face too, but all your sense is gone!"

"You wouldn't dare." He retaliated, throwing his hands up in self-defense.

"Go on ahead and tell him, he's right here and I'm ready to watch. He won't bruise you up too badly."

"Tell me, what?" Ryan asked, knowing he was being kept out of the loop on something important.

"This boy here got it on with your girl last night and he liked it."

"I did not," I lied, "Well, I did, kinda, but if anything, she came onto me, and now I don't know what to think about it."

"What do you mean "kinda", I'd give my left nut just to have 15 seconds with her."

"Wait - what?" Ryan asked, looking a little frustrated with the both of us. *"You and Lexi?"*

"Yeah, It happened right after everyone had left and you went chasing out to get Mark."

"You're serious about this, aren't you?"

"Totally am, dude."

"What *exactly* happened then?"

"You told her to drive us back home, remember?"

Ryan listened, clearly not following along with any

common sense I was dishing out. *"So?"*

"So," I arrogantly said, "One thing led to another and the next thing I knew there we were making out in the front seat of her car for at least fifteen minutes."

"You're full of shit!" Ryan laughed, attempting not to give into reality. *"That didn't happen. You're such a pipsqueak. What would she possibly see in you?"*

"I wouldn't be making this up if my life depended on it, Ry."

"You look upset, bro." Mark relished, making the situation even more unbearable for everyone.

Ryan's face began boiling like a pot of water ready to burst.

"Believe me, it happened. And I'm sorry if it hurts you."

Mark stayed silent, listening, with anticipation with what would play out next.

"I mean, you do remember she kissed me yesterday when we were outside *Guitar Planet* don't you? Y'know, after the way you were harassing me."

"I wasn't harassing you."

"Hey, I can't help it if the girls like the sad puppy dog in me. I have a charm for that sort of thing."

Ryan came up close, preparing to belt me, attempting to scare me away.

"Whoa, whoa, whoa, please don't!" I screamed, fearing for my life. "It wasn't like that at all."

Ryan paused holding his self-control.

"Trust me,I didn't see it coming. We didn't go any further than what I said. Please don't hate me for it."

The telephone began ringing forcing Ryan out.

"I'll deal with you later!" he said before escaping.

"Man, that was a close one." Mark cheered with some disappointment that nothing truly transpired the way he wanted it to.

"Saved by the bell. I can't believe he was that hurt by it. I thought your brother appeared to play macho."

"Yeah, sometimes, but you know that's all an act. He's 100% full of bullshit most of the time."

"Really?"

"Yeah, but nah, you're good. You shouldn't feel sorry for him. He probably had it coming, anyway. It's just funny that it happened with you. You know what I mean?"

"It wasn't like I was trying to start armageddon."

"I gotcha." Mark winked, loving every moment.

"Hey, You two dolts!" Ryan hollered back, gaining our attention quickly.

"What?" Mark answered.

"I have Jeff on the phone - he wants to pick up Lexi and meet up at the mall."

"And your point is, genius?"

"I think I'm gonna head back home." I interrupted, trying not to interfere anymore then I had.

"No, wait, let's hear him out."

"What loser, what are you saying?" Mark called out.

Ryan didn't respond, hearing only the telephone hang up before footsteps pounded the floor.

"I guess it was nothing."

"You two are coming with me." Ryan finally answered, jolting back in.

"But why?"

"We need to clear some things up."

"Actually, this is more of a sibling thing." I whispered to Mark, hoping to hide and trying to flee the scene without being noticed.

"And where do you think you're going, hot lips?" Ryan teased, as my hand barely gripped the door.

"Hey, this isn't my problem."

"Oh, yes, it is!" He said, staring me down, forcing me to change my opinion.

"We have a lot to discuss - me and you. You're coming - whether you like it or not."

Chapter Thirty-Six

I didn't say much during the drive. There was no reason to have to explain myself again. Especially for not being in the mood to show guilt about something I had no control over.

I could swear Lexi was only playing tricks with me but I certainly had no need to feel ashamed about her behavior. If Ryan wanted to pout about it, he had every right to; just don't rain it on my parade.

I kept quiet as he and his shotgun companion continued to fuss up front, almost as if I was invisible to the naked eye.

"I mean, really, Mark, what the hell were you thinking last night with those two girls?"

"It was Friday night, I thought anything could happen."

"It sure did and now look at you, you're out $60 bucks. Thankfully, you don't have a driver's license. They'd have stolen that too, given the chance, then you'd really be shit out of luck."

"What are you, like, dad or something? Stop complaining about it and keep driving. I'm kinda getting sick of hearing your voice. You've been bitchin' all morning. It sucks you don't come with a remote control so I can turn you off when I please."

"You sure as hell ought to wish I was Dad. I mean they saw you coming from a mile away and you didn't even blink an eye to think about any of the consequences. If our parents aren't going to look after you, someone has to, right?"

"But we're still alive, aren't we? Unlike that poor chap in the ditch. Sometimes you gotta live life, don't ya? Of all people, you should know that better than me, right?"

"Yeah, but you also don't wanna wind up dead on the side of the road somewhere, either. These decisions are really all the choices you make that determine everything. Be mindful of that, will you? Before you do something stupid like that again. Next time it *may* be you on the side of the road, you never know."

"That's life, bro, ain't it? You win some, you lose some, so just let the chips fall where they may. You only live once, right?"

"You're crazy, you know that?"

"Maybe, but I'm also young and healthy. So, they're a perfect match, wouldn't you say?"

"You're telling me."

They continued to ramble, trying not to let it interfere with my own sanity, as I sat in the back seat dazing at the scenery being rolled out like credits on a movie screen.

"What do you think, dummy?" Mark turned around looking straight at me hoping for some approval. "You've been quiet since we left the house. You still afraid Ryan's going to kick your ass or something?"

I looked at Mark, not quite answering him, instead fidgeting in my pockets making sure I had some extra cash on hand for whatever we were planning on doing next.

"I think I might've left my wallet at home." I lied, praying Ryan would magically turn the car around and drop me off.

"Sorry, dude, we're already a few miles from your house. I'm not turning back now. Whatever you have on is what you have."

My annoyance arose as I continued to bite my tongue.

"What's the purpose of us going with you, Ry?" I asked, feeling trapped while being held hostage against my will to come along on this joy ride.

"Purpose?" Ryan questioned. "We're performing tonight

and since it's a Halloween event, we need to get dressed up for the gig. The whole band is getting decked out in some "get up" that should help us seal the deal to win this thing."

"Oh, really,"

"So, anyway, we just haven't decided what to do about it yet. We're meeting back up with the guys at the same place we were at yesterday to look for something good. Something that can complete a set. We need to look like *Kiss, if* you know what I mean."."But I thought you guys already chose your costumes for this shindig." Mark interjected, getting his one wisecrack in.

"What do you mean?" I asked, making him explain.

"They're going as Silicon Honey, right? Which is basically what, 4 nerds from Silicon Valley who think they have a chance with girls?"

"Well, from my vantage point," I teased, "The only two members getting any experience in that general area are Darrell and Frank. I saw the way they were smooching up last night. They're like pros out there compared to you two."

"Wait, what?" Mark asked, wanting in on details.

"You should have seen Jeff."

"Why, what happened?"

"You remember that girl he was trying to hook up with before we walked into *Hard Luck* last night?"

"Yeah, so? What about her?"

"Well, I saw Darrell making out with her after I came out of the bathroom stall and I think it kind of ate him up. He was drowning himself at the bar getting really depressed about it, encouraging me to express some male bonding."

"Like he was sulking in his beer, sad?"

"Yeah."

"No way, you saw him like that? I don't think I'd believe it unless I saw it for myself."

"It was kind of sad, really."

"I did figure Jeff was out of his league with that chick, anyway." Ryan concurred, clueing us in on Jeff's brief yet troubled history with flirting. "He's a good guy and all but he has a lot to learn about hooking up."

"What are you talking about?"

"I mean he was raised in an environment that was pretty strict so coming out now can be much of a put on that some may be uncomfortable with."

"You're one to talk, Ry." Mark challenged, "I mean just look at all of us."

"What about us?"

"We're teenagers too. Don't you think we all have the rest of our lives to get completely frustrated over women?"

Ryan pondered his thought, refusing to accept the idea that his little brother may be on to something.

"I don't know about you but I was doing pretty well until your bozo friend back there screwed everything up."

The pressure to respond to his rude remark became unbearable but I chose not to.

"But that's alright now, everything will get straightened out, won't it?" He flinched his eyes directly at me wanting to prove his point.

"Dude, watch the road, you remember what happened last time, don't you?"

"I'm a good driver, no need to worry, son."

"I'm not your son, idiot, now watch where you're going before you kill us all."

Ryan backed off, focusing himself to concentrate on the road ahead.

"Seriously, though," I asked, wanting to get in on one of the things that had been bugging me about his new taste for success. "What the heck does *Silicon Honey* even mean?"

"Beats the hell out of me," he replied. "It was all Darrell's idea."

Chapter Thirty-Seven

We arrived at the mall a little before a quarter to twelve with the aching for food beginning to rumble.

"You, okay, man?" Mark asked, watching me rub my hand around my stomach like something was ailing.

"I actually am getting kinda hungry to tell you the truth."

"Really? It's not quite lunchtime yet." He monitored, looking down at his watch to judge the time. "Didn't you eat anything this morning before you left your house?"

"Yeah, but it's been that kind of day so far. Know what I mean?"

"Quite hectic and unpredictable, right?"

"Yeah, nailed it, so maybe we should pick up some fast food before we go out looking at costumes with the crew. Y'know chill out and take a breather."

The sudden change in ulterior motives made him double think his actions.

"I don't know. What do you say, Ry?"

"Well there's actually a food court over there," he pointed while scanning the area. "You guys can meet back up with us when you're finished. After all, I got the keys and you really can't go anywhere without me, can you?"

Mark and I braced as Ryan, once again, continuously showboated his authority status. "It would actually work out better for me to get away from you two clowns for a little while, anyway."

"Y'know you can't live without us, Ry." Mark remarked, knowing his brother's only true joy in life was causing friction and pain between them.

"See you ladies later, then. Peace out!"

"Wait a minute, hold up," Mark yelled, as Ryan stormed ahead of us, "Is Jeff even here yet? The parking lot looks empty as hell."

"Are you sure Halloween is tomorrow?" I countered, stirring up the pot of antagonism.

"They can meet me inside, morons. There's no reason I shouldn't get a head start without them, right?"

"If you say so, bro! Just don't try on any of the outfits without adult supervision."

"Screw you, guys!" He yelled back, before walking out of the picture completely.

"Man, Mark, why do you put up with that guy? He's a jerk."

"Hey, you have a brother too, don't you? It's just the nature of the beast, I guess, to have a mortal enemy that ticks you off daily. They can't control us, it's human nature to be slaves to our upbringing, ain't it? Isn't it best to just fight back whenever we can? Wouldn't you at least agree with me on that?"

"What the heck are you talking about?"

"Aren't you trying to be a writer, dude?"

"Yeah, so? What's your point?"

"Well, then, you should be more up to date and alert on the matters of sociological behavior within the family, right? It'll give you a good chance to create good dialogue when you're ready to plot stories for the future."

"Since when did you become some kind of expert on the subject?"

"Expert? It's simple common sense. Ain't it funny too how all these geniuses we learn about in school tell us nothing more then what we already know, ourselves? Sometimes I think school is nothing but a ripoff. I almost feel sorry for the parents who pay to have their children put in private schools."

"How come?"

"How come, you ask? I mean, really, just look, we're getting an education paid for by the taxpayer and in the end it's all useless knowledge, right? Sure they might get a better job but is the money really all worth it? Didn't somebody once claim it as the root of all evil?"

"True, but money is survival, ain't it? You kinda need it to get by."

"Maybe so, but how much do we really need? Shouldn't we give people their fair share? I'm getting sick of all these wall street types sticking it to us."

"How old are you again?" I asked, thinking I was talking to some 1960s radical who was on the verge of starting some leftist Revolution.

"Age doesn't matter, man. It's the truth, ain't it?"

"That's really not up for any of us to decide."

"Well I have a big problem with that."

"Are you turning socialist or something?"

"What is it with you, does everything have to be political in nature? It's not like I'm trying to run the country. These are just my opinions. Give me a break!"

"Well, yeah, it kinda does, actually. It's called living life, Karl."

"Karl?"

"Karl Marx, don't you get it?"

"Yeah, I get it. Anyway, for me, personally, I only need enough money that can get me by."

"And how much is that, Einstein?"

"As much as I say."

"Good grief." I yawned, feeling I was losing all hope with this conversation.

"And who may I say are you, now - Charlie Brown?" He chuckled.

"Jesus, Mark, I didn't think you could be quite the philosopher."

"I'm not, I just happen to stumble upon genius when nobody expects it out of me - it's quite Shakespearean, really.

Isn't it?"

"I'll say. I almost fear you now with any power you may hold."

"Ah, please don't think that, man. You'd know I'd never do anything that would jeopardize our friendship, right? And besides, I really wouldn't want to put myself on the same pedestal with Jesus Christ or some dead commie bastard - it's more fun playing - "

"Oh, look - speak of the devil." He waved, confusing his profound wisdom with the car that was rolling by us. "Here he comes now."

"Who, the devil's advocate?" I mocked, getting in on his joke.

"No, it's just Jeff, you idiot. Well, actually, you may have a point if I think about it."

"But I thought he drove a pickup?"

"I think he was only using that to haul the instruments they had. Y'know to have more space for things."

"Yeah, I guess that makes sense. Maybe this is his mom's car?"

"Yeah, maybe," we giggled, "Nothing would surprise me anymore."

We waited as the car parked, strictly eyeing the passenger who tempted our vision.

"It looks like Lexi is in the car with him."

"It looks like it."

"Hey, why don't you ask her if she wants to come and join us and get a burger."

"I don't know," I shrugged. "I already feel uncomfortable about the whole thing to begin with. That would just make things weirder."

"Well, then, maybe this is your opportunity to make things right. Ever think about that?"

You like to put me on the spot, don't you?"

"Pretty much, but in all honesty, you did better than I did last night. I say go for it; besides, Ryan wouldn't know about it."

I looked at him as if he was out of his mind.

"Well, actually, he would, but at least you would be able to see her and have a final meal before he kicks your ass into the ground."

"Mark, sometimes I do wonder about you."

"I'm just sayin' as a friend, I'd understand."

"Okay, maybe, we'll play it by ear. I don't want to make it seem forced."

"Yeah, I get it."

"By the way, I thought you told Ry you didn't have any money on you."

"And you believed me? I told him that, hoping he'd drop me off. I really didn't want to come with everything that happened."

"Well, then, maybe, this might just be your lucky day, then." He said as Jeff approached.

"Well, we'll see about that, won't we?" I gulped, fearing the worst could still happen.

Chapter Thirty-Eight

"**W**hat are you two idiots up to?" Jeff asked, recognizing us hanging out by ourselves, probably looking for an excuse to cause mischief. "Didn't we have enough of you two last night at the bar? I, mean, shouldn't you boys be at home resting up like the little babies that you are? You were up all night after all, right? Your poor mommies weren't worried sick after they found out where you guys snuck off to, were they?"

"No," Mark answered, refusing to let the pandering get the better of him.

"Oooooh, watch out, now!" Jeff incited, becoming childish in nature. "You might go postal and I wouldn't want to have to use my backup to fix it."

"And what backup is that, you dope?"

"You know precisely what backup that is, Mark. And I'd be afraid for you if I had to use it."

"Jeff, can you stop being an ass for once in your life and y'know - be normal? There's a term for that - it's called maturity. Ever hear of it? You sound stupid and it gets really irritating having to hear it all the time."

"Yeah, it's not like it's even our fault we're here in the first place," I fired back, becoming increasingly tense with the whole situation at hand, praying too that he would disappear quickly so I could manage some time alone with Lexi, who was still patiently waiting to get out of the vehicle.

"We heard about what happened with you and that girl

you were trying to hook up with and how you probably wouldn't want others to find out about what really went down, would you?"

"Find out about what, exactly?"

"Oh, nothing." Mark bluffed, knowing precisely how to play his hand.

Jeff gazed, displaying an odd face at us, showing annoyance and seemingly folding to our very will - allowing a firm consensus that we'd won in this wicked battle of brawn against the brain.

"Okay, okay, enough is enough, so why the hell are you two bozos really here? Besides giving me a headache."

"Ryan made us," Mark comically answered, segueing the most logical response to his almost senseless question. "Actually, it was more like he forced us to come if you want to be specific about it."

"And what do you mean by that?"

"Apparently," he pointed my way, "He has it out with my friend over here."

My head spun, appalled to note my best friend had sold me out.

"What the fuck, dude?"

"He was going to find out about it, anyway." Mark frowned, throwing up both hands like he was about to get ambushed by the police. "Why don't you just tell him and get it over with? It's not like it's him who you should be afraid of, am I right?"

I glossed over at Mark with severe intent to cause nothing but physical harm to his body, but backed off once I saw Lexi finally making her presence shown to the three of us.

"Seriously, the guy you should be afraid of is inside the Halloween shop right now trying on costumes like the little girlie girl that he is. You shouldn't need to worry about Jeff. He's not worth it."

"What the hell are you guys going on about?"

"Jesus, Jeff, you and Ryan are two peas in a pod, aren't

you?"

"Mark, don't make me smack the living daylights out of you for saying that."

"I'm sorry, but you're always out of the loop on everything and I hate being the one to have to explain it back."

"Out of the loop about what?" Lexi chimed in, possibly observing the fact that my hands were sweating like a pig, intimidated to speak coherently - praying also to God that Mark wouldn't embarrass the hell out of me directly in front of her.

"I must say, Lexi," Mark spoke gently, swaying his words like a used car salesman baiting to attract a sale. "You look quite lovely this afternoon, if you don't mind me saying."

"Why, gee, thanks kid, thanks for caring. I appreciate it." She laughed, playing along.

"I'm sorry but you didn't allow me to finish."

"Wait a minute, where are you going with this?" Jeff interrupted, beginning to have enough of his lip.

"I'm not going anywhere with it. Can't a guy just be nice for the sake of being nice? I want her to know the nice guys can actually finish first for a change, not last."

Jeff's eyes rolled - perceiving that Mark's bullshit stunk like a week's old leftover trash.

"Heck yeah!" I inappropriately shouted, "Maybe you can learn a thing or two from us. We are the mature adults here, correct?"

"No doubt about that," Mark concluded, slapping my hand back, holding out hope that we'd be able to tag team a victory over our familiar foe.

"No one was asking you, stupid. This is between me and Mark - so back off will ya!"

"I think it's sweet," Lexi gestured, giving Mark a high five. "Maybe they're right about one thing, maybe it is you - *Jeff*."

"Tell me you're not taking their side?"

"I'm not taking any side. I'm just examining what's going on and thinking for myself. It's very lady-like - idiot."

Mark and I remained stunned and amazed at how defiant Lexi was sticking up for us.

"You better keep this one," Mark whispered under his breath, sensing a golden opportunity to throw down the knockout punch of victory.

"Well, anyway, we were wondering," Mark continued, ignoring Jeff's entire existence, "Would you mind coming with me and having some lunch with my associate and I?"

"Your associate?" I chuckled, still baffled.

"You know what," she answered, "That doesn't actually sound like a bad idea. I might take you guys up on that."

Chapter Thirty-Nine

I t was weird walking beside Lexi heading to the food court. It wasn't even twenty-four hours since our rendezvous had elapsed but the silence between us continued to escalate; feeling like an eternity had passed since we last locked eyes with one another.

Thankfully, I had Mark as my buffer, helping to navigate and break the uncertain ice that was still thick to the crunch.

"Seriously, what are you doing on a perfectly good Saturday afternoon hanging out with those two losers, for, anyway?" He asked Lexi.

She ignored him, coming to terms with how he wanted her to judge herself.

"I'm not fallin' for your trick, little dude."

"Little dude?" I laughed, enjoying the fact that she was giving Mark a taste of his own medicine.

"What trick?" He gasped, fainting surprised and unknowing. "I'm just looking for a simple answer to sum up the completely absurd."

"You do know that if they weren't flesh and blood, you'd probably not be thinking that way, right?"

"Jeff isn't flesh and blood, mind you."

"I know that, you goof. I'm talking about Ryan."

"Well, I can't control that guy. He is who he is despite me. I keep reminding myself that he had to have been adopted at birth and I'm the only legitimate child my parents had. I'm telling you, my parents are just hiding the evidence from me, it'll be released shortly, I swear. And then you guys will never hear the end of it."

Lexi and I giggled getting in on the cheap humor that may or may not have been true.

As usual, with Mark, one could never quite tell.

"You're a looney tune," I reminded him, believing the banter was getting out of control and a little farfetched to be taken seriously.

Lexi, on the other hand, continued to focus in on his rant, poking holes at his ramblings.

"But, you know damn well when push comes to shove you'll always have his back when need be."

Mark shrugged, accepting her answer while bowing out to let the lone woman win the fight.

"You know what I mean. The whole blood brother pack and all that jazz. I have sisters, too, we're no better than you macho guys, just different genders, that's all.

"She does have a point? I added, alerting a moral truth that couldn't be overlooked or denied, hoping also to gain some points for potential things to come.

Mark, unhinged with my quick wit, decided instead to belt me in the arm - annoyed he was losing the argument and perhaps a solid friendship if things continued to work against him.

"Okay, okay, enough about me then, why don't we just take a moment and talk about you two and what I heard took place last night?"

Lexi stopped dead in her tracks, taking a second to catch her breath, while possibly anticipating for me to say something first, letting the smoke clear the air about his misguided statement.

"Well, it looks like the cat is out of the bag, ain't it, now?" I feared, turning to her, hoping she'd finish the next line as if somehow this was all rehearsed and planned beforehand.

Unfortunately, she remained quiet, forcing Mark and myself to hold our breath with the next few words that sprung out of her mouth.

"How long have you two been friends?" She snubbed, disregarding the question in its entirety and keeping the focus squarely on the two of us.

"Well, let's see," Mark thought, pretending to care about our history like it was somehow meaningful to this discussion. "We were in little league, weren't we? I think it may have been at tryouts."

"Yeah, it was," I frustratedly answered, still angry at him for belting me. "And you tried to knock my teeth out by jamming your frickin' foot into my face sliding into second base, remember?"

"Oh, yeah, that's right. I do remember that, now. Those were some fun times we had back then. You know, you should have been there with us too, Lexi, if you wanted to get the full story about our past."

Lexi shook her head, not really figuring what to say next. "I guess that's just the price I pay for being two years older than you too, I lucked out. Don't worry, I had my own fun without you."

"I'm telling you, though, we were a wild bunch back then. You should have seen us."

"Like you guys aren't now?"

"Well, I guess that really depends on if you think we have fully matured."

"Based on what I saw last night, I'd say there's still room for some improvement."

"Don't worry, we can show you a good time again. I had a blast last night."

"Mark, can you please shut up, already," I cried, raging uncomfortable with his motormouth.

"Dude, I'm just filling her in on what she asked for. Don't be upset with me about it. Get angry at her."

"Sorry, Lexi, this isn't like us at all."

"Oh, I see," she observed, perhaps painting us as nothing more than a bunch of wannabe rebels looking to be cool. "You boys are quite the odd couple."

"You can say that again."

"Maybe that's why you guys get along so well."

"I'll say, He's my yin to my yang."

"Hey, but wait, don't judge too quickly, there, miss." Mark disputed. "I mean, we were what, eight or nine when we met? We were just your typical little boys doing stupid boy things, right? You can't fault us too badly for that."

"For once, I have to agree with my colleague. It was just stupid fate that made us friends in the end."

"You know, what," Mark concluded, "I'm actually getting kind of hungry. Maybe all this yapping had something to do with it. I'll just shut up now and figure out what to eat."

I looked at him, leaving him with only one comment left on my mind.

"It's about damn time!"

Chapter Forty

"Have you guys decided what you want to order yet?" Lexi nodded, skimming through the menu directly in front of us, waiting for our cashier to take it.

"I don't know. I'm kind of getting sick of eating the same old thing. We should've gone somewhere else if you ask me."

"Mark - you're the idiot who didn't even want to come to begin with. Stop your sobbing and make up your damn mind, already, will ya?"

"I know, but all I'm saying is, do you think they are still serving breakfast? I'm kind of feeling that more right now for some reason. I have an aching for something with dairy."

"I'm pretty sure they closed breakfast at 11 so your kind of out of luck, kid."

"Maybe I'll just buy a milkshake, have the best of both worlds then, that won't hurt, right?"

"Dude, just get whatever the hell you want before I have it in my mind to slap you silly and throw you out of the joint."

"Jesus don't have a cow man. I don't want you turning violent over here."

"A cow?" I laughed. "Why didn't your parents just call you Bart and get it over with?"

"Because the Simpsons weren't around yet when I was born doofus. Get your years straight before you try to make a snappy comeback at me. I'm a pro, remember? I'm actually a natural born genius to tell you the truth and I don't like hearing any rude remarks coming, especially from you."

"Sure, you are. That's why you were the one walking around the school campus last year with a "kick me" sign stitched on your back made courtesy of the football team who had it in for you."

"That *never* happened!"

"That's only what you say but believe me I have proof of the incident from fellow sources who told me they did it."

"No, you don't."

"Wanna bet?"

"I don't have to. I can tell you're full of shit just by looking at your face, retard. You don't even have any friends besides me that matter, anyway. Don't be pulling that sort of crap around here or else you'll get burned."

"Will you two losers knock it off, already?" Lexi implored, focusing on the customers behind us who began to get annoyed with our choice of foul words and obnoxious behavior. Especially the elderly woman holding a bag looking as if she was about to swing it our way without mercy and knock us both out.

"You two boys need to watch your mouth. Do your parents let you talk like that in front of them? I wouldn't think so."

"Sorry, miss, no they don't. We just have a little situation going on now. We didn't mean to startle you about anything. You can just go back to doing what you're doing."

The woman looked away with a stick up her nose, refusing to reply, allowing me to make up judgments about her attitude, accepting instead to criticize Mark so maybe it could help ease her pain.

"Why don't you watch your language when you're around civilized people, eh? I can't be your guardian all of the time and look after you. Stop it, you're embarrassing me."

Mark, hesitant to respond, fumed an obligatory remark under his breath thinking I wouldn't hear it.

"What was that?"

"Nothing," he silently muffled to himself, "Can we please

let it go and get on with our lives?"

"Fine by me."

"Who's paying for this meal, anyway?"

"I guess I am, so make it cheap, will ya? I only have so much cash on hand right now and you're not necessarily the type of person that I'd wish to spend my money on."

"Well, then, what about Lexi?"

"What about her?"

"She's here too, right? Aren't you going to pay for her being that you and her -"

"We'll see," I interrupted, before the red blush reached my face.

"Mark does have a point. No lady should have to pay for their own meal whenever a man is around. That really goes without saying. Wouldn't you think?"

I nodded my head slowly without saying a word - knowing any verbal queue would be futile.

"Thanks, Lexi, It didn't take you long to finally come around to the dark side and agree with me on something. I have to give it to you."

"I know, I'm only hoping I didn't accidentally kill off some brain cells in the process."

"I doubt it - you'll live. It might do you some good in the long haul."

"I severely doubt that, junior."

"I only hope I'll live," I thought, realizing my cash flow was now decreasing by the second. "I only have twenty bucks on me, that better be enough to cover the three of us."

"Didn't I just say I would save you some dough by getting a milkshake?"

"Yeah, but those things are still expensive, aren't they?"

"Dude, stop worrying. You'll have enough. Maybe you should just eat a little light. Go on a diet or something. Save some money for yourself?"

"Whatever, I'm the one that's starving here. I'm going to get what I want."

"Suit yourself, then. Just thought I'd mention it."

"You know you guys really are a piece of work," Lexi smiled. "Who really needs a girlfriend when you have each other to kick around and torment?"

"C'mon, really?" I commented. "There are other benefits for having a girl, Lexi, but I see what you're getting at."

"Sure you do," she winked. "Well, anyway, you boys figure things out quick, I got to go use the ladies room. Just order me number 5 when I come back out, okay?"

"Sure, I'll do it," I answered, as she vanished from sight. "Jesus, that girl sure knows how to walk to the restroom with style."

"You're telling me," Mark whistled in agreement, "I only wish I had her legs."

Chapter Forty-One

"**Y**o, you boys, are you ready to order something off the menu or what?" The female cashier snapped, bitch slapping us back into reality, looking at us funny as if we were recently stripped out from a coma.

"Oh, yeah, right, so sorry about that. We were just preoccupied with other things."

"I can see that." She smirked, possibly alarming herself with whether Mark was coming on to her.

"Are you judging us or something by the way we acted just now?"

"No," she cried with laughter. "Although, I do have some choice words with your lady friend who you both were eyeballing after."

"Wait a minute, you know Lexi?"

"Yeah, she's in my bio class. Her name is, actually, Alexa Charlotte. We're not friends or anything like that, if you're wondering. I just know her from school."

"Oh, really, that's interesting. A girl with two first names. How do you like 'dem apples?"

"That's the least of her problems, in my opinion. I hear she's a bit promiscuous. Let's just say she has a bit of a bad reputation."

"Oh yeah, really, I like that, in a woman. It's a real turn on. Wouldn't you say?"

"C'mon, man, can we just order," I interrupted, hoping the two would quiet down before things got out of hand. "I don't wanna be holding up the line anymore then we've been. It's Saturday afternoon and people are eager to eat something."

"One minute, man. I have to know something first, though."

"Like what?"

"What's your name, miss?"

"Mark, she's wearing a name tag on her uniform. It says Bridgette. Do you need glasses or are you just pulling our leg?"

Mark didn't answer but Bridgette appeared relieved like I was coming to her rescue.

"Excuse me, but can you guys please get on with it?" The elderly woman continued to nag from behind. "There are people waiting."

"Okay, okay - sorry, I will!" I hollered back, uncontrollably. "Will that please you, ma'am?"

"I've had it, I'm going somewhere else!" The woman declared with frustration, walking out of the restaurant with fire in her eyes and leaving all witnesses in shambles.

"Boy, do you know how to clear a room or what?"

"That really wasn't my intention, Mark. I hope management doesn't come out now and kick us out too."

"I wouldn't worry too much about that. That old bag had it coming. We'll be fine."

"You really know how to be kind to the elderly, don't you?"

"That woman?" He shrugged, "I'd hate to be that bitter when I get old. Now, where are we?"

"I think you were trying to ask me out?" Bridgette answered, filling him in.

"Oh, yeah, that's right. So will ya? You can trust me. I don't bite."

"Well, the answer is no," she boldly expressed, "So can I please just get your order before I die of boredom over here?"

"Yeah, man, give it to her. " I complained, "Stop wasting our time. I mean after what happened last night, I'm surprised you still trust the female species at all."

"C'mon, you can't blame everything on one bad

experience. I believe in second chances with the hope that things will work itself out for the better."

"You sure are a fool then, my friend."

"Hey, I'm at least trying here, man, give me a break. It's a hard and risky game we're playing right now with the opposite sex, isn't it?"

"Bridgette," I said, ignoring his whining, "We'll just have the deluxe combo, a number 5 and a milkshake. That won't be too much to ask for, will it?"

"No, it won't. Thank you, Jesus." She praised, in excitement. "I thought you'd never make up your mind."

"We're sorry for any trouble we might have caused. If Mark had any money on him right now, I'd force him to tip you for his behavior but I know you wouldn't want to date a guy like that anyway, he's such a cheapskate."

"Ah, no worries, I wouldn't want that."She smiled, finally getting familiar with us. "It was just nice to have some attention come my way."

"You mean you don't get hit on by high schoolers like us on a daily basis?"

"Well, sometimes I do."

"You should. You're a real catch."

"Hey, wait, are you trying to hook up with me, too?"

"Yeah, bro," Mark wondered. "Stop trying to steal my style and chick."

"What are you going on about? You have no style, which is why we're in this predicament in the first place, mind you."

"Alexa was right about one thing," Bridgette observed with amusement watching over us. "You two are completely hopeless when it comes to finding love."

"Well, we'll just let the hands of time settle that score, won't we? We don't need to hear your little opinion, missy."

"C'mon Mark, let's wait for our stuff and be done here. Good day, miss."

"Fine," he accepted. "Anyway, it was nice meeting you Bridgette. Let's hope our paths meet again sometime."

Bridgette took a deep breath while slightly refraining herself from saying anything negative or off putting.

"We'll see about that, won't we?" She ended, as we walked off.

"So, what else is floating around your mind that needs to come out?" I asked Mark, hanging in limbo, looking for a seat to relax in as we waited for our lunch.

"Nothing much, man, but if you want to know, I'd say, what do you think Lexi is doing in the bathroom right now?"

I looked at him with a face that could make an honest friend upset.

"Watch it, I don't want to hear your perverted thoughts any more than I have to."

"It's not perverted," he argued. "I'm being serious about this. Don't you ever ask yourself why it is that certain girls are in the bathroom for an extra amount of time and yet us guys can be in and out in seconds?"

"That's because we don't care how we look, stupid. It's also all genetics and I don't want to get involved with it."

"Yeah, that's true, chicks are more particular about their appearances and such, aren't they?"

"Hey, is that who I think it is?" I asked, cutting him off entirely, refusing to answer or comprehend any of his ridiculous theories.

"Who?"

"Over there."

"Over where?"

"By the door, coming in."

"Oh, hey, it's Tyler. What do you think he's doing here?"

"I don't know numbnuts, why don't you get up and ask?"

Chapter Forty-Two

I'm not going to say I was surprised seeing Tyler Blackford. It wasn't like it was that unusual but with him, socializing on school grounds seemed more appropriate due to the circumstances of distance.

It was possible he was out with friends, enjoying the weekend without us like any regular kid would. It just took Mark and myself a moment to collect our thoughts, figuring what to say correctly, being that he had caught us off guard.

It's funny, but we really didn't know him well enough to judge for ourselves. We'd figure we'd play it by ear, letting the conversation flow like it always had whenever the three of us got together.

"Hey, wassup, dude?" Mark greeted, going up with a casual fist bump.

"Oh, hey. What's happening, man?"

"Fancy seeing you, here, right?"

"I'd say so." Tyler concurred, overlooking me sitting by myself at the table, waiting for someone to hopefully come by and join. "That sure was a crazy day we had yesterday, wasn't it? Getting sent home early and all. It was fun, though, I'd say."

"Yeah, but we made it through, right? You can't ask for anything better than getting sent home like that. We all enjoyed it."

"Did you guys find out what happened with the bomb threat or who called it in? It was all bogus, wasn't it? I mean that's what I figured but was any of it true?"

"It's a bit of a long story," Mark replied. "But we have other news that happened which might appear more awesome in comparison then that. This actually involves us."

"Really? What did you guys do, rob a bank or something and get away with it?"

"Get real, man. That would never happen. And even If I did, I swear to you that you'd probably never see me again."

"I'm just sayin' though," He laughed. "Anything is possible, ain't it?"

"Why don't you order your food and then come sit with us at our booth and I'll tell you all about it?"

"It must be good if you're that desperate to let it out."

"Desperate?" Mark questioned. "We're friends, aren't we? What are you talking about?"

"I'm just joking, man, Jesus, get a sense of humor."

"Sure, you were. Anyway, are you here with anyone right now?"

"Not really, I mean, just my dad but he ain't coming in. He dropped me off so I could eat something quick. He'll be back in about a half hour to pick me up, though."

"That's good, because, believe me - you'll want to stay around to hear this."

"Okay, alright. Give me a sec. Be patient."

"Cool beans - we'll see you in a few."

"You bet."

"Oh, wait," Tyler paused, giving him an afterthought to take with him before he vanished. "I have some good news to tell you guys too that you may wanna hear."

"That's great, tell us all about it when you get done. Do you see us sitting over there?"

I waved, showing direction as Tyler gestured back.

"Yep, I see you."

"Good, then we're clear to go."

"So, what did you tell him?" I asked as Mark returned.

"He says he has some news for the both of us to hear."

"What does that mean?"

"I'm not sure but he looked pretty excited about it like it was something important that he wanted to share."

"Did you tell him that Lexi was with us?"

"We didn't get that deep," Mark mumbled, hearing our order number called out. "We'll have room for the two of them to tell us everything once they arrive, though."

"Good, now get *my* food." I commanded, eager to chow down before someone mistakenly stole our meal ticket away from us.

"Whatever you say, master." He mocked, getting up, completing the demand. "You do realize you sound like a little bitch when you say that, right?"

"Well it takes one to know one, right? Now scram out of here, will ya, you idiot!"

Mark rushed up, stumbling forward, forgetting to realize that his shoelace was untied.

"I mean look at you, you're a walking klutz! I can't take you anywhere, can I?"

"Don't mock me."

"I'm sorry but it's too easy. By the way, have you seen Lexi yet?"

"No," he answered, bending down to tie his laces. "Oh, wait, I see her coming out of the bathroom now. Maybe you should yell something and let her know where we are sitting."

"No, maybe you should. That appears to be more you, eh?"

"Whatever. I'm not the one who made an old woman get frustrated and walk out of the line like you did."

"Yeah, I suppose it did get heated before. We caused enough trouble as it is, we better not."

"Yo, Lexi!" Mark shouted, getting up and ignoring everything I said. *"We're over here - come join us!"*

Lexi spotted us, feeling unease with the crowd of spectators who were gaining attention.

"Why'd you do that?" I scorned, becoming embarrassed for Lexi and everyone involved.

"Because I could." He snickered, avoiding any eye contact

and heading away quickly.

"It looks like you two haven't changed a bit since I left you." Lexi frowned, coming over. "So, where's my stuff or do I have to beat it out of you?"

"Mark just went up to get it."

"So that was what all that fussing was about."

"Yeah, he's quite obnoxious. He wanted to impress you, I guess."

"Well, I already knew that, dummy."

"Anyway, we have a friend who's going to sit with us. Are you okay with that?"

"He's not Mark's boyfriend, is he?"

"Wow, you're savage! Aren't you?"

"I can play your silly games too." She smiled.

I couldn't help but be sincere, safely betting myself that maybe this was the best time to get a few things off my chest.

"Lexi," I whispered softly, hoping she could hear, "We need to talk."

Chapter Forty-Three

I became choked with fear, this was it, do or die, speak my mind proudly, letting Lexi know directly how I felt, praying too that she was listening. I wanted answers and this time I wouldn't get shut out by an obvious double take to avoid confrontation.

"Here, you go, master, take your stinking order and die!" Mark interjected, disrupting everything as he threw our lunch tray on the table.

"Oh, yeah, thanks. This looks good." Lexi cheered, picking up her food and snatching the ketchup packets that were scattered around.

"What did you get, anyway?"

"A sandwich, Mark." Lexi taunted.

"I know that, but which one is yours?"

"I got the hamburger with cheese, doofus, does that answer your stupid question?"

"You don't have to be mean about it. I was simply asking."

"Mark, I'm surprised with you, you like to dish it with people but never wanna take it."

"That's what I tell him all the time," I chimed in, getting a good sense for my liking.

"I don't know but maybe you two are good together. You seem to know when to gang up on me for no particular reason."

We paused as the silence spoke volumes. I didn't want to react improperly because in my opinion, Mark had a valid point. I just needed Lexi to confirm it, somehow.

Which, for all practical purposes, she wasn't doing, trapping herself inside some type of denial prison that was beginning to tick me off.

"What milkshake did you get?"

"It's banana, Lexi, I like to be nutritious."

"Mark, a milkshake is not a protein shake, you gain weight by drinking it, not the other way around." I sneered, feeling comfortable I could at least murder my best friend with clever insults, releasing tension for the things that weren't being said out loud.

"Oh, I think I see Tyler coming now." Mark waved, signaling him to come over.

Tyler flinched but anxious to greet and talk.

"So, do you want to hear the good news?" He proposed, breaking in, not minding the extra occupant who was sitting with us.

"Yeah, what is it?"

"Oh, hey, it looks like you got company."

"Yeah, her name is Lexi." Mark acknowledged. "We met her yesterday. She's part of the story we need to tell you." He gloated, putting his arm around her and looking to possibly touch her breast. "You're not afraid of her, Ty, are you?"

"Get outta here!" Lexi blushed, shoving Mark away quickly.

Tyler remained skeptical, staring back at me, making sure he hadn't crash landed on an alien planet invaded by moronic men.

"No, Ty, you haven't crossed into the Twilight Zone." I smiled, understanding his confused state. "Come, sit, tell us the good news."

"Yeah, okay, anyway," he shrugged, continuing to tell his tale. "The reason I'm out and about today is because I got this."

He reached into his pocket pulling out something that looked oddly familiar.

"Oh, look, you got one of those." Mark noticed, trying to

judge what exactly it was.

"It's a cellphone , you twerp!" I explained, still baffled by his smug behavior. "My brother got one of those too, Ty. You're going to like it."

"Yeah, they're really neat, man."

"You know you didn't buy that, your daddy did." Mark pouted, making believe people cared what he thought.

"Whatever, man. I've been saving up to get one of these for some time now. It has been on my bucket list all year."

"Well, let me see it, then," Mark pleaded, grabbing it away without warning.

"Hey, what gives?" Tyler reacted with shock. "That's mine."

"I'm not going to break it, dude. I just want to see it for myself."

"Well, then, get your own!" He complained. "They're selling them across the street if you care that deeply about it."

"Where'd you go to get it?" I asked, wanting input.

"I was going to go to RadioShack but Circuit City was nearby and they had a sale so I went over there instead."

"Y'know my dad supervises at the RadioShack."

"Hmm - I didn't know that."

"Don't go telling anyone, though, it's not like you would get a discount." Mark derided.

"Hey, he gave one to Barry, didn't he?"

"Well, yeah, but that's because he was working for him during the summer, wasn't he?"

"Well, yeah, that's true."

"So, who are you gonna call, Ty?"

"Funny you should ask."

"You're not stalking Amanda are you?" Mark drum rolled, waiting for him to take the punch.

"Well, actually, I didn't tell you guys this yesterday but she actually gave me her number during gym before we evacuated out."

You're kidding, right?"

"No, I told her I was thinking about getting the phone and she offered me it up front."

"But doesn't she have a boyfriend? I mean we saw him with her, right? Why would she just randomly give it to you?" Mark debated, feeling his ego was getting bruised. "Unless maybe she was looking for someone to beat you up? Y'know, kinda mess with your head. Girls like to do that, don't they?"

"Mark, you're nuts!" I countered, feeling it best to defend Tyler.

"Well, there is a twist to the tale, Mark." Tyler revealed. "You see, the guy we saw standing with her yesterday wasn't actually her boyfriend."

"You mean that Alex guy? He sure made it appear that way."

"How do you know that?" I interrogated, becoming a police cop directing questions.

"I called her up last night."

"You what?"

"You heard me, and she told me with her own lips."

"So, who is he then?"

"Oh, Alex, he's a friend of hers but he's actually dating her best friend, Carol. He was only there to drive the two of them back home."

"You, see," Lexi laughed, once again mocking us, "You two really are behind the curve."

"There's actually another reason why I'm out today." Tyler continued. "We're going to a matinee in about an hour."

"A what?" Mark replied, hearing a word not fit for his vocabulary.

"A movie you idiot." He backfired. "I told her to meet me at the theater at round 3 or so.

"So, you're saying you still have time to spend with us before then, right?"

"What are you getting at, Mark?"

"After we're finished here," He proclaimed, "We're heading over to the Halloween store to mess with my brother

and his friend. Care to come?"
   "Sure, it sounds fun, what the hell."

Chapter Forty-Four

I sat there, waiting, as the rest of the crew slowly ate up time.

"Boy, do you eat fast, or what?" Tyler gazed, amusingly, noticing I had pretty much devoured my entire lunch in little under five minutes.

"You should've seen him earlier," Mark added, "He was starving half to death, I think I almost heard his stomach explode."

"You may have," I burped, getting a sensation from the sweet taste of Diet Pepsi currently flowing into my system.

"I don't know how you do it, man."

"Do what?" I asked.

"Eat like that. In a hurry, like your life depended on it. I couldn't do that."

"That's right, I forgot, you don't have any siblings, do you?"

Tyler shook his head feeling a tad guilty that he didn't.

"Well, it just becomes second nature to shove food down your throat when you have an older brother who is always on your back looking to steal it away from you."

"I know what you mean," Mark sympathized. "Sometimes when my idiot brother is around, you never know how long it'll be before it gets snatched and I'm, like, dude, there's nothing left. I think it's just out of habit that we do it. At least, that's my thinking."

"I'm kind of glad I'm an only child. I don't have to worry

about any of that harassment."

"Yeah, your life is pampered, ain't it? Makes me wonder if you still wear a diaper underneath your clothes. Should I check to find out?"

"Mark!" Lexi intervened, almost choking from laughter. "Don't listen to these two numbskulls - apparently, you're in a better place, anyway. You're with a *girl*."

"Thanks," Tyler accepted with some shyness showing. "I appreciate it."

"You're welcome."

Mark nudged me as Lexi's flirtation seemed to be persuasive enough, sending mixed signals.

"You better stop him before he gets her too." He whispered, thinking instigation was probably the proper form for revenge to save my dying reputation.

"Is that your phone going off, Ty?" I asked, attempting to ignore Mark's response, fast tracking my ego before any real frustration sparked.

"Well, aren't you going to answer it, Ty?"

"Oh, yeah, sorry guys. Let me take this. I'll be back in a sec. Don't steal my food while I'm gone."

Tyler got up, pacing around as the three of us observed.

"You think that's Amanda calling him back, right?"

"It wouldn't surprise me if it was, Mark. Maybe she's taking a rain check, letting him down easily. It wouldn't be the first time."

"I can't believe you guys." Lexi blazed with astonishment. "Isn't he like your friend? That's the moral support you show?"

"Oooooh, she burned you there!" Mark blew up in shock.

"We're just having a little fun. Don't get sore with us."

"I don't know but when I see you guys all I see are your brothers. You're turning into them sooner than expected. By next year I'll probably not even notice the difference."

"Is that good or bad?" Mark glared, knowing any answer would be thoroughly challenged.

"I think you know."

"Chill, guys." I butted back in, "Here comes Tyler now. He'll tell us what's going on."

"So who was that?"

"It was my dad." He responded, looking a little happier than we'd expected.

"What did he want?"

"He has to run errands and said he'll pick me up later tonight."

"So?"

"That's good news."

"Why's that?"

"I get the whole day to myself. I'll go with you guys and then hit it back up with Amanda afterwards."

"It looks like today may be your lucky day then." Lexi applauded, once again buttering him up while making Mark and myself appear invisible.

"It might be."

"So what movie are you going to see?"

"I don't know yet. I don't even know what's playing to be honest. Knowing her, she might pick a rom-com or something of that ilk."

"Well, my brother and his girl took in a showing of The Six Sense last night."

"Oh, I heard about that one, not sure if Amanda is into scary movies, though. Was it any good?"

"I'm not sure. I heard there was a twist, so, I guess, it'll keep you entertained until the end."

"I'm, actually, surprised that the movie is still playing," Mark disrupted. "Didn't it come out in the summer?"

"I think it did." I answered. "I'm guessing maybe they saw it over at *Dollar Tix,* y'know, the one by the drugstore that plays the movies the week before they get pulled from the theaters?"

"Y'know what movie you need to show her, Ty?"

"If you even think about saying *The Blair Witch Project* I'm going to slap you."

"Hey, now, it was only a suggestion, besides let Tyler

think for himself. You don't own him."

"I hear you both guys but I think I'll just suffer alone with anything she wants to watch right now. After all, the chick is always right. Right?"

"Smart kid." Lexi praised, demolishing our spirit once and for all.

"She's right." Tyler followed up. "I'm sticking with that for now. It's in my best interest."

"Oh, well, whatever you say man. Are y'all ready to head out of here or what?"

"I still have a few french fries leftover. You want any of them?"

"Sure," I accepted, grabbing them away.

"Maybe you should leave a tip?" Mark suggested, maneuvering his body to get up from his seat.

"You don't do that here, you moron."

"Well, the way we've been acting, I figure it would just be a gentle curiosity for someone."

Chapter Forty-Five

I walked out of the food court a little taller and wiser knowing my self-control had mediated within - leaving me relaxed to not punch either one of my two friends with the rage I was still feeling over Lexi's bitchiness about the previous night.

"So, what's the plan, Stan?" Tyler belted with ambition, as the fresh air reached his lungs, mirroring a *Titanic* moment where he felt on top of the world.

"Well, Ty, just so you know - my name's not Stan, so, if you're looking for any direction in life - talk to Mark about that. I can't help you there, buddy."

"Boy, are you a party pooper today. What's with you, huh?"

"Don't mind him," Lexi remarked, clearing her throat from a vicious couch, "He's just that way over what happened between us."

I became stunned - caught off guard, suspecting maybe now was the time she was ready to open-up.

"What's she talking about?"

"Maybe he'll tell you about it." She rushed, poking me from behind and running off before I could fully answer.

"Hey, where are you going?" I yelled at her.

"I'll meet the three of you inside the store, you guys are too slow. You walk like old women."

I couldn't help but smile. If she was a devil, she played one in disguise.

"So *what* really happened?" Tyler hounded, demanding answers.

"It's a long story."

"Well, maybe, now is a better time than ever to tell it. Care to try, sucker?"

"Yeah, go ahead," incited Mark, "Go on Mr. Friday Night, fill him in on the details and our escapades."

"Mr. Friday Night?" Tyler questioned.

"Well, if you really want to know - Mark, myself and Lexi all went to *Hard Luck* and we had a pretty good time together over there."

"You mean the bar? But you're under age. How did you guys get in?"

"Well, we did have our sources."

"What, you mean like a fake ID or something?"

"Not quite."

"My brother got us in," shared Mark, filling him in on some minor specifics.

"Oh yeah, that's right. You were telling me that the other day, weren't you? Your brother is in a rock band with some older guys."

"Well, technically, yes, he is, but their big gig is actually not till tonight. Yesterday was just an appetizer and he invited us to come along."

"He didn't invite us," I recalled. "If I remember correctly, you begged him to take us because we had nothing better to do. You more or less debased your own humanity for it."

"You can keep telling yourself that but that's not true."

"That's cool either way, guys," Tyler confirmed, keeping our story straight and also becoming a little jealous that he wasn't physically there to witness it. "But what does any of that have to do with Lexi?"

"So," I explained, "That's where the story gets interesting and takes a funny u-turn."

"Did you guys get lucky or something?" He laughed, possibly wishing for a rhetorical response.

"Of course, we did," rejoiced Mark, eager to embellish my story at a moment's notice.

"You see, Ty, my brother, Ryan, was actually thinking about dating her until Mr. Smooth over here swept her off her feet and beat him to the punch."

"You see," He pointed, "He was making out with her last night in her car after midnight."

"Is that true?" Tyler questioned.

"Yeah, well, kinda,"

"Congrats, then, man."

"I only wish it was that simple." I told him. "Until just now, she wasn't even bringing anything up. I really didn't know what to make of the whole situation. She's been keeping me in the dark if you know what I mean. Being a real *bitch!*"

"Gosh, I hope Amanda doesn't turn into a monster like that when I see her this afternoon."

"All I can say is good luck. All they do is give us mixed signals and it's very irritating."

"Mark, your brother must have been pissed once he found out, right?"

"You should have seen him this morning. I swear I thought he was going to go postal on his loser ass."

"Don't listen to Mark. It's all a misunderstanding between us that I know will get squared away."

"Let's hope he's a little calmer by now, though."

"I think he is. He's been warming up all day for tonight, showing he's game, he's probably not even paying any attention to us anymore."

"I hope you're right."

"Besides, he wouldn't cause a scene with Lexi around, would he? We should be fine. We shouldn't be worrying."

"I guess deep down he's just like the three of us." added Tyler.

"What do you mean?"

"Any girl willing to date him would probably make any man feel a little happier inside, right?"

"Yeah, I know you're right about that."

"So what about you Mark," he continued, "When are you going to get a girl and join the club?"

"Don't worry, it'll happen soon. I've been noticing lately how Michelle Pebler has been stalking me around in the halls."

"In your dreams, dude." I laughed, knowing he was simply throwing out a line.

"It'll happen, watch, come Monday, I'll have her eating out of the palm of my hand. You guys will just have to wait and see."

I didn't attack him in front of Tyler about his recent episode, strictly obeying the bro code to never rank out a friend within fellow company.

"Well let's just hope that it does." Tyler smiled, reaching the entryway into *Halloween Havoc* and opening the door for us. "I really am interested to see what your brother and his friend picked out."

"You bet," Mark answered, looking around and glossing over the many costumes they had on display.

"They may pull it off, but then again, it might just be something stupid."

Chapter Forty-Six

We browsed the store for a while before catching up with our fellow comrades, checking out the cosplay that the other customers were exhibiting in the back.

It felt strange, being there, in the presence of all that youthful excitement, transferring the three of us back in time to express some past holiday dress up of our own.

"Say, remember that time when we went as Ninja Turtles?"

"How can I forget?" I told Mark, getting my hands on an old school Michelangelo mask hanging up on the display rack. "Instead of candy we told all the parents to give us pizza slices."

"And if I remember correctly, one of them actually did, right?"

"I think so," I recollected, "It must have been pizza night or something and the family was like, "Eh, here you go kids, if you want it, you can have it."

"It must have been an elderly couple. I mean what normal people in their right mind would have done that?"

"Yeah, I guess that makes sense now. At the time, though, I was like *that* was totally awesome!"

"Remember too how we refused to say "trick or treat" but "*Cowabunga!*" anytime someone would open the door?"

"Oh, yeah, I almost forgot about that. And you kept scaring them away with your ridiculous karate moves."

"I can't express how much those lessons paid off." He

laughed. "They probably thought it was cute or something, so they let it slide."

"How old were we again?"

"I'd say what, about nine or ten at the time?"

"You'd think we could pull that off again if we wanted to?"

"Nah, they'd probably just think we were crazy ass teenagers, attempting to relive our childhood."

"What about you, Ty?" I asked, directing him into our banter. "We didn't know you back then when we were younger. How was it for you growing up? Do anything out of the ordinary?"

"I actually had it pretty good."

"Pretty good," Mark teased, "Your momma didn't help you with your costumes, did she?"

"Actually she did."

"Who were you then?" I questioned before Mark could roast him.

"I went as Freddie Kruger for three years straight."

"Oh, really?"

"Yeah, I had this old red-green shirt and figured with a little makeup maybe I could make something out of it."

"That's pretty cool," Mark approved. "Did you know anyone who'd go as Jason or Michael Myers to complete the trifecta?"

"I was friends with a kid named Chris Dickens and Kyle Owens back then and yes we did. It kinda took our parents by surprise."

"Were they afraid that the costumes would rub off on your personality somehow?"

"I don't know but we were three children dressed up as serial killers so that was maybe a possibility of being a little concerning."

"Whatever happened to those two?"

"Well, Chris was part of a military family, so he always tended to move around a lot. I'm not exactly sure whatever happened to Kyle, though, he just seemed to disappear on me one day without any real notice.

"That must have felt weird."

"It did but then I met you two and the rest became history."

"I don't know though," I judged, thinking over his Halloween selection of yesteryear. "If I really wanted to go as someone scary I think Hannibal Lecter would've been a better choice. Wouldn't you think? I mean the guy was a freaking cannibal. He ate people."

"Yeah," Mark agreed. "He would come in chained up with that stupid thing around his face."

"Wait, who's Hannibal Lecter?" Tyler frowned, thinking we were talking gibberish nonsense.

"You're telling us you never saw *Silence of the Lambs?*"

"I mean I've heard of it but never saw it."

"Dude, you're really missing out then."

"Yeah, really, man, that's a great flick."

Tyler remained speechless as he watched the two of us butt heads.

"Wait, you only watched it because you had a thing for Jodie Foster." I argued, knowing instantly that would shut him up.

"So, your point is?"

"Besides Hannibal, that whole movie was basically her fake Georgian accent and some transvestite trying to make his own coat of many colors."

"You mean that wasn't her real voice?"

"No, dimwit, that's why it's called acting. She was playing you like a fool."

"She pulled it off pretty well, though. That's why she won the Oscar, I bet."

"I guess so."

"Wasn't she also in some other film before that where she played like a child prostitute or something?"

"Yeah, *Taxi Driver.*" I answered. "You know, my dad still refuses to even acknowledge that film for what it almost did to

Ronald Reagan."

"What are you talking about?"

"The Assassination attempt."

"Oh, yeah, right, that creepo was stalking her in college, wasn't he?"

"Something like that, I suppose. And he wanted to win her over by doing something drastic like killing the President on National TV."

"What a complete wackjob."

"You're telling me. I guess it's not for us to understand the mentally ill."

"Hollywood does know how to fuck with our minds - that line between fact and fiction is overly blurred. Leaving anyone open for those crazy misinterpretations that the filmmaker creates on their own behalf."

"That's pretty much it. It's nothing more than one gigantic propaganda machine feeding from the people who can't think for themselves."

"Boy you guys watch too many movies." Tyler critically noted, focusing back after we were slowly going off topic.

"Well, what else are we supposed to do?" questioned Mark. "It's the 90s, so other than playing video games, movies are like our only other pastime, right?"

"But you two are like encyclopedias."

"I know," I added, "We have so much useless knowledge floating around our brain it's probably scary to the average human to try and comprehend."

"I would have to agree, we have so much trivial insight we'd best belong on a game show where we could at least win some cash back for it."

"That wouldn't be such a bad idea." Tyler thought. "Maybe you should grow a 'stashe?"

"How come?" Mark asked.

"Someone's gotta play Alex Trebek, don't they?"

Chapter Forty-Seven

J okes aside, I could tell we were in the waning hours as the store appeared empty leaving only the mature section left to explore.

Teleporting us into a cheap answer of what looked like a semi-qusi sex shoppe, getting targeted in the crosshairs of no man's land where even the familier became a cloaked investment of the devil. And, as usual, my friends had no problems touring this new bastion of human perversion with unabashed interest and total ignorance.

"Do you want to be the female socket or the male plug?" Mark gagged, handing me the infamous plastic outfit still safe in its wrapping like an unused rubber condom. "I dare you to open it and try it on for yourself."

"Put that back, you idiot before someone sees us with it. We don't need to cause a scene."

"Get a hold of yourself man, it's not like I'm holding weed - it ain't gonna kill you. And even if it did, it might actually be a benefit."

"Well, I don't care."

Mark stayed stern hoping to see if I'd crack against my good nature.

"Don't you need to have two people for this, anyway?"

"Not if you want to jerk off with it." He joked.

"Get real, you idiot!"

"The changing room looks vacant. Maybe Ty wouldn't mind joining you to see how it fits? Would that help?"

"No way," Tyler refused, looking unamused at Mark.

I could tell he too was becoming unsettled by his mischief.

"Well Lexi is over there," Mark waved, getting her attention. "Maybe I should grab her. Would you want me to do that instead?"

Once again I begged him not to but in typical fashion he ignored my order, allowing just enough time for her to ponder what exactly the three of us were doing by ourselves near the dressing unit.

"What are you three stooges up to?" She hollered, locking eyes and looking directly at whatever I had fidgeting in my hands.

"Do you need assistance with that or something?" She laughed, judging my appearance, looking as if maybe I was about to faint in public from complete humiliation.

"Here comes your girl," Mark jabbed, waiting to see how I would handle this scenario up close and personal, no strings attached.

"We were just playing with this." I shyly remarked, attempting to cover everything up before she noticed.

"Oh, my goodness, you guys *are* nuts!" She said with shock as the label flashed before I could succeed with the impossible endeavor of hiding it.

"Do you want to try out the female one?" gloated Mark, praying she would go along with the juvenile gag.

"Is that all you have on your mind?" I questioned, pretending to be appalled, thinking too that Lexi would be on my side.

"I'm surprised that it's not on yours." She chuckled, feeling the peer pressure mount.

"See, bro, Lexi doesn't mind going in with you, do you?"

"We'll, actually, it is a bit derogatory but it's all in good fun, ain't it? This costume only works *if* a real man is wearing it with me, right?"

"Holly crap," I gulped, assuming nobody heard.

"See," Mark approved, clapping, "What do you say now, hotlips? You don't want to be an odd man out now, do you? Go in and try it on. It's not like you're going to wear it tonight. *Be a man!*"

I looked around - scooping the area first, catching Jeff and Ryan a good distance away and still debating what they had up their sleeve for their own primetime attire.

"Lexi, did you figure out what those two knuckleheads were going to do tonight?"

"They didn't really say," she sighed, becoming impatient. "It's more than likely they might just ditch the effort and do something else."

"If I were them," interrupted Mark, "You know what I would do?"

"What, genius? Put flowerpots on top of their heads and turn into Devo yelling, "Whip *It*?"

"Well, actually they could," Mark suggested, "They were nerds too, weren't they? But my thinking was more like they should do what the *Red Hot Chili Peppers* did and go full naked right on stage."

"Wait a minute - didn't they at least have socks on when they did that?"

"Yeah, sure they did." He laughed. "That gimmick didn't last long before it streamed out of control and somehow ended up on *Rolling Stone* magazine."

"That's just it, though. I'm not sure if they're *man* to enough to even try something that shocking in front of a crowd. Couldn't they get arrested for that?"

"Yeah, you're probably right. I don't think we need the cops to raid the place for indecent exposure."

"That would really be something, though, right? You probably wouldn't hear from either of those two again once your parents are forced to go to the police station and bail them out."

"If you put it like that, maybe it wouldn't be such a bad idea. I could go a few weeks without seeing Ryan or Jeff around.

Talk about having some peace and quiet. I'll take that any day of the week."

"Well, here's your chance to let them know how you really feel," Lexi cautioned us, watching them question our commotion as they barged over.

"What are you doing over here with these *losers,* Lex?" Ryan heckled while twisting his brother into a funny pretzel headlock.

"Hey, man, that hurts!" Mark cried.

"It's just a little love tap, bro. Don't go barking up a storm. Well Lex, why are you with them?"

"You don't own me," she backfired, losing complete control over the male bonding she'd been hampered by all day.

"C' mon!" She flicked my way, "I'm getting sick of all of this bullshit with everyone. Do you want to try this outfit on or not?"

My instinct was to scream no but the increased intensity made my mouth utter something entirely different.

"*Good!* Then let's go sneak in so we can get outta here."

Chapter Forty-Eight

I was surprised by how Lexi had treated Ryan. It was possible to suspect that some trouble in paradise was brewing and the cards were in fact on the table for me to play.

It wasn't that difficult to assume the obvious - she was a teenager, very attractive and looking for a quick hookup with any guy brave enough to ask. She saw her opportunity and within hours of meeting the poor bum - the true reality finally sunk in. He had reached *loser* status and I was left in the shadows, waiting to pick up the pieces.

At least that's the way I figured it. And who's to say I wouldn't have been correct in that thinking? It wasn't easy to stash a babe and to keep someone of that caliber for any measure of time once the love potion of being a rock star faded - seeming hopeless by any stretch. What she needed was a comforting arm - someone who knew better and could show her the difference.

Snapping back from this pleasant idea of romantic intrigue, my palms were sweating. Here I was getting changed in the same room with someone whom if you'd had told me months ago would be in my presence not a mere inches away, breathing in the same air right next to me, I would have checked myself into a clinic for my own sanity. It just didn't seem real. It had to be a dream.

"Here, hold this," she demanded, handing me what was left of her soft drink.

"You didn't finish this yet?"

"Nah, I didn't really have time. Besides, the ice cubes were beginning to turn into water. I can't stand to drink it when that happens."

"Yeah, I know what you mean. That's disgusting."

I took the cup, placing it on the floor but not before watching her get undressed to the satisfaction of my own deepest desires. If hearts were floating across my eyelids - they were surely seen by this spectator who might have thought I had died and gone straight to Heaven.

"I guess you've never seen a semi naked woman before, have you?" She delighted, gaining my affection.

"No, not really," I hesitated to reply. "I don't have a sister so I really wouldn't know all the trappings of what exactly that's all like."

She judged my response unsure with where I was going with my rambling.

"Well don't go having a hard on while you're in here, please. That wasn't the point of this. If you want to do that, take it elsewhere."

Her straight talk startled me, leaving me breathless and out of any words to respond. I wasn't sure if I was attempting to flirt with the lady or the tramp. It seemed at that moment it didn't matter one way or another. She was an unleashed creature frying up from within.

"Kid, we made out yesterday in my car. It's alright, you can talk with me. I don't bite. Well, not yet, anyway. Care to test me?"

"I'm s-sorry," I stuttered to say, revealing the utmost fear raised in my voice. "I just don't want anything to happen here, y'know, causing trouble with Ryan who for every practical purpose can kick my ass for just laying my hands on you accidentally."

"Don't worry about that guy. There's really nothing happening between us. I'm going out with him tonight but by Monday I'll probably just break it off. It's nothing personal, really. You saw the way we were fighting in the car before, he's just not my type. I only wanted to have some fun this weekend. That's why I'm with him now. You understand what I mean, right?

I nodded in agreement as any lovesick fool would.

"But does he know about any of this?"

"Beats the hell out of me, to tell you the truth, I had more fun with *you* yesterday."

My eyebrow raised with suspicion, along with some other parts, stunned to hear what was being said.

"This is actually a pretty big dressing room to fit two people in, isn't it?" I responded with an oblivious nature to erase what I thought I just heard, for the sheer embarrassment that any words uttered next would make her question my chivalry towards women.

"Y'know, you're actually a pretty attractive kid. You shouldn't let any self-doubt or your idiot friend tell you any different. There'll be plenty of girls eager to eat you up when the time is right."

"I'm only a freshman. I guess maybe in a few years things might turn around."

"I'm going to guess even sooner," she said smiling, placing another kiss on my forehead with the lipstick stain freshly cementing that I was awarded my red badge of courage.

I couldn't contain it any longer. My hands began floating around her shoulders with panic setting in that If they were placed anywhere else on her body an illegal flag would have dropped causing a possible 15 yard penalty and a loss of down.

"You're more sophisticated than I thought," she giggled, sensing the attraction was at its leveled peak. "Any other place would have gotten you a slap."

My lips uncontrollably smacked over her mouth, unwavering with anticipation that I was stupid enough to risk it all in one full swoop. In those moments of potential death, I heard the cowboy inside me holler, "it was best that if I were to die, I'd do it with my boots on."

"Oh, hell," she wavered, switching on her charm as we relived the exact same episode from the previous night - this time with complete fulfillment that this quick fling was turning true. Hoping too that nobody heard any of the grinding and groaning suggesting foul play at work.

"Don't take forever in there!" A voice echoed through the door causing me to jump out of my skin thinking maybe I was caught by my friends.

"Somebody else has got to use this room too!" The voice was female - sounding more like a parent who was annoyed that their child had to wait in line while two immature minors made out in the clutches of the darkness.

"Hold your horses, will ya?" Lexi yelled, sending the woman away and the child crying.

"This really isn't like me." I retreated with little force, brushing Lexi off before things got out of hand and the store manager came strolling in to monitor the situation.

"No, wait, what are you doing?" She flinched, not wanting to quit.

"This just isn't right." I said with pity and frustration.

"What are you saying? Do you not like me or something?"

"No, that's not it. You're freaking beautiful."

"Well, then, what is it?"

"We're in a dressing room for Pete's sake. I don't want it getting out. At least not like this. Y'know, give me a day or two to clear things through and get things right."

"You're friends already know, don't they? What good is that going to do?"

"It's not them I'm worried about."

"I told you before, you shouldn't worry too much about Ryan. He'll get over it in time. You need to grow some balls and be a *man* about this."

"But you don't even know my name if I remember correctly. You only know me by my brother, Barry. Isn't that the truth?"

"Maybe, so, but I have time to figure you out, stupid.

You're not that complicated. In fact you're quite square. All you're missing are some Clark Kent glasses."

I smiled continuing to hold her, taking in a deep breath, happy with the notion that she was at least sticking up for the cause.

"I really don't want this getting out, not yet. Lex. Will you at least do this for me?"

She looked at me, a bit unflattering but willing to accept the ultimatum being presented.

"If that's the way you feel about it then I guess we'll do it your way."

Chapter Forty-Nine

I had survived my first true battle in this dangerous competition with the sexes. It was war and more than just getting through it, I could claim a solid victory.

Persuading Lexi to hold off was a brave move and figuring what to do next seemed like an eternity of endless planning and late-night calculation but I was equipped for any challenge that was afoot.

"So, overall, how do you think we look?" I reacted, stretching my legs fully while getting situated in my attire as the plug became parallel to her socket.

"It looks like we were made to be together." She giggled as the sexual innuendo continued to bubble underneath. "Did you want to go outside and show it off to our guests?"

"God no," I fantasized. "Before we go any further, I think I'd like to have some surge protection of my own."

"Well, do you?" She clapped, breaking my frame of thought for what I hope would someday occur.

"If you're not going to say anything then you can just watch me walk out without you. I'll be unplugged and not turned on. Trust me, this won't look good on your part."

"No, wait, I'm coming." I screeched, pulling up my pants, preparing for all the humiliation that awaited from the potential mob of spectators.

We exited, but with minimum suspicion on the part of people's faces, except for the usual suspects who were ready to fire any questions and critiques my way.

"So, how'd everything go in there?" Mark addressed, tempting to ridicule, but becoming quite surprised that we may have pulled it off better then he'd hoped.

"What's that on your forehead," he smudged, smearing my lipstick stain, looking to focus on another matter entirely.

"You two really got it on there, didn't you?" He said with his jaw dropping and his ignorance showing.

"Hey, this was all *your* doing, wasn't it?" I winked, facing Lexi, possibly coming out of the closet faster than I wanted to about our relationship.

"So, what, are you two going to wear this tonight at the gig? That would really make things interesting for everyone around, wouldn't it?"

"I don't know, Lex, what do you think?" I suggested, thinking it over, swinging my head around quickly as Ryan and Jeff both made their acquaintance shown.

"I thought you were going as the *Bride of Chucky?*" buzzed Jeff, who stood looking and wondering why his best friend's girl would be assisting someone like myself.

"I actually think this works out better." She answered, knocking Jeff off his keister, giving me the perfect opportunity to mount a clever comeback and spit it right back into his face.

"You wish you were me right now, don't you?"

"Not really," he joked, knowing precisely that Ryan was about to lay the smackdown for messing with *his* woman.

"Hey, how come you're doing more with this pimply-faced little boy than you are with a real man like me?"

Lexi assessed Ryan's immature smugness - measuring it by responding with a classic line I never would forget .

"He's more of a man than you'll ever be."

Ryan, taken aback, couldn't hold it, his face contorting and becoming red with his veins bulging forcing Jeff to pull him aside before he became completely unhinged.

"Hey, I don't want you heading for a stroke." He comforted, wrestling a brotherly bearhug showing support.

"I really don't want you looking like a jerk in front of her man. You'll never have a chance with the chicks if this gets out. You know how reputations go around here. Once they get tarnished it's over forever. You might not get another chance until after high school or something."

"But I swear," Ryan whined, "What the hell is she thinking? Choosing that twerp over me? He's not even a sophomore yet. What is he doing that I'm not?"

"They're women, what the hell do we know, right? They're complicated as *fuck* to guys like us!"

I couldn't hear the commotion but I could tell by the way they were communicating like two jealous feens - I had kicked the hornet's nest and ruffled some feathers the wrong way. I had slayed Goliath and it was driving them both crazy.

"Wow, Lexi, you had some nerve telling off Ryan like that." Mark praised.

"He's lucky I didn't kick him in the balls." She laughed with some light amusement, attempting to sound like a typical woman scorned.

"You're quite vicious!"

"I wouldn't say that," she dismissed. "As I told Chase, I'm only with him for the weekend so nothing was ever stitched in stone to begin with."

"Yeah," I nodded, like I had already begun taking orders from my future wife. "Ryan, just needs to relax for once in his life. We'll get everything squared away in time. He shouldn't be throwing some temper tantrums for everyone to see. After all, aren't we the younger siblings here? Shouldn't he be the one setting the example for us? It just looks sad. Don't ya think?"

"Let's just hope that you're right," Mark skeptically approved, shocked to even notice his old friend begin to build some self-confidence for himself.

"Looks like they're coming back," he warned. "Let's try not to start anything."

"Okay, Chase," Ryan fisted with anger. "Here's the deal, If you want Lexi then your ass is walking home. I'm not driving you back."

"C'mon, man!" complained Mark, sticking up. "That's not fair at all. You shouldn't be so bitchy about this. I'm sure he probably didn't even mean anything by it."

"That's okay, Mark, I don't need him."

"But how are you getting home?"

"Jeff will bring him," Lexi demanded, knowing her word was stronger than anything the two of us could've mustered.

"Do I have to?"

"That's who I'm looking at." Lexi scolded, turning stone cold, numbing his brain to comply.

"Do what she says," Ryan frowned. "I need time to cool off. Maybe it's best that way."

"I guess I'll see you guys later then," Tyler added, almost forgetting he was still around to witness the meltdown.

"Oh, yeah, have fun with Amanda at the movies and don't forget to tell us everything on Monday."

"No problem," he said, departing, leaving the rest of us to get on with our day.

Chapter Fifty

"I'm not your *chauffeur!*" Jeff fussed as Lexi and I walked towards his car without a clue of where he wanted to take us.

"I wasn't asking you to be." I responded, "All I ask is for you to take me home before things get even more chaotic than it has."

"Like it hasn't already turned into a shitstorm by what you two have done? Things were going swell before you guys decided to break everything up."

"Jeff, don't be such a spoil sport." Lexi intervened, getting anxious and still annoyed with his wise cracks. "Drive me home first, though, alright? I can't take any more of your hounding."

"I was already planning on it. You're closer, anyway, it would be stupid of me otherwise, wouldn't it?"

"I wouldn't know," she teased. "I don't know how your brain works. I don't understand *moron* the way you do."

"Hey, you want to come in and stay for a while?"

"You know I can't, Lexi." He reluctantly responded. "I'm heading back to Ryan's place to figure out our plan on what to do with our look for the main event. There was really nothing much at the costume shop for us to pick from. We're going back to the drawing board and basically starting from scratch on the whole thing."

"I wasn't asking you, anyway, dummy." She insulted, flicking him off, gazing instead at me.

"Wait, you mean him? That twerp?" You really are crazy."

"Why not? He can come and meet up with my sisters at the house. Get to see what life is like on the other side of the tracks. It'll be an experience."

"But what about your parents?" I asked, chiming in, intimidated by the offer she had placed at the table.

"You don't have to worry about them, they're never home. Most of the time it is as if they don't even exist."

"Yeah, I know what you mean. Mine are the same way. Did you tell anyone about last night?"

"No, not yet, so here's our chance to fill people in."

"So, you're saying that if I *do* come over, I'm going to be getting *the* third degree from all of them, right?"

"It was going to happen sooner than later. Why not just get it over with? Are you not equipped to handle a pack of feminine hijinks all at once?"

I studied her question, blanking with the possibility that I was a bit naive with what I was about to get into and overwhelmed with whether I could handle the pressure that awaited on my behalf.

"Are your sisters younger or older than you?"

"Let's see," she thought. "Rebecca is a year older and Brittany is, I believe, around your age. Do you know her?"

"I can't recall anyone with that name in any of my classes."

"That's because she's only in middle school right now. She started a year late. Sorry, I forgot to mention that. It's actually a long story as to why that happened but we don't have the time to go into any of that. I just need you to know one thing."

"What's that, exactly?"

"Rebecca's boyfriend may be staying at the house."

"Why does that matter? He's not homeless or something, is he?"

"You're a funny guy," she smiled, feeling relaxed by my comment. "It doesn't really matter, I guess, but there's something you need to know about him before we go any further."

"And what's that then?"

"He's a *pothead*, you may smell him when you walk in. He's quite disgusting, actually. I really don't understand why she puts up with him or why she even continues to date him."

"Has he been arrested yet for possession of the stuff?"

"Not yet, he would be put in jail, though, if he was, that would be a better place for him to be for all of us, considering. He is a bit shady but I guess that just comes with the territory for being a user."

"I'm assuming he probably dropped out of school, correct?"

"Yep, he's a real *loser* in every sense of the word. My sister has really low self esteem issues and just figures she can't find anyone better. He's not bad looking when he's not stoned but that's a rarity in itself."

"How'd she meet him?"

"Where else? At a bar doing the same thing you and your friend were doing. It's quite easy in a small area like this to find the lowest of low in terms of dating standards. Especially when you have beer goggles on while doing it."

"Should I take offense to that statement?"

"You could," she laughed, "But you were actually raised with a clean slate from what I've seen. That's actually quite odd these days."

"I guess I was brought up right. My brother could be a bit of a trouble maker but I don't think he'd ever stoop so low as to how you're describing this guy."

"Yeah, your brother is actually pretty cool. I don't know him that well but I've seen him around. Who's he dating, anyway?"

"J-Jill," I stuttered, "Jill Walker, do you know her?"

"Doesn't every guy?" She groaned reminding herself that she wasn't the only school flirt in this same proximity who wanted to expand her expectations on certain men. "I thought she was dating some other guy, though."

"She was but Barry picked her up on the rebound. At least that's what he is claiming."

"I see," she said, studying my story, almost alarming me that he may be in danger. "I don't wanna start any trouble here, but I've heard rumors that her former boyfriend may have knocked her up and is now playing the denial card. Typical, right?"

My fear arose. Her statement fit the narrative from the previous night to the tee.

"Where did you hear that?"

"I don't know but you know how it is, the word gets around."

"**Can you two please stop talking and get in the car before I die?**" Jeff begged, beginning to feel out of place with our continuous mumbling.

"Don't worry Jeff, we don't want *you* feeling uncomfortable with us while we're talking cute in front of you." Lexi taunted, giving him a silly face.

"Good, because in all fairness, I'm still team Ryan. This *dope* doesn't belong in our league or even in this conversation."

"Don't listen to him," Lexi said, rolling her eyes. "You'll be alright."

Chapter Fifty-One

I scratched my head, continuing to think what Lexi had said. I needed assurance that my brother was okay but with the lack of any portable device in my hand, the only outreach was to picket her with the hope that she could help and assist in some way.

"Is it possible that I can use your phone when we get to your house?" I pleaded, sitting in the back seat, attempting to place my arm around her shoulder like any other typical dating couple.

"What for?"

"I need to check up and let my mom know where I'm at."

"She knows you're out with friends, doesn't she?"

"I told her I was staying with Mark for the afternoon but I don't think she'd expect me to be back any later than this."

"So, what's the worry then? She ain't gonna miss you, is she? She knows you're a teenager, right? It's the law for you to break the rules at your age. Don't be stupid."

I didn't want to jump the gun, politely suggesting the reason was simply out of love.

"Sure, whatever you say. You can use it once we get in. I mean it's not like we don't have one."

Blowing a sigh of relief, I quieted my mind.

"How come neither one of you wanted to ride shotgun with me up front?" Jeff interrupted, getting all up in our business.

"Jeff, stay in your own lane, will ya?"

"What's that supposed to mean?"

"You know what," Lexi cracked, turning her attention instead to the radio station and the news that was coming across the dial.

"Hey, can you turn that up, please? I want to hear something besides your voice before I accidentally shoot somebody in here."

I looked around, getting nervous that she was serious. Jeff too obeyed, silencing himself in a manner that suggested an avoidance to bother any woman who seemed on the verge of total meltdown.

"Jeff, can you switch stations?" I begged, getting a lump in my throat not wanting to hear what the news anchor was revealing on air and trying also to focus in on Lexi's obvious assets that were directly in front of me, making my hormones move.

"Yeah, I'm sorry, dude, we just hit a bad time, nothing is really on right now since we reached the top of the hour newsbreak. I'll change it for you. There's normally something good on the classic rock channel.""You should know," Lexi nudged, preparing herself for the bad car karaoke that was doomed to occur in a matter of moments.

I looked down at my watch, getting a clear view at the time, it was already 4 pm, the day was flying by and I couldn't have imagined how lucky I have been thus far.

"Why don't you have a CD player installed yet?" Lexi bitched, making Jeff's face burn red.

"I'm old school just like my papa. If you want all those finer luxuries you should be hitting it up with Ryan and going back with him but that's just my two cents, missy. So stop your sobbing and wait there until I drop you off."

"Well, your two cents aren't worth much." She giggled, glancing back at me and puckering her lips for something possibly romantic.

"Okay, you two, here we are now get out!" Jeff barged, halting my heart rate to look out the window and get a good sense of where exactly I crash landed.

"You live here?"

"You weren't expecting the Taj Mahal were you?"

"Not really... I guess. This looks... *nice.*"

My eyes scanned the premises of what some might judge as a white trash paradise, getting a long look at the tool shed with an ax hanging on the door and the doghouse nearby with a phantom creature waiting in the shadow. I sputtered to picture the horror that awaited if I exited the vehicle improperly.

"Oh, you have a dog?"

"Actually, it's our dad's - it's a Pitbull, he got him at the junkyard, the rumor was he was chasing away too many of the owner's customers and he was like you can have him if you want."

"He looks quite fierce, don't you think?"

"My dad trained him that way."

"He did?"

"You know why, right?"

"I can only imagine, I guess."

"To scare away the many boyfriends we send his way."

"And how many is that?"

"Right now, I think we're up to six. You would be lucky number seven."

"Should I be afraid of that?"

"Only if you break it off with me," she warned, making her way out of the car and towards the mutt for a pet. "So, are you coming or what?"

My brain signaled caution ahead, but my libido answered otherwise.

Chapter Fifty-Two

"**H**e's not going to bite you," Lexi patted, feeding him the last bag of discounted doggie treats she had stashed. "Come on now, don't be shy and come over here."

I didn't make any sudden move, fearing not to trigger his hunting instincts with what looked like the face of a small lion licking his chops, possibly fantasizing about the next full stomach meal on his plate.

"If you can survive the meet and greet with Dick Grayson here, then, you'll have no problem being welcomed into the family."

My eyes widened, getting slightly adjusted to his environment, my shoes still stuck in the mud from the slush from the previous night's rain and my heart pounding rapidly with fear that it would turn into mincemeat by the fangs of his sharp needled teeth sipping with spit and dripping straight onto the ground.

"You named your dog after a Batman character?"

"Well, the "dick" part is obvious for many reasons, of course, as you can tell, but yeah, we thought most people would get the twisted humor behind it."

"It's actually kind of cute."

"Yeah, I know," she agreed, "Now get over here and pet him, otherwise I'm going to unleash him so he can sniff you for loot. And boy, you won't know what hit you if that happens."

My gut continued to quiver inside but I accepted, hoping

she was only bluffing. Gently gliding over, rubbing the pooch, gaining approval and relief that nothing drastic conspired.

"See, was that so bad?"

"I'll be honest, I have a dog too. Just not one that looks like it can rip me to shreds."

"Oh, you do, don't you?"

"Yeah, my mom gave it to us as a sign of maturity. I guess it was a way for her to judge our true character by sticking us with responsibility in the form of an animal. I think it was a backhanded compliment to do that to us."

"Yeah, I can see that." She nodded, unleashing the hound as Dick's tongue cleansed my face while slobbering his approval in large doses.

"You probably needed a shower anyway," she smiled, overlooking an unwanted parked car in front of the driveway. "Yep, damnit, he's here, alright."

"Who, who are you talking about?"

"Turner, that douchebag boyfriend I was telling you before."

"Oh, yeah, him. Can I ask how Dick treated him when they first met?"

"I'm not sure they have yet. It's funny, but most dogs have the ability to detect bad odor coming from fakes and phonies and he fits the bill."

"I gotcha."

"Y'know, Dick grabbed one boyfriend I had by the seat of his pants and was pretty lucky - he swallowed his wallet causing him to run off, burning rubber, accidentally blowing out a tire in the process and ended up driving down the road on just his rim."

"Are you joking about that? That sounds crazy and a little out of this world."

"Why would I joke about something like that? It was funny as hell. Rebecca has the photo somewhere inside the house if you want the proof. Do you want me to go grab it?"

"Nah, I guess I believe you," I said, shrugging off the

stories of her many failed suitors, neglecting the fact that I had rushed out of Jeff's car so quickly that I had forgotten to snatch our Halloween outfits from the back seat.

"Did you take the costumes before you got out?"

"Oh, crap, I knew I forgot something." I admitted, praying this error in judgment wouldn't cause my ultimate downfall. "I left them in there, we'll have to hit up Jeff before we go back to *Hard Luck* tonight and remind him about it. I doubt he'll torment us about it. But then, you never really know with that guy."

"Yeah, I guess we can do that, later." She sighed, looking past me and back at the 1992 Honda Accord, clouding her judgement. "Right now my mind is just focused on other things."

"This Turner, guy, he's not dangerous, is he? I mean, can he cause trouble being here?"

Lexi didn't speak, taking time to justify her true feelings about the bum.

"They've been dating for less than a month, so I can't tell but I think he is, at least, I think he's dangerous enough to affect my sister's future."

"Is she planning on going to college?"

"Between the three of us, she's actually the smart one. I'm just the one treading water. I don't think any of us are college bound, but I do want to see her live, at least into her 20s."

"That's a low bar too set for oneself," I thought to myself. "Live fast, die young, I suppose."

"Is she "using" with him?"

"I think so, he's always out of cash looking to swindle money from anyone who puts pity on him like some Charles Manson freak who can influence young women to do whatever they want. I know for a fact he was trying to steal the tip money that she had made as a waitress from the jar sitting by the dresser. She'll deny it of course but something just ain't right every time I confront her about it. I think she's shielding him from all the bad consequences and sad realities she placed herself in. I guess I'm just trying to look out and protect her in some fashion. There's nothing wrong with that, is there?"

"I don't think so," I said, offering my opinion, coming to terms with some familiar sibling sentiment. "I think it's very sisterly, actually, what you are doing."

"Thanks, I try not to let it show but I can't help it, y'know?"

"Well, what do your parents think about all of this?"

"That's just it. Our parents really aren't the type to set boundaries for us. They're not the parental type, if you get my drift. You should be lucky, your parents from what I can imagine still care about you, right?"

"To some degree," I chuckled, "We are getting older, though, this is my first year in high school so I guess maybe now is the best time for them to be moderately concerned."

"True, you were telling me you wanted to get in contact with them."

"If that's possible, I would. Just to touch base."

"Yeah, you can when we get inside."

"I don't know if I should ask but has Turner ever made a pass at you?"

Lexi grimaced, insulted that I would ask.

"He's still alive, isn't he?"

Her confidence, consistent with her flawless charm, intimidated my manhood.

"I don't know who to be afraid of more, you or the mutt?"

"Maybe it's best you *never* find out." She giggled, controlling the power structure that was orderly put in place. "Hey, did you hear that?"

"Yeah, kinda, what do you think it was?

The sound muffled, sounding like a woman moaning in the distance.

"Wait here." She ordered, leaving me alone as my dynamic sidekick continued to detect the smell of food all over me.

"I'm going to find out what's going on."

Chapter Fifty-Three

I continued to wait with Dick, not knowing what to expect; a smokescreen igniting in an eerie fog of war. The noises, streaming from the back of the house with the window open, more than likely assumed the worst, that Turner was having his way with Rebecca and help was becoming urgent.

Lexi's unexpected arrival, leading to a rescue filled with vigilante justice to aid and assist.

My heart racing, skipping a beat with the clanging of metal doors crashing into the open space and the howling wind blowing through the trees into the clear October sky.

Their parents, away - nowhere to be found. The youngest, possibly with friends, clueless and unaware of the fire ablaze and I was left holding the leash of someone else's pet struggling to contemplate how far I was willing to go before I told Ryan he could have her.

I knew I shouldn't judge but a weekend trip down these parts made me consider my humbleness. Barry may have been a jerk for most of my life but I could never visualize any criminal element, enforcing an arrest and lockup.

In a way, I felt sorry for Lexi, she was no different than me, quite practical with common sense holding a watchful eye towards those she loved. She was diligent, trying to solve problems the only way she knew how, on her own.

"What are you standing around for? We gotta get a move on." She yelled, sprinting out the front, charging with raw abandon, flashing some shiny keys around her finger like she was resurrecting the kindred spirit of outlaw Bonnie Parker, subjecting me to play alongside Clyde Barrow.

"What was going on in there?"

"Turner and 'Becca were having sex on my bed, can you believe those two? I saw it and it made me lose my nerve."

"So that's what all the shouting was about? I thought, maybe it was a bit more serious than that."

"What - you mean like rape?"

"Well, yeah," I fidgeted, not wanting to sound an alarm.

"Nah, that wasn't the case, although nowadays, any woman can claim it and more or less screw a guy's life over it just by leaving a mark on her body."

"I know, I hear about it all the time from my dad, they call 'em *feminazis.* They want to control every aspect of the women's movement against men."

"Wait a minute, your dad's a dittohead?"

"That's funny that you even know that."

"Why's that, you'd just assume my family were all a bunch of commie Democrats? I'm not ashamed to admit I'm the black sheep in my politics."

"That is courageous of you to say. Most just get blacklisted for speaking out."

"Well, thank you, but we still gotta get out of here before more shit hits the fan. Me and Turner just don't get along so it's best we scram before he notices what we're about to do."

My eyebrow rose - skeptical of her remark and it's true intent on what was transpiring.

"So where's your car?"

"That's kind of it, you see, it's not here at the moment."

"What are you sayin'?"

"I'm telling you that the car wasn't mine. It was my mom's. Both she and dad are out of town this weekend, if you haven't already figured that out. One of my relatives died, they're taking a road trip and won't be back anytime soon. That's why it's all chaos up here. You kind of have to stay with me, I'm taking this all in as we go. It ain't easy."

"So, who's keys are you holding in your hands?"

"Who do you think?"

My mind scattered with the possibilities for the next saga of this outlandish excursion. I was already on a path flirting with human disaster, now it appeared grand larceny skated near the tip of the horizon.

"Wait, a minute, no way!" I refused, getting a strong inkling of where her mind seemed to be focusing.

"What are you chicken or something? He's not going to notice, at least not for the next hour or two. Everything seemed to have cleared down in there, him and 'Becca are alright - It just troubled me that it was in my room, I mean, Jesus, rent a cheap motel or something. He's buying all this weed, you'd think he'd have some extra cash on hand to wet his pistol in an unknown location away from any of us. I'm telling you, the guys in this area are nothing but scum and lowlife trailer trash - please *never* turn into any of them."

Her ultimatum - piercing, filling me with doubt on every level of what to believe next.

"So you're saying we should just take his car and go? But where?"

"I don't know, just on a quick joy ride, it's only to teach them both a lesson, once he comes to his senses, which he probably won't since he's stoned out of his mind and basically an idiot at heart, he'll know not to fuck with me again."

"But what if he calls the cops? Lexi you're committing - "

"Don't worry about that, I got enough dirt on that bastard that it would be the least of his worries to even consider. I'm doing this to protect my sister, she's too scared to see any reality staring her in the face."

"I don't know. I'm not sure about this."

"Man, you worry too much," she sighed, looking down at my pants, possibly checking for any stained marks leaking through. "If we get stopped, we can always say that a friend of my sister's loaned the car to us."

"You mean like we're running an errand?"

"If you want to call it that, trust me, they'll never know the difference. So, I need to know right now, are you with me or not on this?"

I stayed paralyzed, numb and dazed, clearly stuck in the middle between a hound that could kill me and the owner who would make him.

"Dick, you know what to do," she called at him, causing a severe lapse for any sound reasoning I could salvage before envisioning his fatal fangs sinking into my gut, eating me alive.

Chapter Fifty-Four

There I sat in the passenger seat of a semi stolen vehicle, with a girl, who for all practical purposes, hostaged my heart, held it at ransom and floored it into smithereens from the heel of her foot steaming with sweat swerving onto the highway like a Duke straight out of Hazard County.

She wasn't letting up, keeping me in suspense with the pedal to the metal, driving off in Turner's ride, still paranoid that he might be after us if I accidentally glanced out from the rear view.

There was no turning back. I was a rebel, maybe not in the same vein of Waylon Jennings but certainly in the moment of writing my own verse of Waymore's Blues. What happened from here on out was strictly out of my hands 'en route towards some symbolic heroic outlaw legend.

All that was left was to figure out who would be brave enough to play my part in the film version of my life, if I could only be so lucky to have one made.

"Jesus, you look like you've seen a ghost," Lexi frowned, noticing my nerves continuing to fester - as if all this excitement was beginning to be too much for one kid to handle.

"I don't think so," I denied, wanting to sound like this imaginary chase was up to par.

"Then how come your knuckles are so white holding onto the dash like that?"

"I'm cool, I've just never been this far before."

"What do you mean by *far*?" She laughed, sensing my immediate shyness and inexperience getting exposed.

"Well, for one thing, we rushed out forgetting to contact my parents. I wanted to call up my house to make sure everything was in order. I really wasn't planning on hijacking a seven-year-old Honda Accord from a deadbeat whom I never met simply to please you and your dog who was on the verge of attacking me."

"You really are a big mama's boy, aren't you?" She smirked, beginning to sound a bit anal. "What you need to do is to relax. Why don't you check the back seat and see if he has a flip phone or something that you can use if you're that worried about everything."

"Do you think this idiot would have enough cash on hand to buy one of those?"

"How the hell should I know but with the amount of weed he stashes, I know for sure they don't give that shit out on credit, right?"

Her logic aside, I was beginning to confirm that I was in no man's land - a place where the brain fell under the spell of a woman's allure and anything I said simply died on deaf ears.

"Okay, I'll check and see."

"Also, check what's in his glove box. See if he has any extra loot hanging around that we can borrow if we need it for emergencies. I mean you never know, right?"

"When you say borrow you really mean never return, correct?"

"Well, no shit, Sherlock. What do you think I am, a millionaire? He won't remember what the hell happened to it so stop asking such stupid questions and do what I say. Jesus, why can't you accept the fact that this is fun and you're having the time of your life? I mean, seriously, what would you be doing without me right now? Lying on your couch playing with your balls or something, watching scrambled up porn on cable trying to figure out if you just saw big tits on the screen?"

From what I could tell - chatting with Lexi was becoming risky. I was no more or less her slave, taking orders from her every whim and want, but if you were to ask me today if it was all worth it, I couldn't help but think she was right and I was just out of my element.

"*Holy shit!*"

"What, did you find something good in there?"

"There's at least $500 in small bills here."

"That's more than enough, I suppose." She smugged, looking pleased with her decision about possibly robbing the jackpot.

"I didn't realize crime could pay so well." I thought, riffling through the wad and listening to the slapping sound of financial freedom ringing in my ears. "He's such a dope that he could probably make $1 million and nothing could save his ass from destroying himself."

"Well, Junior," she winked. "What are you waiting for, take it and stick it in your pocket before you grow a conscience, every little bit helps if you get my drift."

"You want us to steal it right out?"

"Once again, I repeat - duh! It's his loss, don't think otherwise and grab what you like, just save some extra for me too, will ya?"

I was tempted to obey. It wasn't everyday a big chunk of dough just happened to land in my lap without notice or strings attached. This was the kind of scene one would watch in a crime picture where some actor like Al Pacino would blow his fortune by building a drug empire, turning kingpin, all the while finding his only solace with his little friend nearby to help distract from his ultimate downfall: a Colt AR 15 Assault Rifle.

I guess I couldn't help it, I was in danger of becoming someone I wasn't, but then, I was only fourteen, scared to death that the woman next to me would embarrass me to hell if I acted out of character.

"*That frickin' dillweed!*" Lexi screamed, gaining my

attention fast, stopping on a dime, suspending me backwards against the cushion padding.

"What's going on?"

"We're running out of fuel in this damn thing."

"Well, what did you expect?"

"I guess not much, but he could have at least been considerate enough to fill up his tank."

"Considerate?" I thought, thinking she had lost her marbles completely. "This moron didn't even know what had hit him yet."

"You know what," she suggested, springing to mind a plan of action. "I have an idea."

"I'm afraid to ask what that might contain."

"It's nothing out of the ordinary but let's go find a gas station and leave the car parked there. It would clear us from any involvement with this jerk."

"Are you crazy? What about us? Where are we going to go?"

"I don't know, but, hey, Freddy's Mart is about a mile up the road from *Hard Luck,* ain't it? We can drop the car off there and walk the extra mile over, if you want. I mean we are going to go there anyway, right? What do you think about doing that?"

I fluttered to grasp at straws, thinking maybe she was onto something that could at least get us off the hook for the time being while we pieced together our silly fable .

"Fine, I'll go along with it," I accepted. "But only under one condition."

Lexi didn't speak, choosing to hear me out before getting the quick chuckle from my next response.

"Wouldn't it be kind to at least fill up his tank before we go?"

Chapter Fifty-Five

There was a story my brother told me once that somehow sprung to mind. At the time, I could swear he was telling it to blow off steam but now, looking back, I could be wrong about his true intentions.

It was something he had done with his friend when he was a freshman, making it hard to believe that he too was no different than me, only a few years separating us from the same game we were both playing.

The incident occurred when I was over at Mark's house one Friday evening. He had told me beforehand he'd be out with Nick, his childhood sidekick, cruising for excitement - in a beat up van Nick had recently purchased after he had finally gotten his driver's license. Albeit, a few years older than Barry, due to some unfortunate circumstances of having repeated the second grade twice - the two were inseparable.

The account, from his vantage point, began like this - they were out of town, ditching to tell their folks their exact location - leaving me as the only buffer between them and their somewhat known whereabouts.

It started, oddly enough, when Nick got a beep on his pager. The number came from a girl he'd been communicating with, whom if I believe correctly - lived a good distance away and had never actually met in person - hence this road trip to get a good sense for the certain things they went out searching for.

For those too young to remember, this endeavor took

place long before wireless online dating reached its zenith and hooking up happened in a matter of seconds behind clever texts one could send with specific emojis enhancing the mood - no, this was during the era of chat rooms, where the hip mingled and interacted with complete strangers over AOL modems waiting for any dial tone to reach its connection before signing off - leaving any suspicion of who was on the other end thrown out the window.

To make this long story short, Nick politely asked Barry if he wanted to come for the ride, lending an open ear to dish out pointers when he was ready to fly solo on his lustful fling with girls.

By accepting his offer, the expedition began. And as any idiot could foretell by using a crystal ball, it was doomed straight from the start.

First came the flat tire that literally drove them off the road, realizing neither knew the proper way to change one; the anticipated wait for help from a simple samaritan seemed like an eternity. And, of course, back then, there was no magic mobile app that could save the day and rescue them from complete humiliation of looking like two stranded knuckleheads standing alone, becoming useless - thumbing the next hopeful driver for any further assistance.

This is where things turn a bit juicy for our lonesome couple. After about fifteen minutes of waiting and having no success by any fellow patrons, Nick - already frustrated with it all, ditched the effort and walked the half mile to the local mechanic whom he figured could assist. It was only a miracle of luck one happened to be in the area after spotting him before disaster struck.

"Wait here," Nick nagged, attempting to let my brother think he had everything under control. The way the evening was turning - it appeared scripted straight from the pages of a slasher flick and all that was left was for the bogeyman to claim his territory with a few kills of his own.

"How long are you going to be?" Barry hollered, not

getting a firm response before disappearing into darkness. He was tempted to follow but played his part as the car's watchful babysitter.

He remained vigilant, counting down the minutes until the most unbelievable circumstance transpired - a babe, a brunette with piercing devil eyes, drove up, asking if he needed a lift. His thought process escalated fast with only the imagination running wild - not thinking twice before throwing caution to the wind and hopping in like any other lovestruck fool being manipulated by the love potion being sprayed his way.

He knew it was wrong but he didn't care. If he was going to die by such an accident of fate - he'd figured he at least had enough survival skills in him to fight off a loophole somehow if push came to shove.

"What seemed to be the matter?" She addressed, looking at him as he edged his way into the car. Sitting comfortably in his seat while sliding his hand across for the seatbelt to click in properly.

"My buddy and I need a tow, can you help us, please? We'd really appreciate it, ma'am. He's up the road, you can drop me off there and I can wait with him. You wouldn't have to go far, that would be all."

The woman, slow to speak, appearing timid, lowering her guard to reel him in slightly for the trap being set - decided not to listen, instead let her vehicle do the talking as Barry and Nick locked eyes for one last time, turning horrified when they blew by each other like a bat out of hell.

"Hey, wait! Where are you going? You just passed - "

"I'm sorry, honey, I can't do that," she dismissed, pedaling past and leaving him in the dust. "I saw you on the road and decided maybe you needed comfort. I have no use for your friend and what I'm about to do with you next."

Barry, trapped with anxiety, between desire and common sense had stepped past the threshold into some kind of vampire land - letting himself be taken into parts unknown where danger dared to strike and being bitten was the name of the game by any young bloods.

"I'm not kidnapping you," she eased, hoping her voice could salvage him from unbuckling his way forward towards freedom and out to the police station.

"Then what's your plan?"

"I don't really have one. I have the car for the night and figured I'd just go out and spin it around some. See what the nightlife had to offer me."

"You did this purposely?"

"Wouldn't you?"

"No, you're a crazy son of a bitch!"

"That's what the last hitchhiker said," she laughed. "Then I had to get serious with him and boy he didn't like that. I think he might have wet his pants."

Barry panicked, her motives beginning to pressure his reality on things fearing now that maybe there was a shotgun hidden in the trunk along with the rest of the bodies.

"Where were you two heading, anyway? This is pretty much a dead area down here, there's never much excitement."

"Well, Nick, my friend, whom we passed, we were on our way to meet somebody."

"You mean, like a girl?" She mocked, knowing full handily everything Barry was about to say. "That guy didn't look like the type who would be straight."

"Nick? No way -"

"Relax. I was just joking. I mean you're all the same - only after one thing."

"Like your kind isn't?"

"We are too, I guess, but we have you guys cornered to hide us from it. I mean if you want to blame anyone, then blame the Bible. It's all there, right?"

"What, you mean like Adam and Eve?"

"Exactly!" She shouted with joy. "Look, I'll make you a deal, honey, if that's what you really want. I won't beat around the bush with you any further."

Barry listened, adapting himself, accordingly, hearing her proposal.

"There's a local midnight diner coming up that I wouldn't mind stopping in for a quick meal if you want a bite to eat. It can help you get your story straight before I drive back. Do you want to go with me?"

"But I don't have any money."

"I'll be nice about it."

"Well, then, that's fine I suppose." He answered, accepting.

And that my dear readers concludes this sad tale of woe.

Of course, one could figure, she lied, departing without paying, leaving Barry stranded at the diner without a clue of how to pay it back before eventually calling up somebody to help get him untangled from the web he had weaved.

Chapter Fifty-Six

"Did your brother really do that?" Lexi paused, coming to terms with whether or not my tale had any merit of truth.

"That's what he said but then who can really believe any of it, right? All siblings exaggerate their lies so they can feel they achieved something monumental in another's eyes. It's all a power balance with growing up and a lot of it is complete bullshit, right? I just thought the story had some similarities to it."

"I get it, we're all human - we all want to one up the next guy in status - but really, a chick "just happens" to pull over and pick him up, give me a break. I mean what drugs do you want me to take to believe that garbage?"

"I mean, I got you, didn't I?" I smirked, underplaying her own line. "I do know Nick came back and picked him up after he got his tire fixed and he was pretty pissed about it, really. They kind of stopped talking to each other after that whole incident."

"I guess karma's a bitch then, right?"

"You can say that again. That's the price one pays, I guess."

"That's for sure."

"So what's next for us?" I enquired, getting back to business.

"Well you were the idiot that wanted to fill up Turner's tank, remember?"

"Yeah, so?"

"So do that," She replied, getting out of the car and slamming the door. "I'm going to go inside and get a few snacks for the two of us to share between now and then. Do you want anything in particular? Don't hold back - it's not like it's our money we're spending."

Her declaration made me consider the obvious.

"Grab me some Ho-Hos and maybe a cola. We need some fuel too, don't we, if we're going to be walking after this? Buy a lotto ticket while you're at it also. That's the easiest way to blow a good chunk of change, ain't it?"

"Do you want me to feed the homeless too while I'm at it?" She continued, laughing at my absurdities.

"If it can help bring out world peace I see no reason why not."

"Oh, I hear you," She shouted back, finally entering the store, leaving me at the pump, figuring which nozzle to pick.

"Hey, you," a man's voice reflected my way coming from the other side of the island dispenser. *"Was that your girlfriend you were talking with?"*

My immediate instincts inside jumped, thinking maybe this was an illegal drug heist and I was the uninformed stooge getting cornered without any knowledge.

"Who's that?" I thought, looking around, trying to familiarize myself with the stranger's tone and appearance.

"I'm Dan," he greeted himself, appearing too casual for someone I'd never met. *"I heard the two of you talking, you're really one lucky dude, I couldn't imagine having someone like that by my side."*

The man looked somewhat overweight, possibly in his late twenties, already balding to some length, so the compliment felt fair in comparison to what was expected.

"She's not mine quite yet." I remarked, hoping this conversation wouldn't last longer than its required minimum. The last thing I needed was finding out this nut was nothing more than a Michael Myers surrogate, ready to claim victims for his own Halloween night massacre.

"Oh, really?" He shrugged off. *"From the looks of it, I'd say you have it in the bag."*

"Thanks." I smiled, hoping the kind gesture could distract him from talking any further.

"Oh, I'm sorry, by the way, I didn't mean to startle you."

"Ah, it's no biggie - I don't mind the chatter. This actually isn't even my car. I'm just filling her up for a friend of mine."

"I gotcha, That's cool of you man." He said, sending me his pleasantry.

Obviously, the guy had no idea what was going on.

"I know it may sound funny, but I swear I know you from somewhere. You look familiar to me."

He studied my face, checking every dimple, before concluding.

"Weren't you over at Hard Luck last night? I think I remember seeing you over there on stage. That's right - you were doing the karaoke, weren't you? You were good."

I was frightened. It wasn't every day I got recognized for such fame and glory. Maybe this fool was nothing more than a low-level groupie only looking for a petty autograph from a living legend.

"I'm heading over there after this," he added. *"They're having a Halloween spectacular tonight and there's live music all around, I'm going to bring some friends with me - are you and your girl going to go? I could try and save you a table or something when I arrive."*

"Sure, that's where we're heading too." I answered, attempting to blow him off without sounding mean spirited. "It was nice meeting you, man, but I have to get going. I don't want to keep my girl waiting inside. She can be a bitch about things, y'know?"

"Yeah, that's cool, I understand." He nodded with sympathy, looking ahead at the gas price displayed on his monitor before officially allowing me to exit. *"Can you believe that, though - nearly $30 just to fill this little piece of shit up?"*

"What can I say? Blame it all on the economy, right?"

"You can say that again," he nodded. *"I don't mean to sound conspiratorial over it, but if we don't get a handle on things in the Middle East, things are just going to get worse for us around here. And you know what will happen next - all hell will break loose and we'll be left paying the cost for years to come."*

"Jesus, you sound like my dad." I chuckled, comforting his radical theory.

"He must be a wise man."

"He would like to think so." I teased, thinking it to myself. "Sorry to rush, once again, but I really do gotta go. I'll see you tonight and if I see you, we can continue our talk."

"Sure thing, bro! And whatever you're doing with that chick in there, I'd say, keep doing it. She's hot as fuck for my blood and I wouldn't know how to contain myself if I was you."

I left before anyone else was taken aback by his brashness - jogging my way forward to check on my beauty before he lassoed me back for seconds.

"Who were you chatting with out there?" Lexi scolded, looking out from the door, noticing the vehicle finally pulling away, possibly thinking either that I had dodged a bullet from a creeper or wrongly flirted with another woman who could instantly send me into damage control.

"Just some random dude who noticed me last night at the bar."

"Oh, wow, you got a stalker!"

"I never thought of it that way but, yeah, maybe I do. That's quite something, ain't it?"

"He wasn't like an undercover cop or something - digging you for info to why you were there, was he?"

"Nah, he was nice and actually wanted to save us a seat when we arrived."

"Oh wow! Was he that blind to not even notice you look just a tad underage?"

"Why would he care? The guy looked hopeless enough. He congratulated me over seizing you."

"As he should," she gloated while grabbing the last

handful of chocolate sweets from the rack.

"Wow, how many of those are you taking?"

"As many as we need, dummy."

"I'm surprised you're a big junk food addict. I thought women looked after things like their figure?"

"Hey, if we're going to blow all of Turner's money, wouldn't you think it's best to at least get the things we want and celebrate a little? I'll worry about *my* figure another day. Jesus, you can be a bore."

"*Hey, do either of you want this last leftover slice of pizza,*" The store clerk offered, figuring he too had an open opportunity to steal more money from us.

"Yeah, we'll take it." She rushed over, grabbing it from the trey.

"So, what's all this going to cost us?"

Lexi dropped all of the goodies on the counter as the clerk rang everything up.

"It looks like it's gonna cost you guys $27.87."

"That's not too bad." I thought, considering we packed a heavy load.

"Plus you owe me $25 on pump #2."

"Well," Lexi grabbed me, "Give him the money, stupid."

"Oh, crap, I think I left it in the glovebox. I gotta go back out to the car and get it."

"Well, do that then and hurry up!"

Her smart-alecky sensibility began to bug me. I knew I was in over my head but none of that mattered. I was playing the part of lovestruck fool.

I hurried back to the vehicle, opening up the cubbyhole, only to notice a few hundred went missing.

"*What the -*" I freaked, sending out bad vibes, discovering my stupidity of leaving the door open - potentially for that prick to rob us blind before vanishing to *Hard Luck.* Our loud voices seemingly luring him to be skeptical and curious about our unclaimed fortune.

"I'm surprised he left us $100." I thought as I stuck the

rest of the twenties in my pocket. Lexi wouldn't worry about my miscalculation only if I found a decent way to hide it from her sight.

"Jesus, what took you so long?" She fussed, opening the door back up, welcoming my return.

I didn't answer, putting $60 on the counter as the clerk raised his eyebrow in suspicion. As if a kid like me would have enough money to pay off such a large bill.

"Here's your cash, Steve." Lexi flirted, glancing over at his name tag.

He rang up the order, giving us our change.

"*My name's actually not Steve,*" He corrected using a strong Indian accent. "*It's really Saketharaman - In India, it means, "I'm a lord."*

"Oh, really?" She questioned, placating his ego.

"*You may not believe me but it's true. I was once a king of my village before the government kicked me out, losing favor with the ruler. I thought it was best to leave before I lost my head. The kind of people that are over there are not real pleasant when it comes to matters of -*"

"Come on, we've gotta get going," I pinched Lexi, warning her to hitch before this psycho started reminiscing about his storied past.

"*You two be safe out there.*" He cautioned as we exited with his blessing.

Lexi's mind, not paying attention, planning yet another opportunity to make Turner's life a living hell.

"Hey, I got another brilliant idea."

"I'm afraid to even ask what this is going to entail." I quivered, alarming myself for yet another inevitable decision to be had on our part.

"I have his keys, let's just say that I drop them on the passenger seat and lock the doors with them inside. What do you think will happen?"

"A possible tow." I thought, not wanting to show her the support she craved.

"Yeah, I know, it's genius isn't it? We need to do it!"

Chapter Fifty-Seven

My legs ached.

The rocks stapling my shoes as I continued the dreaded walk down to *Hard Luck* on foot.

The breeze, beginning to be a bit contagious, fearing somehow being outside too long would lead to the common cold; with flu season around the corner, it was that time of year for one to play hooky.

My new lease on life made me want to reconsider such temptation of satisfying that need. It was true, I was only a freshman, but the way things were heading in this first semester alone, seemed I was on the fast track to something good and I didn't want to lift the accelerator to slow it down.

I hadn't revealed to Lexi yet about the misfortune of accidentally squandering the extra cash but the gratification she was showing for one upping herself on Turner put her in an elevated state of nirvana, making it easier to judge whether or not the time was right to open up the can of worms.

"Just imagine the look on that douchebag's face when he sees his car missing and not only that, he has to go down and get it back after it gets towed away. That'll teach him something, right? I can only hope my sister appreciates all the shit I try to do to show her my love and affection. Man, ain't it just a little fun being evil?"

Lexi's enthusiasm was overshadowed by the pain stinging at my feet.

"What's wrong with you, kid? You act like you've never

hiked a freaking mile before? You got something in your shoe? You need your mommy to come over for support?"

"I'm not sure, really, I think I might." I replied. "With all these little pebbles around here anything can slip in. I also don't think I came quite equipped with the right kind of kicks."

Lexi looked down, judging the footwear and snubbing her nose over at the Chuck Taylor's I'd been flashing with style.

"What are you doing wearing those, anyway? Are you attempting to go back to the future or something? Those damn things are so uncomfortable, aren't they? They have no soles on them."

"I thought they were hip. All my friends were talking trash about me not having them so give me a break. I wanted to fit it. It wasn't like anyone told me how this day was gonna end up."

"I'm surprised that you actually wanted to fit in with the crowd. You look to me to be more like the kind of person that struggles to be a nonconformist their whole life. You know the type: the loner who ultimately dies... y'know, alone, with no kids or any connection with humans."

It was weird hearing her say that. It was as if she had reached down into my body, grabbed at my soul and read out my autobiography directly while coming to terms with the idea that maybe it wasn't a pretty story to be told.

"Well, I'm not in the mood to wait around, slowpoke. I'll meet you up at the place. You'll need to catch up if you want to see me. I'll see you again *if* you decide to get there on time."

"Also," she reminded, "Don't forget the loot, we're going to need it tonight to have some fun."

I thought for a second to tell her, opting not with hope that maybe future circumstances could change the narrative as the night progressed.

"By the way, Lex," I yelled, "May I just ask how the hell we are going to get back home without a car? My house is literally 20 miles away from here."

"Did you forget, stupid? You do have friends coming over.

They have cars, don't they? They'll drive you back, besides we still gotta get a hold of Jeff somehow and let him know about our costume. I still think the two of us can pull that plug/socket thing off with just the right hint of attitude."

I watched as she gradually departed from the picture, blowing me a kiss before filling the empty void with only the survival skills I had to complete the rest of the journey on my own.

The weather, now playing a mild factor, once again, spraying a light drizzle, hinting to be another night of potential rainstorms in the surrounding areas. The forecast becoming unsure with itself about dictating the proper mood.

"Not again," I thought, taking a moment to bend down and unlace my laces for safety purposes.

The cars, now whistling past fast, storming on through, watching some of the drivers take notice, honking their horns, igniting a howl from the wolf who came out in full character on this crazy weekend of the year.

"*Hey buddy,*" a man signaled to me, rolling down his window. "*You wouldn't happen to know where I can pawn off this surround system I have stashed in the back of my van, here?*"

I looked at him, thinking he was nuts, possibly attempting to bag me in his ride for an upcoming documentary on the whereabouts of missing children.

Not wanting to spoil his fun, I played along with the knowledge that my mom told me to never talk with strangers.

"I really don't know." I answered, not trying to reveal anything, "It's probably best if you just ask someone else. I'm not really the one to be asking about that. I don't really need one."

"*You want to come in and see for yourself? It might change your mind.*"

"Not really." I ignored, as he quickly hit the road, fearing maybe a policeman was on duty doing his nightly guard watch. My assumption being he didn't want his face to be too cleverly revealed for a lineup accusation if I was called in. In any event,

I survived another brief dash with death making head waves to reach my destination without a mark.

"There, finally, I made it." I said as the neon lights displayed brightly across the *Hard Luck* banner, making for yet another evening of unpredictable mayhem and possible disaster to follow.

Chapter Fifty-Eight

It hadn't been twenty four hours since I stepped off the hardwood floor, noticing a difference in the set of locals inhabiting the establishment as I walked in.

My initial instinct was to spot Lexi but for some odd reason, I couldn't find her, possibly in the bathroom powdering her nose, gearing herself up for the night ahead.

The time was still early so being greeted without the fear of getting kicked out was refreshing. I scanned, hoping to find some familiarity as I watched Darrell fill up a glass for a customer seated at the bar.

He spotted me quickly with a wave and a humorous gesture to come over.

"Hey, Mr. Friday Night, you come here for seconds?"

Breaking the ice, I made my way towards the seat - not unusual seeing some question my age as I sat down and pleaded for a drink.

"Are your two *loser* band mates here yet?"

"Not yet," he smirked, looking and detecting if I was bluffing about the beer. *"We're still about two hours away from set up time. I'll give them a call in about a half an hour and see where they're at. I wouldn't worry - you were with them today, weren't you?"*

I nodded, keeping the small talk alive and at a minimum to not disrupt the others.

"I did bring over our new addition - you see that babe by the jukebox?" Pointing to his trophy girlfriend who looked as if she

came straight out of an early 1990s music video: flannel shirt, pierced nose ring, dyed hair - you name it, a cross between a teenage Courtney Love and Shirley Manson. The Seattle scene, apparently still alive and well even with all the evidence, pointing to the contrary.

"Yeah, that was the chick you were with last night, wasn't it? The backup singer."

"Oh, yeah - I forgot you saw us making out. She's a knockout, ain't she?"

I didn't say anything about Jeff's heartbroken episode, keeping any feud that could lead to a possible breakup with the group to myself.

"So, what's going on right now?" I asked, watching some roadies set up the stage.

"It's Saturday, so we allow a lot of our locals to have open mic - they'll be done before 8 when the real party begins. You can just sit here and chill a bit. Order some food, y'know make believe you actually came to have a good time."

"I appreciate that." I said, feeling a safe connection with him. "By the way, have you seen Lexi?"

"Who?"

"The chick I was here with last night. We came in together."

"Oh yeah, that's right. I forgot about her. I saw someone come in and head to the restroom. I think that was her. I'm not really sure though, you know how it is, they all are alike. You can't live with 'em and yet you can't live without them."

"With Or Without You, right?"

"Yeah, right, like the song. Good catch!" He laughed, judging whether he wanted to add it to their set list.

"That's what I figure. We've kind of had a hectic day as it is. I just think, for now, sitting here is therapeutic enough."

"Are you tempting me to give you a drink or to listen to a sad sappy story? I mean look at you, you're getting older as we speak, before you leave tonight, you'll be aging at least twenty years."

"Come on - It's still early, give the kid a brew! He ain't gonna

get drunk on one piss of alcohol tonight." A man argued, taking my side on the matter. *"He doesn't even have a license. What's the worst that's gonna happen, stumble on the side of the road and get a ticket for lewd behavior?"*

"*Sam,*" Darrell sighed, "*How could we survive without you?*"

"You couldn't, now do as I say and let the boy have a night he won't forget."

"*But he already had one of them last night with my permission. Jesus, who do you think I am? His guardian?*"

"No, actually, just a good person." I teased, hoping that line could sell it.

He reached down, pulling up a glass, ready to fill the order.

"Nah, just give me a bottle, I'll make it easy on you. A Budweiser will do."

He looked puzzled, not commenting, doing instead as I said.

"*I was gonna treat you with a nice mix but, whatever, the customer is always right.*"

"So are you guys gonna dress up tonight?"

"*I'm actually not sure yet. In my opinion, our music is killer enough to impress the judges. We really don't need a stupid gimmick.*"

"Well your girlfriend looks like she belongs in a time capsule."

"*Yeah, you're right.*" He laughed. "*I miss the early 90s, all this nu-metal crap that's out there just doesn't do it for me. I mean look what happened with Woodstock this summer.*"

"Yeah, I saw that on MTV. Seriously, what the hell is our generation coming to?"

"*Who knows? I think what is fueling people up is all this bubblegum pop that's out there. Sooner or later this clash was going to happen - the writing was on the wall, wasn't it? I mean, we went from smells like teen spirit to actual teen spirit. People were gonna get pissed off sooner or later.*"

"All that hippie bullshit of peace, love and dope really

went out the window too, wouldn't you say?"

"You're telling me. The dude that was promoting that shitstorm was the same loser who did the original back in '69 - y'know before inflation hit the fan and the price of water didn't cost you $4 bleeping bucks."

"God, that is true. I almost forgot about that and all those porta potties, what a waste of human feces. It didn't go to shit like that in '94 when they did it back then."

"Yeah, well, a lot can happen in five years. Just tell that to any major corporation that wants to make a quick buck by selling out the youth of America by dropping them off in the middle of nowhere then jerking them to buy their junk with their own price tag stamped on it for profit. Capitalism at its worst if you ask me. Like you said, man, peace, love and all that other crap ain't selling these days. It's all a business being played out by the few feeding off from the hand of the many. It's just human nature, I suppose to see ourselves eat each other alive."

"Are you too young'uns talking about good ol' Woodstock?" Sam interrupted, filling us in on his own historic past about the event. ***"Y'know I may be just an old hippie to you two but I'll tell you what - I was there when it all went down and it was beautiful, man."***

"You mean you saw Hendrix?"

"You're damn right I did."

"Well, explain it to us, grandpa. And please - don't leave anything out."

"Oh, you bet!" He toasted, rambling on about his flower power experience. ***"It was Day Three of the festival. A Sunday I believe, I was shaking up with this unbelievable brunette from the night before, you know what I mean - sexy as fuck, a bush for a puss. I don't think I ever saw her again after that but that's not the point. I used her, she used me, like the Bob Seger song said. We were both stoned out of our minds, still wasted humming out some tunes from the likes of Janis and The Who when I first heard it calling to me."***

"What did you hear, old man? The sound of the police coming

to arrest you?"

"No way, man! It was that smokin' guitar playing out the Star Spangled Banner directly to the half million of us who were there to witness it firsthand. Even though the fact was that I was a microscopic distance away from the legend, it didn't matter, but I tell you, man, you had to be there to get it. That sound pierced into my soul. It was one of those lifetime things, y'know?"

"Hold up - hold up, Wait just a minute. I need to know one thing before you go any further with this piece of hippie folklore."

"What's that?"

"With everyone stoned out of their minds, as you claim, who the fuck had the analytical ability to count that many people? Isn't it possible they were all just seeing some double vision?"

"Yeah, I know what you mean, Darrell." I added, "That line must have been all gibberish nonsense to get the masses to accept it as legit."

"There was a movie made if you two don't believe me - I mean you don't have to take my word for it; people came, you can see it for yourself."

"Yeah, I've seen that movie," Darrell said, slowly losing interest, glancing instead up at the television looking at the football scores on the ticker.

"For Pete's Sake, Michigan is trailing!" He jolted, as if he was losing money on the game.

"Who are they playing?" I asked.

"Indiana," he cried. *"They're a freaking basketball school, not a team in competition for the Big Ten title. Geez, what gives?"*

"Any team can come to play. It's all about school pride, right? That's the one thing that separates it from the pros."

"Yeah, well, right now I'm out $100 bucks until they can come back, so I really don't want to hear about school pride."

"Who did you bet?"

"You're looking at him," Sam smiled, relishing in Darrell's displeasure. *"Don't forget, you still owe me from last week too."*

"Oh, give me a break! That game didn't count, that one was on point spread."

"Well, you can just pay me for my beers, then." He laughed. *"That'll settle everything."*

Darrell didn't respond, letting him win his case.

"Anyway, I gotta get a move on."

"You're not staying for tonight's main event?"

"I can't," He sulked, swallowing his last drop of whiskey. *"I got a wife that's home that keeps complaining I'm staying out too late over here. I wish you boys luck, though."*

"We'll definitely miss you man. You're one of the few that know how to cheer us on."

"Yeah, well, that's just me helping out."

Sam got up, finally patting me on the back, before making his exit.

Chapter Fifty-Nine

Paul Westerberg once wrote the perfect bar anthem outside of *Piano Man* when he penned the alternative rock classic, *"Here Comes A Regular"* - a bittersweet ballad of loneliness darkened with the backdrop of such mellow lyrics as *"Summers past, it's too late, to cut the grass, there ain't much to rake out in the fall."*

Sitting there, underage, scooping out the scenery from these uncompromising fixtures that autumn evening - I sensed the mood shifting as it swayed across the room, counting down the minutes to the costume contest that awaited and the *Battle Of The Bands* that held the fate of my friends in its hands.

Lexi was still nowhere to be seen, leaving open the opportunity to catch the eye of the perpetrator who had stolen my money at the gas station, managing a small gap in time to suggest a quick walk across the floor to claim it back, with only fear of having my arm relocated in the process of retrieving it.

"Do you know that guy?" Darrell squinted, looking confused with why my eyes were focused at an angle towards him.

"Technically, yeah, I do."

"Care to explain then, bro?"

"Well let's just say you're not the only one that lost a shitload of money today."

"What are you ranting on about?"

"You see that guy sitting over there has about a couple

hundred dollars on him he got stashed in his pocket from the car we robbed."

"What the hell are you saying? What car did you rob?"

"It's a long story but I'll sum it up like this: so take some mental notes if you'd like."

"That's funny, I would never consider looking at you as a thief."

Darrell remained amused, allowing me to clarify myself before falling to the floor from laughter.

"Lexi and I kinda stole this dope addict's ride after she bear witnessed to watching him have sex with her sister in their room."

"Whoa, really? Talk about scaring a person for life. Was her sister hot, at least?"

"I wouldn't know. I was waiting outside, guarding her pitbull, when it all went down. You see, she dashed out quickly, stealing his keys, becoming wanted bandits without any assurance of what could happen next to the two of us."

"So you're saying that she threw you into the whirlwind of criminal deceit, didn't she?" He laughed. "Don't worry - That's typical for any woman to do. More than anything else, that's what really makes you a *man* in their eyes. I'd keep them peeled, man."

"Yeah, I know, right? " I sighed. "Anyway, we found this guy had about $500 loaded in his glove compartment from weed dealings but I left it in there not thinking twice to take it for myself before that jerk over there overheard us and swiped it when we weren't looking."

"Holy shit, for real? That was pretty stupid of you not to just grab it yourself, I mean, I definitely could use some of that dough if I got my hands on it."

"My mind wasn't exactly there- y'know, I never had a day like this before. Everything spinning so fast. It's been a long weekend, thus far, and the damn thing isn't over yet."

"Well, what can I do to help?"

"I'm not exactly sure but anything will do. You want to

throw him out of the bar for being an asshole? Y'know, just to make me feel better about the whole mess. You have the power to do that, right?"

"I'm not sure, dude." He sighed, "Without real proof, man, it's kind of topsy turvy if you want to know the truth. Besides, with what you were telling me, you might be in a bit of trouble if word gets out about what you and Lexi did. The last thing I want is to have cops around here scoping out the place and asking questions about it. You two better know what you're doing before you go any further with it."

"Yeah, I hear you. That's kind of my fear at the moment, though, I'm a little shell shocked about what to do next. I'm kind of in a pickle, you see. I haven't even told her about losing the cash yet. She's probably gonna curse me to the grave or something when I do. It only seems logical from what I can gather about our relationship thus far."

"Yeah, women can do that." He giggled, "Welcome to the world of never ending paranoia. They're always going to be watching over you. You're never really free anymore once they have you under their mind control and place you in their stranglehold."

"So what should I do about it?"

"I don't know kid but here's your chance to find out for yourself. I think that's her coming over here now."

I turned, looking ahead before Lexi slapped me on the forehead.

"What have you two been yapping about?"

I was hesitant to reply but my conscience couldn't hold back.

"We kind of have to talk."

"Hold up, buckaroo!" She snapped. "You can't be saying that kind of crap to me."

"Saying what, exactly?"

"We *need* to talk. I operate the car in this relationship and if there's anyone that will be saying that shit, it will be me."

"But this is kind of serious."

"What can be so serious? I mean, Jesus, you're only, what, 14 years old?"

"Well, remember the money Turner had in his car?"

"Yeah, so, what about it, you did grab it for us, right? Where's my share?"

"That's kind of it," I said, shaking my head, pointing across to give her direction to the culprit who had it. "That guy over there has it."

Lexi, baffled by my incompetence, glanced over to see for herself.

"Who's he supposed to be?"

"He's the guy at the gas station. He must have overheard us talking, opening the front door, which was unlocked, and took the money straight from the glove compartment after I walked away."

"So you're saying he stole the money?"

"Yeah, well kinda, but he was nice enough to leave us with $100."

"Well, whoopdedoo! What could we possibly do with that?"

"Actually, we just spent that when we ate those goodies on the way over."

"Why don't you just go over there and ask him for it back? This is your problem, kid, not mine."

"That's just it. I'm afraid."

Lexi, annoyed by my cowardice, tucked in her gut to deal with the matter herself, walking away angry with an agenda of rage building up.

"Leave it to a woman to do a man's job!" She belted, before striking revenge at the target afoot.

Chapter Sixty

I was never big on confrontations. The way Lexi's eyes bolted with fire suggested I shouldn't be in the way in matters of her vendettas.

The drama-filled lifestyle she seemingly craved appeared never ending, going from one toxic situation to the next, almost as if she didn't have a care in the world about the consequences that followed. All that mattered was the end result and the selfless belief that she was doing her job, protecting herself while providing some solace for her entire family.

I only wish I could be so courageous. My spine, basically jello, a jenga set ready to crumble in a heartbeat's notice, wasn't up to the challenge.

I sat there, glued, watching the drama unfold before my eyes, unsure how far she was willing to take it before she let this fatso really have it.

He may have been big enough to scare me away but hell hath no fury like a woman scorned or in this case, a woman pissed entirely at the world who wanted that money for herself.

"I have to say," applauded Darrell, looking on, "You have it to give it to your girl. She's got guts. That dude won't know what hit him, once she gets through. It's not the size of the punch that will hurt but the psychological damage she'll inflict that will sting him like a bee for years. He'll never see a beautiful woman the same way again. If he doesn't already."

"Yeah, but what's going to happen if a fight *does* break out between them?"

"That's not going to happen. No idiot, especially a dude like that, would ever put a finger on some chick, especially in this bar. They'd be too chicken to even try it with someone like me behind here ready to pull the trigger, trust me, by tonight's end, you'll get that money back. If not in your pocket, especially in hers. And from there, all bets are off on what she'll do with it. "

"That's my thinking."

"Why don't you go over and assist? Y'know, scope out how things are going, gain a pointer or two. I mean you're always learning when it comes to understanding women, right?"

"Are you crazy? I'm trying to keep a low profile as it is. Getting a black eye is the last thing I need to worry about right now. I mean, c'mon! What insurance do I have? Would you want to help pay for any damages I would get in the shuffle?"

"Oh, hell no! I'm not spending a dime on your scrawny ass." Darrell laughed, entertained by the animated excitement. "Well, it looks like you might not have to worry about any of that after all."

"Why's that?"

"She's coming back over now with the verdict."

"Really?"

"Yeah, look."

"That was quicker than I thought." Darrell chuckled, proving his intuition correct as she greeted us.

"Yeah, it was a piece of cake, really." She smiled, noticing the anticipation on her return.

"So, what exactly did you say to him to get him riled up?"

"Nothing. I just told that loser that if he wasn't going to fork over the cash, I'd have to get tough with him and do something even more drastic that he wouldn't like."

"And what exactly did that entail?"

"Nothing, really. I just bluffed a little and told him directly that by the time the night was through a piece of his anatomy would be chopped off to pieces and fed to my dog."

"And he believed you?"

"You bet."

My mouth dropped, stunned by such earnestness.

"Men are such wimps in these cases. They play it tough on the outside but I always figure they are nothing more than a bunch of pansies who when given the chance, bail on a dime and come crawling back to their mommas looking like lost souls. It's quite typical of them, really. I've been around long enough to figure out how the game works with them. When God created the dominant species he really had the woman in mind. It's just society telling everyone else otherwise. Y'know what I mean, right? Hollywood writers in a male dominated environment telling us what to think. It's all male Chauvinist bullshit if you ask me and if you don't get wise with it, it's more than likely that crap will eat its way into your system and have you brainwashed in no time."

Darryl and I remained silent, not getting uptight from her defiant stance. It wasn't like we were in any mood to face a challenge with an attack dog already racing at us.

"I just can't believe you went full scale Lorana Bobbitt on that jerk?"

"He had it coming, anyway. I wouldn't want to be him tonight. I figure he'd probably wet his bed or something before he turns in."

"I can only imagine that." Darrell pondered.

"So where's my cut of the money?" I asked, fishing to get back on her good side.

"After what I had to put up with, what makes you think you should be getting any of it back? From my point of view, it all belongs to me, right? I went over there and claimed it back. You'll just have to deal with your losses."

"She has a solid point," laughed Darrell.

"Take it, I was uncomfortable holding that amount of money anyway." I bickered. "It's best if you just squander it away for yourself. At least then I don't have to worry about it anymore. My hands are cleaned."

"Oh God," Lexi shrieked. "Looks like we got more trouble on the horizon."

"What are you going on about?"

"The badges are finally coming for us."

"The who?"

"She's talking about *the cops dude!*" Darrell hissed, sounding frantic.

"Oh boy," I whispered, ducking my head, for shelter from the potential storm ahead. "That doesn't sound good."

Chapter Sixty One

"What do you think they're here for?" Lexi asked, calming her nerves before pausing to let me answer.

My brain blanked, spinning in a loop, thinking up all of the crazy shit that her silly rhetorical question posed.

"Well, for starters -"

"I guess it really doesn't matter." She interrupted, rushing away as quickly as possible without hearing my answer, almost as if I wasn't even there.

"How'd you like that?" Darrell chuckled, amused in the bitterness at how she left me hanging.

"Well, what did you expect? I mean didn't we just have this conversation not more than a few minutes ago, remember? They're women - they'll do that and then leave us hanging with the check."

"You're right about that," he sighed. "I just hope they don't go around snooping, asking too many questions."

"What do you think they want?"

"The cops normally come by, especially with what's been happening lately. We've been getting a lot of underage assholes snooping in."

"You mean like me?"

"You bet, so it's best that you scurry too before they ring your neck out of this joint for questioning."

"I think you mean *your* neck too, don't you? You'd be in deep shit too if they found out."

"I'm not worried, kid, it's been typical, as of late, I even know the officer by name. He's been pretty chill about everything but with what you've been telling me tonight, it's best that you scram now before I have to tell some lame ass excuse to cover for you. I hate it when cops try to corner me with crap like that. It really doesn't make me look good and besides, the last thing that I want is them ruining my night."

"I appreciate that, man." I smirked. "I'll be in the bathroom waiting until everything blows over. I don't want anything on my conscience."

I sheepishly got up, scanning the floor quickly, hoping not to make eye contact with the officer who was already beginning to glance around at some in attendance.

"The safest place on earth." I thought, pushing open the bathroom door and blocking my mind from the harsh reality that was waiting in the rear view.

"Gosh, they don't do anything to clean this place up, do they?" I cringed, disturbed by the foul odors still surrounding the room from the day before. "I mean not a mere twenty four hours and this space still reeks as bad as it did when I left it."

"Anyone in here?"

The urinals seemed empty but feet were underneath one of the stalls.

"Your little girlfriend is a *bitch!*" A man's voice echoed through the wall, scaring me.

"Who's that?"

"You're worst nightmare!" The voice raised after opening the door to reveal his identity and suspect now that I wasn't even safe inside this smelly sanctuary.

"What happened to your lip?" I asked, getting a good look at the gas station thief straight in the eye.

"What do you think happened, turd?"

"You're saying Lexi did that?"

"If that's what you want to call her, yeah. She punched me right in the kisser and took the money straight outta my pocket."

"Well in my opinion, you deserved it, dude. I didn't come in here to feel sorry for you, *Dan!*"

The man gazed into my eyes, testing my immediate strength.

"I don't want to hurt you, kid. So it's best if you get out before I begin to have other thoughts that might make me think otherwise. I have a machete in my car and I wouldn't want to use it on your scrawny ass.""

"You don't scare me," I countered, feeling almost insulted that he even tested my patience on the matter. "Now get out of here, yourself, or I might lose it too."

My heart jumped, shocked those words came out of my mouth coherently without a stutter to note. What had Lexi done? It was as if my confidence level was lifted beyond belief. It felt good being on cloud nine, earning another solid victory.

"Okay, I've had it," The man bulged, leaning forward, tugging at my shirt, fist in the air, ready to land me a right jab.

"*Holy shit!*" I freaked, ducking before my face became a black and blue piece of bathroom graffiti. "*What the fuck?*"

"You're lucky I missed," He joked, possibly thinking he was doing this to teach me a lesson.

"Yeah, well, I don't need to worry about that, do I? You punch like a sissy, anyway. I'm also not the one who has to remind myself how much of a loser I am trying to rip off kids on a perfectly fine Saturday night for no good reason at all."

He stood there, without a clever comeback to refute, brushing his hands across my shirt instead attempting to simplify some tranquility between us.

"*It's not over!*" He fussed, before slamming the door to exit.

My knuckles, now turning white, my face numb, full of fear with anxiety showing all over, becoming unbearable to control without freezing dead.

I made my way out of the premises, looking chill and praying the police storm had passed. I caught a glimpse of Lexi standing with Darrell by the bar, making her own presence shown along with the officer who appeared at the moment to be acting friendly.

I couldn't face it any longer. I had to come clean and take my lumps if we were compromised. It was the only justifiable thing to do, face the consequences and take it like a man.

"Are we safe?" I thought, approaching, figuring things didn't appear as bleak as I had been picturing it.

"They're actually here for you, kid." Darrell warned as I watched everyone immediately gaze in my direction.

My stomach plummeted, I was about to faint to the ground.

A new nightmare was upon me now.

Chapter Sixty-Two

When I was a child I had a dream. It was one of those things you don't realize how traumatizing it was until years later when a heavy dose of irony strikes you dead on and puts you on a full scale psychological crisis that one never saw coming.

It was late at night, I was in a car crash, probably no younger than ten years old at the time with someone whom I couldn't recognize driving the vehicle.

I always figured it was my brother but I could never get a good glimpse as to who it was before my father woke me from terror.

"Son, it was only a bad dream." He'd calmly remind me, as Barry lay above me on the top bunk, without a scratch on him, peaceful in his slumber.

"But it seemed so real."

"Dreams are like that sometimes."

Dad had a way of making me understand things by telling me exactly why they were.

"But how?"

"Don't expect me to know everything, son, but that's just the way it is. As we sleep, our brain still works and those dreams that we have are nothing more than our mind working overtime when our eyes are shut. I heard a writer once say to an audience member, " I get a lot of my crazy and silly ideas when I sleep."

"Really?"

"Yeah," Dad nodded. "He continued also by saying that these dreams are like gateways to our inner imagination. They tell us stories that we could never see when we are awake and sometimes they may appear real because we live inside what he called a trap door that he describes as a mirror between truth and fiction."

"Seriously?" I pondered, thinking that was a pretty strange synopsis. "What does he mean?"

Dad laughed, "You'll probably understand it better when you get older, right now you should get some rest yourself, you have a big day coming up tomorrow and I wouldn't want this to spoil it."

"I would like to be a writer too." I said, as he attempted to tuck me back in.

"I know, son. I've seen you're quite the reader lately. Most kids your age, I'd say, would not be so consumed with all of these books you have scattered around. I'm surprised that you don't play as many video games like your brother."

"C'mon dad, you know all they do is rot your brain. That's not me. I want to manage to be smart."

Dad continued to chuckle as Barry's eyes began to wake above us.

"Looks like we woke you up, huh?"

"Not really," He yawned, pretending to be asleep. "I heard you too the whole time."

"I'm sure you did." I snickered, feeling a little uneasy with his cynicism.

"C'mon, now, spill it," Barry kicked, "What were you dreaming about, really? It wasn't about me now, was it?"

"It kinda was."

Both dad and Barry looked on with anticipation with what I would say next.

"I wasn't out there slaying dragons or some stupid crap like that, was I?" Barry egged, making me lose my focus. "I mean I'm too old for such childish nonsense."

"No, idiot!" I belted. "It was serious than that."

Dad could tell we were beginning to get on his last nerves, cleverly leaving the room before the two of us duked it out like prizefighters.

"I'll let you boys discuss it amongst yourselves then. I better be going." He bailed before closing the door behind him, leaving us in complete darkness to talk it over.

"So what was it, troll? What had *me* on your mind this late in the night that you had to have dad come in to rescue you?"

"You and I were in a car crash together, bro. And I don't think either one of us survived it."

Barry paused, without any retaliation on his behalf. "Like for real?"

"That's what it was."

"But I don't even have my driver's license yet you bozo. How can that be?"

"I don't know." I answered. "All I know is that the person in the dream looked older and you're the only person that's older than me that I know of, so it had to be you, right?"

"Not really, I mean it could have been anyone. Or maybe it was someone from your future? Have you ever thought of that, genius?"

"I don't know Barry. I mean it felt so surreal. Y'know like in one of those movies where everything just spins out of control and you wake up going what was that?"

"What do you think?"

"I say your nuts." He laughed. "Dad's right, though, you have an active imagination. I wouldn't think too much of it if I were you, just get some rest. I'm not going to die anytime soon and even if I were, I'd probably kill you before I let anything happen to me, right? I'm the oldest, there's no way I'd die young."

"You're so full of brotherly love, aren't you?"

"All the time," he joked, before fading back to sleep. "Don't worry, bro, you know such dreams don't ever come true. That's why they're called nightmares. They're only made to scare us."

"Yeah, well, maybe you're right about that."

I hoped for once, he was.

Chapter Sixty-Three

"**A**re you okay, son?" The officer snapped, waking me from what for all practical purposes could have been a mini coma.

I was dazed, confused and winded by all the commotion. I couldn't move my body.

"You're coming with me, kid." He ordered, without allowing me to explain.

My heart, now speeding at a record pace, unheard of in my lifetime, was turning frantic and out of control.

They had caught me dead on and now I had to be whipped and sent away to the death chamber.

"What about her?" I begged, pointing directly toward Lexi, who was looking innocent about the whole thing.

"She has nothing to do with this." He paused, confused with why I asked.

"She's part of it too, ain't she?"

"Not this time."

"Then what's this all about?"

"I got called in from your mom who told me you might be over here. Not sure how you got in considering your age but we'll deal with that for another time."

"My mom?" I shivered, shocked with how she was brought into the conversation. "What does she have to do with any of this?"

"I'll tell you all about it when you get into the car, you're heading down to the station with me, anyway, to clarify everything, so I'll fill you in then."

My initial reaction was to remain silent. I was already way over my head, the last thing now was to have this officer pull me aside and read me my Miranda rights like any other hard nosed criminal.

"Hey, what's really going on?" I thought to myself, as the bubbling whispers began to spring up inside my head, making me alone and uncomfortable.

With the moon turning full, I couldn't deny the strong sense that something was immediately wrong. I was getting a cold tingling in my stomach that warned me that maybe the nightmare I had been foreshadowing all evening was turning true.

"Hey, where are you heading?" Asked Mark as he tried to approach waiting outside with both Ryan and Jeff, ignoring an answer once he caught a glimpse of the cop ahead who was dangling his keys standing by for orders from someone on the other end of his walkie-talkie.

"Holy shit!" He mumbled, vanishing quickly.

"Okay, son, get on in." The officer demanded, treating me like some punk kid who might as well have been put on parole.

"You look like a normal kid so I'm just going to lay it on you quick. Is that okay?"

I almost felt like I needed to not respond, dragging this whole episode out until I felt comfortable enough with it.

"Hey, kid, are you listening to me?"

My adolescent self refused to talk, hoping that whatever came out of his mouth would not have any lasting effect on me whatsoever.

"Your mom seemed very worried about you when we told her what had happened and she was desperately needing to get in contact with you somehow to make sure you were safe and out of harm's way. We really had no other way of reaching you until she suggested that you might be hanging out at the bar."

"Really?" I thought, letting my internal fears remain checked without overreacting further.

"Right now, she's waiting with your dad so you will be able to see them both when we get over there."

"Okay," I said as my voice finally cracked, frightened with where this was leading.

"You're what, 13 or 14?" The officer assumed, possibly beginning to feel a bit sorry for me.

"Something like that."

"Well, It's not going to be easy for me to tell you this so I don't want you to think I'm not being sincere."

It's funny how perceptions work. If I had been plastered with tattoos or a nose ring, he may not have been up for the challenge to be so polite. In any event, I braced myself for the next sentence that came out of his mouth. Bad news I could accept, life changing devastation on the other hand would be something completely foreign.

"Your brother was killed last night."

I took a moment to digest the news. If I had been trampled by a thousand pound elephant, I would have been better equipped for survival than the silver bullet that pierced my heart in that instant. I was shattered.

"Do I need to pull over or something?" He waved, as my face began to bulge open like a water balloon, bursting in no time flat.

"Okay, okay, hold on!" He shouted, pulling the vehicle over just in time before the smell of puke scented the air. "I hope that makes you feel better. It's not easy for someone your age to have to go through something like this. I know that when I was about your age, I had a friend who lost a sibling with something similar. It crushed him pretty deep that I don't think he ever truly got over it. In fact I think he became an alcoholic years later. "

I got appalled by his lack of empathy. I could only think maybe this wasn't his first rodeo having to explain such tragedies to others, probably spending decades going around town on the job dishing out sympathy calls to all the less fortunate souls who were unfortunately put in the position I was placed.

"I'm sorry that I had to be the one to tell you."

"Nah, it's alright." I forgave, hoping he'd just shut up before I accidentally committed murder.

"Can you at least tell me what happened, exactly?"

"At around 1 am," he commented, "I got a call stating that a vehicle was turned over by Bilter Ave."

"What do you mean turned over?"

"Flip flopped," he rudely implied. "Yeah, apparently, part of a drinking incident. Don't worry, though, we got the assailant. He was honest with us when he was picked up after his car stalled out of gas. I guess we were thankful he was driving a clunker and didn't bother to check his fuel light. It saves us a bunch of time trying to catch lowlifes like these."

"Can I ask who it was?"

"Technically, I'm not obliged to disclose that information to you son but I can see by the look on your face that it is hitting you hard."

My face remained pale waiting for anything to help cushion the blow. Hearing this officer audition for stand up sure wasn't doing anyone any favors.

"Brett Andrews." He answered.

Deja Vu returned. It was the name I didn't want to hear, the one I had been dreading and the one that changed everything.

Chapter Sixty-Four

There was a time when all I listened to was country music. I wouldn't stand for the sad depressing stuff my dad would shuffle through but it almost seemed instantaneously my world had been shut down and colored black into tragedy strummed by the howling sounds of Johnny Cash, three chords, and the lonesome truth whistling it's way into my ears.

Barry was dead and there was no way of bringing him back. It was as if not only the music had died within me but the entire band had departed from the stage, leaving without an encore. There was nothing but a cold and bitter taste eating me and the night could only get worse.

Could this really be? What was left but to crumble to the floor, taking my broken heart to the dump where it festered into oblivion, having the rats chew it out till all that was left was empty hole that begged for the forgiveness of the cruel things I might have been guilty of to cause the aching pain.

Why wasn't I there when I suspected danger? If only I had followed my gut and not my hormones maybe I could have changed things. It was all a battlefield of regret and the casualty was too hard to control without breaking down completely.

I walked into the police station as dad sat motionless in a chair. I was nervous to approach, his eyes covered with tears as they swam underneath his face with his clenched hand distorting my view.

In all my years on earth, I never once saw him come unglued in such a state of shock and despair. It was unbearable to watch and I felt I needed to comfort him.

"Where have you been?" He asked, swallowing his gut, sugar coating his pride, fearing it would show as we spoke.

"I was with Mark and his brother all day. I told mom before I left the house that I was planning on spending my weekend with them. She didn't seem to make a big deal about it so I went along."

Dad listened, coming to his own conclusion as to whether or not my actions were punishable.

"What were you guys doing at the bar, anyway?"

"Mark's brother invited us to come watch, they were participating in an event tonight. We all thought it would be fun. I also met a girl and wanted to impress her. Can you blame me?"

Dad studied my face, leaving open space to not be too overly critical, possibly allowing himself to let fate play its course and not be too judgmental over the night's events.

"Is that where you were last night too?" He figured. "Your mom was telling me something about that before."

I didn't want to feel like I was disappointing him by verbally saying yes, so I nodded, thinking that would be best.

"Where's mom at, now?" I asked, hoping to sway the subject.

"They took her into another room for questioning and to possibly get a look at the body to verify. We're going to be here for a while. It's been a long day, we're all just trying to deal with this thing the best that we can."

I could tell dad was struggling to adjust and frame his words correctly. Barry's death only frayed at the fabric of our nuclear unit, being placed in a position where all of us had to deal with the tragedy on our own solid ground.

"You should go on and get out of here. Let the cop that brought you here bring you back home. This is no place for you. There's nothing wrong with holding onto your innocence for a little longer. The only thing left in life now is sorrow and grief and I don't want that for you, son."

I wasn't sure if dad knew the full story of what had happened but I was in no need to rush things. The details would eventually come out and all the tabloid hoopla would be front and center soon, so, now was clearly not the time to push any buttons.

"Did the police officer fill you in on what exactly happened?" Dad asked, turning my own theory around on itself.

"He told me mostly what went down, that Barry was involved in the crash and that they caught the guy who was responsible for it."

"Did he tell you who it was?"

I didn't burst out the name, fearing an unsettling moment would transpire but dad seemed equipped to not mince words.

"It was Jill's ex-boyfriend!"

I was surprised dad knew, unaware that he had paid attention to any of the people included in Barry's social circle.

"The cop was telling us that he confessed to stopping by her house last night, almost stalking the two of them in the process when they got into an altercation."

"You mean Barry got into a fight with him?"

"Not quite sure." Dad said. " But it led to this guy getting drunk and following Barry home where he did what he did."

I shrugged, remaining in disbelief, trying to piece the puzzle together while attempting to follow the narrative. I knew dad was confused too, and more so, I couldn't provide him any explanation for his own solace.

"What are we going to do now?" He asked, in an almost uncertain rhetorical fashion.

I couldn't answer because growing up, as it happened, began that night.

Chapter Sixty-Five

I didn't want to return home. In fact, it was the last place I wanted to be. I wanted so badly to take dad's advice and postpone this deep loss but I knew it would only be short lived.

It didn't matter anymore what went down at *Hard Luck*. I knew that whatever happened, I would get notified by the weekend's end and the news would fail in comparison to the larger scheme of things that had occurred.

I attempted to focus on clarity. I needed to relax but the difficulty only sprang when I heard the message Jill left on our answering machine.

"I'm deeply sorry that I put your family through this." She sobbed, as her voice muffled over the receiver. *"I feel so awful for what Brett did and I have only the deepest condolences to you and your family right now. Please don't hate me, I didn't wish for anything like this to happen. You're in my heart and prayers. I really hope that in time you can forgive me for this..."*

I was at a crossroads, listening - on one hand, I wanted to believe her, but my underlying assumption now made me look at her in a different light entirely. As if the evil that came upon Eve in the garden of Eden had tempted my brother and trapped him in a no-win situation where playing bait was his unfortunate and ultimate undoing.

It wasn't fair for anyone, especially for him. He was only seventeen, a lifetime still awaited and thanks to a selfish and stupid accident of bad luck in timing, it was over and the only

Greg Zimmerman

thing that remained were the chills of regret and silence from all the living who were involved in the mix of the confusion.

I retreated to my room to think. I didn't know where else to turn. My soul searching could be refined under these four walls. A place Barry and I once shared and now, in only a matter of minutes, a place that seemed like an eternity of memory that time had erased.

I laid on my bed, turning on the radio dial, hoping the music could drown out some of the pain.

It did nothing.

I turned over towards the bookshelf, thinking maybe I could use my imagination to escape from the pit I was drowning in.

It was all useless.

There was no story on earth that could replace the feelings and sorrow that was trapped within. I was alone and the only way out was to find my own answers to the madness. It wasn't going to be easy.

It's only a shame there wasn't a book for understanding the meaning of life. I figured everyone lived about the same, they get a reasonable childhood handed to them, maybe a broken heart from some boy or girl and if lucky, they survive it all and find some way to create the same amount of chaos for their offspring so the cycle has this symbolic refuge to repeat itself for the generational shifts that occur across most family circles.

It was naïve to think life could work in a way where everyone lived without tragedy. It wasn't Peter Pan. Even Peter had to grow up and leave Neverland behind, or if memory serves, he never did.

Wendy was the wisest who knew that time was limited and growing up was just a process one must achieve before accepting the keys to adulthood.

Lexi, in my short time with her, matured me to see life in a manner that suggested not everything was what it seemed. That the true beauty wasn't found in the outward appearance of others but in the sacrifice we have to hold and lift each other up no matter the circumstances. Her family struggle only enhanced my knowledge in how the world really worked. In essence, I began to see things introspectively, understanding certain relationships with a more human form, that not everyone was perfect and the only people who mattered most were the ones who never cheated you to begin with.

I understood Mark would *always* be Mark. Our friendship over the years would last, even if there were speculation running about that he'd drop out of high school the moment some playboy bunny came chasing after him through the halls asking for potential suitors.

Mark was funny that way. He'd bite you on the ass one minute and then be kind enough to hook you up with the person who could best help you cheat on your SATs.

Jeff and Ryan would continue their uncompromising and alluring bromance together. Their safe yet good hearted natured bond, regardless of the way they were towards me, would be compatible with my growing support system one needed while traveling through the curvy roads of adolescence.

Maybe Mr. Barrera was right. A writer can only examine their existence, search for its meaning and then share it. I knew I wasn't a great writer yet but maybe these experiences outlined something for another time upon reflection. The building blocks for growth and self discovery for one to accept the mantle of such *childish* maturity.

I always wanted to tell Barry I loved him and yet because of time and our undercutting for personal gain, I couldn't.

It's funny now, but sometimes, telling the truth is harder than simply writing a good story.

∞∞∞

Epilogue

O ne of the reasons I felt compelled to write this novel was because I came across an old homework assignment my brother had completed about a person he felt needed an "authority figure" around.

I'm not really sure why this deep thinking was assigned but he must have been in middle school at the time when it was written because the way that I'm described in the piece made me look way too young and very impressionable, making it almost silly to think he was writing about someone else.

His creative sense hadn't developed to show the true intentions on how much this task could help benefit him, leaving only to write it as an afterthought for another day.

He probably hated doing it, being nagged by some teacher to complete the required work or else be on the verge of repeating the grade for another year.

I remember those times when he would struggle with his classes. Saying typical juvenile stuff like this is pointless. Why am I doing this? How is this ever going to affect me later on?

It's funny now, but I kinda knew the way he thought about it, he'd be staring at that blank page for hours with a pencil in hand, ashamed he would have to go into the pillar of his soul to say something nice for someone he tormented daily.

So it's pretty obvious that this masterpiece of Shakespearen art was rushed as if to say, this is the work you wanted, so pass me, please, so we both can get on with our regularly scheduled lives.

I think that's as much explaining as I can give. So here it is, a little piece of my childhood on full display, helping to shape the wonderful story you just read.

And if you're wondering afterwards, what letter grade he achieved, this beauty landed him a fair and pretty remarkable, C -.

Dear Little Bro,

(Or Booger, as I call you at home in front of your face)
This is your big bro, Barry. Hope you're doing ok. You'll never guess what I'm stuck here being assigned to do in English class. Write about you!

Yep, I have to write 100 plus words and pick somebody that I know (who?) I can help guide as a mentor. I'm not exactly sure why this matters - it's more than likely that before this is all said and done - I imagine you'd be helping me figure things out. (If that even makes any sense.) I mean, look at me, I'm a mess - holding on for dear life to pass this class, rambling my sentences so the word count can add up so Mrs. Heller won't notice that I'm just trying to stall.

I mean, what do I know about life, anyway? I'm 13 years old - I just reached my teenage years. Isn't that the time when all parents begin to get worried that their little children are out and about exploring the dangers of the world? Exposing themselves to all sorts of peer pressure and whatnot.

I understand I will be going through this before you so maybe it's best that I'd be the one giving you "the warning" about things and some sound advice so you won't repeat some of the same mistakes I'll be making. So look - what do you know? Maybe this is part of the "mentoring process". You should lead by my example!

Anyway, hang in there, kid. You still have a few more years before you reach the same level of flux. Middle school will most likely be a drag and high school will be in another league of its own. I have faith, though, that things will work out for us both. It's a long roller coaster and the best that we can do is just enjoy the ride before we throw up from having too much fun and excitement.

    Take care, (See you at home)
Barry Chase

It's a shame Barry didn't live to see the day I'd use him as a focal point to build my narrative. It's possible he's out there laughing all about it somewhere in parts unknown or having a cigarette with the big guy himself. It's better like this, though, I assume; needing space to have the last word and build self-esteem for myself.

But I aimed to do him justice.

I hope I didn't disappoint.